MW01700812

Off Track

Alice Griffiths

Copyright © 2009 Alice Griffiths

All rights reserved.

ISBN: 978-0-9813017-8-5

ACKNOWLEDGMENTS

I could not have written this book without the help and encouragement of the people in my life. A big thank you to, my writing group, Margaret, Bill, Judith, and Cathie for their thoughtful critiques, to Jeanne for her helpful "how many words?" emails as I was writing the first draft. To my sister Jacqueline who has always encouraged me. To my parents who taught me my love of reading. To Sue who said "what a great idea" when we decided to start a publishing company.

And, to you the reader. Thank you for purchasing this book, I hope you enjoy the read

1

"What the hell" Madeline said, turning the page in her diary. "Simon, get in here."

At this time in the day, she should have been in a meeting. It was right there, her first appointment. 10:00 am discuss the deposition for the Michaels case. It was 10:05. No one was in her office, except her. She could clearly see across the tops heads in cubicles, that the glass-lined room across the busy office floor was empty.

"Simon," Madeline shouted, shriller than before. "Where the hell are you?"

"Here," Simon answered as he came through the open door. "What's the problem?"

"Where are the people for the Michaels case?"

"They canceled," he leaned across and opened her desktop Outlook icon. "Look, I sent you an email. You should really check your emails before you freak out."

"Great, thanks for the lecture. My crackberry needed charging. Anyway, I like paper notes; they don't run out of power and turn themselves off. Can you just remember to leave me a note on my desk next time there's a schedule change?" Madeline flicked a bright red fingernail to the desk as if to point out the exact spot the message should have been. "You know I don't check emails first thing."

"No prob," Simon nodded. "I can do that."

The lights went out with a snap and sudden cessation of the underlying buzz of electric power. "Damn, now what?" Simon looked around as though someone would answer.

The only light came in from the bank of windows along the east wall; it was raining, as usual, so it wasn't enough to light anything past the first row of cubicles.

"Shit," Madeline said. "Do you think it's another drill? If it is, I am so not going down. Go find the floor warden and tell him I'm unwilling to leave."

"Uh," Simon hesitated, "you remember the last time when they made us leave and then wouldn't let us into the building until everyone else was back at their desk because we held up the drill?"

"Yes," Madeline reconsidered. "You're suggesting we just go along? Like sheep?"

Simon shrugged. "It's up to you but it might be faster in the long run." The emergency lights flickered on. "And, if it's not a drill, do you really want to die here?"

"Yeah, yeah," Madeline picked up her black Coach purse and pushed Simon ahead of her towards the stairs. "Get going. I'm right behind you. Where the hell is the warden anyway? If this was a real emergency we would be dead waiting for direction."

Simon led her towards the stairwell and double-checked the sign on the door, "We're taking the green stairwell." He looked at the people starting to drift toward the refuge area. "If we go now, we'll beat most of these people down stairs."

Madeline looked around and couldn't see the fire marshal. The marshal was probably doing a sweep of the floor to confirm everyone was leaving. After four bomb threats in two months, people knew the evacuation process inside out, assemble in the refuge area and wait for instructions on which of the two doors to take. She stepped out of the four inch heels and picked them up. Now she stood five foot two and had to look up at Simon's five eight. "Let's get out of here." She said, giving Simon a not so gentle push toward the door. "If we get down fast enough I can get a Starbucks for the wait. If we go right now, I'll buy you a latte too."

Simon pushed open the door to the stairway as a voice came over the speakers. "Please wait for instruction from the floor warden. This is not a drill. Please make your way to the refuge area and prepare for evacuation. Do not return to gather your belongings; do not remove your shoes. Please wait for instruction."

Madeline gave a small chuckle as she let the door close behind her. She hiked up her black, pencil skirt and hurried down the stairs behind Simon. The soft buzz of the emergency lights almost covered the sound of voices on lower floors. Madeline felt the dusty dryness catch in the back of her throat as her breath sped up with the exercise.

"Hey," she managed to say without allowing the cough out. "What did you find out on the Juneson file?"

"Are you serious? You want to debrief as we run down eleven floors?" Simon turned his head and grabbed the handrail to stop from falling down the stairs. He saw Madeline's nod and rolled his eyes. "Okay, the investigators found out Michael Juneson kept three different accounts stashed away from his wife and mistress. According to an online calendar we found he was planning to leave the country on Friday."

Voices floated over the clack of the doors opening as people from each of the twenty floors started their journey down to the safety of the street. Evacuees gossiping and guessing about the cause of the alarm filled the previously clear stairwell.

"Damn, stop talking, people will hear." Madeline said.

Simon motioned her to the left side of the stairs; the new people were filing down the stairs close to the right wall. "Keep left and keep moving; that was the sixth floor." He reached behind him to take her hand. "Don't get separated from me. We can finish this at the Starbucks across the street."

Madeline felt her pace increase and tried not to fight for control. Keeping her focus on moving and getting out of the building, she looked at the door as they passed, "fourth floor, almost there."

"Uh huh," Simon stopped as a large man in a black suit stumbled through the door to the third floor.

The alarm continued to sound as the building emptied one floor at a time. The dry click and shuffle of twenty floors of work shoes echoed off the walls of the stairwell. Body heat pushed up the temperature and raised a thin coating of sweat on Madeline's forehead. "Two," she counted out. Then the emergency lights blinked twice and went out. "Damn and blast it to hell."

“Keep moving, we’re almost there,” Simon gave her hand a quick squeeze. “Look the emergency team is here already.”

Madeline looked up and saw a faint light ahead; its flickering was odd, but reassuring. A sudden shivering itch ran over her body and she pulled back on Simon’s hand.

“What,” he turned back to her. “You can see the steps, don’t worry.”

“Okay, just give me a second.” She took a breath and the itch calmed.

“You got it man. I’m right behind you.” Simon looked back at her again. “We are supposed to follow this guy, you ready?”

She felt the other bodies in the stairwell push against her and hugged the wall a bit tighter as she tried to speed up.

“If you let me fall, I will make your life a living hell, Simon.” She struggled to keep her balance at the speed he set. Simon’s tug pulled her to the left around the corner of the stair. The press of the other people vanishing as she moved.

“What’s going on?” She tried to pull Simon to a stop but he kept her moving. She could see the light shine on one wall then another as their guide swung his arm. The walls changed from slabs of concrete to bricks; she felt dampness chill her skin. “Where are we, Simon? Where is everyone else? If I don’t get a latte soon I’ll start screaming.”

“Don’t freak out. I can see light just down the corridor. The door is open, we’ll be in Starbucks in a few minutes and you can buy me a vente mocha to apologize for your yelling.”

Madeline laughed, “I’ll get you your mocha but I won’t apologize and you know it.”

They walked through the doorway and she felt cool grass under her feet. Then the sight of tall trees made it to her brain. Her little inner voice screeched, something's wrong!

"What the…," Simon let go of her hand and spun around. "Where the hell are we?"

Their guide walked to a small group of people in the middle of the clearing. He threw back the hood of his coat and ran his hands through dark blond locks. The rest of the group consisted of a woman, four men and eight horses. The blond man turned to face Simon and Madeline, bowed, and beckoned them over.
Madeline turned to go back through the door and saw what had made Simon stare. A tree occupied the place the door should be, a massive tree, a tree so big it would have been a tourist attraction anywhere else, like that tree in California you can drive through. There was no door. No outline of a door and no hope of a return to the office building they had been evacuating mere seconds ago. She turned again and faced the group across the clearing.

"What the hell is going on?" she stalked toward the woman who sat on her horse staring down at Madeline. The large, muscular, blond god smiled at her, his blue eyes fixed on her face. "Who are you? Never mind, just send us back or tell us how to get back, and we'll forget all of this. If you don't, we are going to sue that smile off your face pretty boy."

"Madam," he bowed again and Madeline blinked in disbelief. "May I present the Lady Arabela of the Summer Lands?" He gestured to the haughty woman on the big red horse. "And, I am Sir Jode Montgomery of the Lower Plains. I offer you my service and my protection for as long as you need it."

Madeline felt fog creep at the edges of her sight. She was way out of her area of expertise a new experience for her. "I don't need protection. I need to go back. Open the freaking door in the tree." She felt her cheeks burn and her throat tighten. In her peripheral vision, she saw Simon step forward.

"Simon DiPalma, executive assistant. It is a pleasure to meet you," Simon stood feet together arms relaxed at his sides; he nodded his head slowly as an approximation of a bow. "This lady is Madeline Victoria Higginbottom of Brown Wilson and Jones attorneys at law."

"Simon," she spun around and marched back to him, finger pointing at his chest; all her anger and fear focused on him. "Don't act like you are at a cocktail party. We've been kidnapped."

Simon took Madeline's arm and pulled her until she started moving towards the group. "Just play along" he hissed to her. "There is no way we're going back through the tree. These people seem to want to be friends, and until we figure out what's-what we need friends. Hey, it might just be fun."

"Fun? You asshole, how am I going to get on one of those horses in this?" She pointed to the tight fitting black skirt that narrowed at her knees.

2

The woman, Arabela, said something to one of the other men and he adjusted the saddle on a black horse allowing Madeline to sit sideways and balance by holding the front and back of the saddle. Simon scrambled onto the back of a grey horse and then the group set out. Two men held the reins of their horses tightly to lead them; all Simon and Madeline had to do was stay in the saddle.

Madeline listened to the quiet words spoken by the welcome party. She glanced at Simon and they shared a shrug.

"It looks like no one is going to talk to us. Any ideas?" He asked. The look on his face bothered Madeline, he was smiling and his eyes were scanning the forest around them. Was he enjoying this?

"No, and stop having so much fun. We are getting out of here as soon as I have a chance to negotiate our release." She swatted at a flying insect, it swerved around her hand and flew at her face. "Damn, bugs." She tried swatting it again and almost lost her balance.

"Take care, madam." Sir Jode dropped back from his position beside Arabela. "It will not harm you. It only seeks to understand what you are."

"What I am is angry. Why won't people talk to us? Are you some kind of spokesperson? Who do I talk to about a ransom?"

"A long list of questions," he smiled. Madeline's heart flipped but her temper put it back into place.

"So, how about some answers."

"In good time," he put up his hand to forestall her next set of questions. "Others aren't speaking to you because they cannot speak your language."

"But you can," Simon joined in before Madeline could snap out the same question. "Why is that?"

"Another good question, are all of your people so full of questions?" Jode waited for an answer.
Madeline jumped in before Simon could speak. "Yes, and until we get some answers we won't stop asking. Look, buddy, you just took us from home and brought us into this hallucination. The least you can do is give us a clue about what's going on." Her tone was as calm as she could make it. She was well aware that the anger burning a hole in the stomach was showing as a blaze of red across her cheeks.
"I speak your language because Lady Arabela has provided me with a temporary translation skill. The others have not been so transformed." He turned his head as Arabela called his name. The only thing Madeline understood was Jode the rest was a liquid bubble of unfamiliar syllables. Jode excused himself and rode forward.

Madeline realized she had been gaping in astonishment and snapped her mouth shut. She turned to Simon who was shaking his head. "Um," she paused to try to compile a coherent sentence through her fury and confusion. "Temporary translation skill… what do you think… I mean, do you have any idea what's going on?"

"Well, from the pain in my ass from this damn saddle I'd guess we're not sharing a dream. I don't know of any drugs that would give us the same hallucination." He shrugged. "I have no idea, but I think it might be a fun ride as long as it lasts. Why don't you just play along?"

"Are you really suggesting we should just go with the fucking flow?" Madeline grabbed the saddle again after losing her balance when she threw both hands out in frustration. "We're somewhere, or some when, only one person can talk to us and he's at the beck and call of princess freaking Arabela. By the look of it, the plumbing and the medical practices will be medieval. There will be no TV, no movies, no MP3s no real entertainment. There will be… Shit, what about my clients?"

"Chill, someone will take care of the clients." Simon tried to reach out to pat her arm but quickly took hold of the saddle when the horse stepped the opposite way and he started to slip to the side. "Look, you don't have any control. This isn't a courtroom, you can't reason your way to a win. This is something else. Until you can find a way to control this, yes, I'm saying go with the flow."

He turned his gaze back to the surrounding trees. "Think of it as a spa retreat. Maybe a bit of rest and disconnection from work will do you good."

The sharp scent of pine cut through the ripeness of the horse smell and filled the air making her look around at the scenery. Simon was right; it was like the area around Lake Louise where she'd attended a law course last year. It was all a bit raw and fresh for her taste, as though the earth had just finished the upheaval of forming the mountains looming over the top of the forest in front of them. The trees were too big, she expected to see one lift its roots and start walking along beside their party.

Madeline straightened her back and tried to maintain balance with her stomach muscles. She took riding lessons as a teenager and she tried to recall what she'd learned so she'd be able to ride without the trainer reins if she could get her hands on some more appropriate wear.

As they passed, the travelers occasionally set a flock of birds into rattling flight, or surprised a group of what looked like deer into a bounding escape. Most of the time though, the only sound was the creak and jingle of the horse tackle punctuated by airy horse snorts.

"Chill, go with the flow." Madeline muttered. "I guess it's not a bad tactic. But just wait until I can speak to people. Someone is going to regret bringing, me here."

"I am truly sorry to have upset you." Jode's voice broke through Madeline's muttering. "We will be at the castle soon. Lady Arabela has instructed me to inform you she will perform the translation spell on you as soon as we are able to find some privacy."

"What does that mean? I'm not sure I want someone putting a spell on me."

"It is nothing painful," he paused. "And it will only work if you wish it to do so. The spells Lady Arabela casts are what we call sympathetic spells. It requires the permission and involvement of the recipient."

"I have no reason to believe you." Madeline could feel her blood thickening in her veins at the thought of giving control to someone. "How do I know she won't make me cluck like a chicken and dance the tango?"

"Why would she wish to do that? If she requires entertainment, she will call her troupe of dancers, I'm sure they know this tango you mentioned, unless you are a dancer?"

"No, I'm a lawyer. A very good one," she said, making her tone cold and intimidating.

"That word is unfamiliar. Tell me, what do lawyers do in your world?"

"I thought you could speak my language." Madeline frowned.

"Yes, but not as you do," Jode smiled at her again, the grin half covered by his thick moustache, his blue eyes sparkling. Madeline had never seen eyes actually sparkle. "The spell allows me to understand your words as if you were speaking my language. Some words do not exactly translate and the spell lets me know when it hasn't been able to find the right word."

"How?" Madeline's curiosity was taking over. She wanted to know how it worked because it was going to be cast on her.

"I hear the word lawyer as negotiator or agreer but it's not sure which. What does a lawyer do?"

"It's my job to help people settle disagreements. I also help people make contracts so they are protected if something goes wrong."

"Ah, a mediator, negotiator and scribe, we have separate jobs for each thing." He nodded to himself. "Now I begin to understand why it was you the vision found for this quest. It is a good profession for a woman of such passion. You must be a formidable opponent."

"Quest? What quest?" Madeline ignored what seemed like a pick up line; this man could not possibly be trying to flirt, could he? She felt a pang of disappointment with the thought that he might not be.

"Lady Arabela will tell you the tale later."

"Okay, okay. How is it that I can understand you?"

"The spell changes the sounds of the words as my mind forms them. I speak your language, which is why you can understand me." He pointed to a peaked slate roof poking up through the forest to their right. "We are almost at the castle, see there is the roof of the mews."

"Well, I'm about ready to get off this freaking horse. What will happen when we get there, will Simon and I be put in a dungeon?"

He laughed a rich chuckle, causing a tingling in places that made Madeline want to squirm. She told her libido to go back to sleep. This didn't feel like a good place for casual sex; and even if it was, she was too worried to enjoy a romp.

"No," he answered. "I do not know why you would think so. Lady Arabela will give you each a room, clothing and servants to attend you. You are not prisoners you are guests who may be of great service to Lady Arabela and her people."

"Does she need someone to defend her in court?"

"Not in court, no. Now I must not say more. I must return to Lady Arabela and escort her into the castle. I will await you in the hall for the feast this evening." He gave his horse a squeeze with his legs and trotted back to Arabela.

"What did he say?" Simon had taken advantage of the slack in the horse's reins to give Madeline and Jode some privacy for their conversation. "Did he tell you why we're here?"

"No, I think we're just going to have to wait." She nodded towards the roof in the distance. "I figure we'll be there in an hour and when I've had a chance to get the feeling back in my butt we'll get our answers."

Simon laughed. "I pity them. Have you considered holding off for a few days. This is like a vacation. We can check this world out; maybe there's more than bad plumbing and poor doctoring going on. This magic thing could be a hoot."

"Hoot! What are you talking about? Any time we spend here is wasted time. What? You think we can learn spells and take them back home and bewitch people?" She reached out, tried to smack his arm and almost came off her horse as it stutter-stepped.

"No, I'm saying maybe it will be good for you to have an adventure. You are way too tightly wound these days."

"You know it's partnership time at the firm. If I'm not there I can't have a shot at it."

"Is that what you really want?" Simon asked. "Those guys are as stiff as eight-hour old corpses. You aren't easy to work for, crap you are a pain in the ass, but do you really want to be committed to the old farts with corner offices?"

"I've been working towards it for years, since law school."

"You never wanted to do anything else?"

Madeline looked around at the changes in scenery; they had left the forest and were riding through a wide valley of grass and wild flowers. There was a lake jutting out from the corner of the last line of trees the water shining off the small waves. Children were running along the edge of the water, throwing a ball back and forth.

"Yes, but it's too late now. I need to get back and make partner. And, I don't care if I'm a pain in the ass to you. It only matters if I win my cases. That's what my clients and the partners expect." She looked away from Simon, trying to end the conversation.

"Okay, keep your hair on. I get it." Simon nudged his horse closer. "I wanted to be a musician, had a band in high school. We were pretty good. I only took the executive assistant job to pay the bills. The main plan was to keep up with the band and make my future as a rock star."

"What happened?" Madeline was always intrigued by other people's life plans.

"Like Bryan Adams said, one of the guys quit, he joined the armed forces and ended up in Afghanistan, the drummer got pregnant, and then married. That left me and Wings, the keyboard guy."

"Why didn't you just find someone else?"

"Wings got scooped by someone else, and I got busy. It's hard to build a whole band." He clicked his tongue. "Maybe I'll try again when we get back."

"Yeah, let's hope we get back."

Jode and Lady Arabela trotted back to them. Arabela spoke to Jode in the same flow of syllables; he nodded and turned to Madeline and Simon.

"Lady Arabela asks if you would prefer a view of the lake or of the trees."

"I'd prefer the view of the building next door to my apartment," Madeline said through gritted teeth.

"Lake," Simon jumped in before she could continue.

Jode relayed the answer and Arabela nodded before taking the reins to lead the horse.

"Jode, buddy, I can take my own reins, the lady doesn't need to lead me." He reached for the reins. "I can ride."

Arabela looked at Jode for translation and shook her head. "It would be better if you allowed her to lead the horse until we arrive at the castle."

Simon shrugged, "No problem. I guess you don't trust me not to run away."

"Not at all, where would you go?" Jode gave that toe-curling chuckle again. "Lady Arabela is concerned for her horses. They are all trained to respond to signals from knee and hand as well as from the rein. You could inadvertently give a signal and have the horse buck you into the lake, which would not be good for the horse."

"Oh, great, are we supposed to follow you around on a leash the entire time we are here?" Madeline shifted slightly in the saddle.

"Not at all," Jode answered, appearing unruffled by her waspish tone. "Simon, can learn the signals tomorrow in a couple of hours, I notice he has already started guiding the horse. You, I'm afraid might need more lessons than he does. Do you ride? Is it only the skirt that makes you look so uncomfortable?"

"No, the damn saddle makes me uncomfortable. I can ride a little, but not well." Madeline didn't like to tell anyone she didn't know how to do something. “Is there a different way to get around?”

“For our quest? No, everyone will need to ride. I can teach you tomorrow, if you are right about your skills, you should be able to ride enough to not hurt yourself or the horse. You will improve with practice; you will need to wear riding clothes, though.”

He spoke to the rider holding Madeline’s horse and she felt a small tug on the reins before it started to trot. She grabbed the saddle tightly and screamed at Jode. “A little warning would be nice.”

“Please, accept my apology,” he said, she could see a glint in his eyes. “I will remember next time. We must arrive at the castle before the sun goes down. It is not a good thing to be out in the dark unless you are familiar with the land.”

3

Madeline felt relief as they rode through the open gate of a grand house built of stone. Hanging banners flapped in the breeze and added flashes of color to the grey walls. At the sound of the horses stamping their feet and snorting, people came out of doors and around corners to help them dismount and take the horses back through the gate. Madeline realized the stables were not inside the walls, only people lived in the safety of the enclosure.

She watched as Simon limped after Jode through the open door. Madeline knew she was going to feel the effects of the ride as much as Simon. She slid her feet into her shoes, lifted her purse from the pommel of the saddle and straightened her skirt before attempting to walk after them. To her embarrassment, the stiffness of her back and thighs made it more a hobble than a walk.

Stepping into a wide hall where a long table covered in cloaks and gloves and other clothing stood, Madeline took a deep breath and inhaled a sweet smell of furniture wax, flowers and unfamiliar food. Jode's tall silhouette came into focus in the dim light; he was bent over talking to Arabela, who barely came up to his chest. Simon stood to the side in the shaft of sunlight streaming through a window, his suit showing the wear of their journey in the creases and dust smears.

As she watched, Simon stepped forward. Arabela reached up, touched his forehead and spoke a few words. When she removed her fingers Simon spoke to her and she answered.

"Bloody idiot," she muttered, then stepped towards the trio.

Simon stepped forward anticipating Madeline's argument. "Just let her put the spell on you and don't make a big deal about it."

"How do you know it hasn't done something to you?"

"I don't, but it's much easier to talk directly to people and not through Jode."

"What does it feel like?"

"It's warm where her fingers touch and then you start hearing whispers. All of a sudden, you know what she's saying and it's done. I honestly feel the same, including the sore muscles, as I did before she touched me. I still don't know if I want to go home; I still think you can be a pain in the ass."

"Okay, shut up. If I'm going to argue my way back home, I'll need to do it myself. You're right I can't be persuasive through an interpreter."

Madeline pursed her lips, thinking. She stepped closer to Arabela. "Jode, can she take away the pain from the ride as well?" He translated and Arabela nodded flashing a grin. Madeline chuckled when heard Simon mutter in the background. "Why didn't I think of that?"

Arabela reached her hands up to touch Madeline's forehead. As Simon had said, warmth permeated her skin and Madeline felt peace come with it. There was silence for a second or two; she feared the spell had gone wrong.

"Don't worry," a soft voice came through the silence followed by a wave of whispers like rustling leaves. "It is done." Arabela said.

Madeline realized she no longer felt the soreness in her back and legs. "Thank you." She said as graciously as she could.

"You are most welcome," Arabela said. "I hope you will feel comfortable in my home. Please, let us take you to your rooms. I'm sure you will want to change and, perhaps, bath before dinner."

"Why couldn't you have done that spell when we first arrived? It was difficult to endure the day with only one person to talk to, and ask questions of."

"Ah, that would be part of the reason. I was not prepared to answer questions in the field in front of my men. The other reason is magic can attract attention if it is practiced outside the protections. In my home the priests have built wards against those creatures attracted to magic." She turned toward the grand staircase and wrapped her arm around Madeline's.

The two women ascended the stairs followed by Jode and Simon. "Come," Arabela continued, "I have assigned you each a servant. Madeline, you will be attended by Elise and Simon by John." Two people were standing beside doors. They nodded at the sound of their names. "They will draw you baths and find you suitable clothing. We will meet in an hour to talk, just the five of us in the small dining room. Dinner should be ready for service in two hours."

"Five?" Madeline looked around.

"My priest will join us. We need to speak quietly and privately."

"Why can't we talk now?" Madeline said. She felt manipulated, politely to be sure, but this tiny woman expected automatic obedience and it rankled. "Or, at least why not right after we've had a wash. I don't really want to wait an hour I've been waiting all day."

"My priest has information to add and I trust him with my life. It is a long difficult tale and I am tired." Arabela said. "Before I am able to share our story with you, I need to spend a short while resting then speak with my priest. There may be news that I have not heard."

Simon forestalled Madeline's next comment. "We'll wait until you are ready to tell us. An hour won't make any difference in the long run, Madeline."

"I thank you Simon." Madeline was surprised at the sudden weakness in Arabela's voice; magic must take a lot out of you.

"Is it possible to arrange a snack before dinner; we have not eaten since breakfast. In our world we eat little in the morning and both of us are very hungry."

"I'll have the kitchen send something to your rooms, and perhaps, dinner can be prepared sooner. Please excuse me now I must retire for a short while." She turned to the two people standing at the doors. "John and Elise will attend you and bring you to dinner at the right time." Arabela turned and took Jode's arm and both of them walked down the hallway and passed through a curtained doorway.

Madeline looked at her servant; the woman, looking every inch a milkmaid, was cheerfully waiting for Madeline to enter the room.

"Simon, we should talk about how to deal with this. Can we meet in a half hour?"

"As long as I get a bite to eat I'm good, where?"

"My room, bring your food and we'll eat while we talk."

Elise put her hand to her mouth and blushed, "Madam, that is not proper."

"What," Madeline's patience was drained to the bitter lees. "I can't meet with my assistant?"

"Not in your room without a chaperone," she turned a deeper shade of pink.

"It would be unusual and probably scandalous to meet in your room with a chaperone." John spoke for the first time, his voice deep and resonant not matching his fragile appearance. "If you wish to speak in private it would be proper to do so in a more public place. There is a bower in the back of the house; you may meet there. You will be in sight of people but they won't be able to hear you. Will that suit?"

"Fine," Madeline pushed open the door of her room, "in half an hour, tops."

The room was large and square. In the centre of the east wall stood an intricately carved bed covered in bright linens. The dark wood floorboards gleamed at the edge of patterned wool rug. The walls were made of a warm red wood; panels of it were carved in scenes that depicted battles, parties, and hunts.

Madeline felt the warmth of the room seep into bones she didn't realize were cold. The fireplace was on the wall facing the bed; or, more factually, it was the wall facing the bed. The white stone hearth and mantle carved in straight clean columns that repeated from the side of the fire to the walls, creating a sense of space and eternity, balancing the earthy colors of the rest of the room.

"Please," Elise said. "Take off your clothes and get into the bath. I'll find you something to wear for dinner and by tomorrow you will have enough clothes for your time here." She pointed to an armoire in the corner by the window.

"Um," Madeline tried to bring her wits back from where they had fled at the sight of the regal bedroom. "I don't know how long I will be here. What do you mean enough clothes?"

Elise took Madeline's shoes, placed them in a box, and then tried to tug off the jacket. "For tonight you will wear a dress and slippers. By tomorrow, the seamstress will have made two riding outfits with a cloak and two more dresses. Please, remove your clothes, or you will not be ready to meet your young man."

Madeline shrugged out of her clothes and stepped into the tub of steaming water that was waiting in front of the fire.

"Good," Elise said handing Madeline a pot of soapy goop and a rough cloth before gathering the clothes and shoes. "Tonight you will have to sleep in borrowed night clothes; tomorrow night there will be a nightgown and robe made just for you. Do you have a family crest for the seamstress to incorporate in the clothing?"

"Uh, no, we don't go in for that much where I come from." Madeline sat in the water, hot but not dangerously so.

"Well, not to worry. What colors do you prefer?"

"I like green and black. Why?"

"I'll ask the seamstress to use those colors and you will be known by the combination."

“Okay,” Madeline didn’t want to talk about clothes any more. She just wanted to soak and then get some answers.

There was a soft knock on the door. “That will be the seamstress,” Elise said and went to answer it. She walked back into Madeline’s line of sight with her hands full of dark blue and white fabric, a pair of black sequined slippers on top. “If you wish to eat you must hurry.”

“I suppose,” Madeline stood and looked around for a towel. Elise handed her a rough square of homespun fabric and helped her out of the tub.

When she was dry, Elise showed her how to fasten the ties of the dark under-dress and to wrap the white over-dress properly around. Madeline noticed there were delicately embroidered stars around the edge of the white dress. She felt weird without underwear but at least the dress was tight enough across the chest to hold her up. The slippers fit snuggly and she wiggled her toes hoping there was not a long walk in her near future.

“How did you know what size I needed?” She asked as Elise started to brush out and braid Madeline’s red brown curls.

“The seamstress saw you when you arrived. She only needed to know your height and general build to give you this style of dress. I’m sorry the shoes don’t fit well, your feet are a little larger than expected.”

Madeline didn’t bother to get upset at the foot size comment, the calming influence of having her hair dressed after a warm bath was making her purr internally.

“There will be shoes here tomorrow made from a pattern of the ones you had with you. They do fit better than the slippers, I hope.”

"Yes, those shoes were made for me." Madeline felt a pat on her head as Elise finished tucking in the last braid. "Are you done? Can I meet Simon?"

"Yes," Elise handed her a small pot of red paste. "Rub this into your lips. It will help keep them smooth and will brighten your face."

"Wow, magic world lipstick." Madeline used her pinkie to rub the paste into her lips. It tasted sweet and carried a faint scent of violets, or something like violets. "Thank you."

"My pleasure," Elise gestured to the door. "John will carry the food to the bower. Enjoy your evening; I will be here when you return to help you change out of your dress."

"You don't need to do that; I can undress myself." Madeline patted Elise's arm. "You should go home and get your rest."

"This is my home," she pointed to a curtained off alcove next to the door. "I sleep here. You will not be alone."

"Oh, I'm used to sleeping by myself. Don't you have a family to go home to?"

"I have been assigned to wait on you. Are you unhappy with me? Did I distress you when I commented on your shoes?"

"No, don't worry; I'll be fine. I'm not used to having a servant. It's fine. I'll see you after dinner."

Madeline opened the door and saw John walking in front of Simon holding a tray covered with a cloth. Simon was dressed in black leggings and a red tunic; the look flattered his lean body, and his expression showed he knew it.

"Wow, Maddie that looks great on you."

"It's Madeline," she snapped and then regretted it, "thanks, you too. I just hope I don't have to get used to this. And, I'd better get my original clothes back so I can go home looking more normal. Especially those shoes," this was addressed to Elise, "will they survive the process of making my new ones?"

"Yes, madam," Elise curtsied and stepped back into the room.

John led them down the stairs and around to a small door in the side of the great hall. The sun was almost down but there were torches placed to give enough light to allow people to stroll before retiring. John showed them to a bench surrounded by a frame of vines carrying the same violet scent as the lip balm; the flowers looked more like roses than violets.

"I will return in time to escort you to meet with my Lady." John placed the tray on the bench and lifted the cloth. There were two mugs of red wine, an assortment of fruits and nuts, and slices of thick brown bread piled beside sausages. A pot of something that looked like butter sat in the middle. Two knives were the only cutlery in sight.

As soon as John was out of sight, they dug into the food, sipping wine in between mouthfuls. "Okay, what did you want to talk about?" Simon said around a bite of sausage.

"We need to decide how we are going to approach this. I want to go home as soon as possible; if we agree not to cooperate maybe we can get home tomorrow."

"Hold on, I don't want to go home that fast, maybe not at all."

"What if you have to go so I can?" Madeline finished the last piece of dried fruit; it tasted of apple and had the consistency of an apricot, then sat back with her wine in her hand.

"Well, from my side of it, what if you have to stay so I can stay?" He put the last bite of bread in his mouth.

"I don't want to look at it through your point of view. What is the big attraction here?"

"It's a new adventure that's enough for me."

"What would it take for you to help me get home?" Madeline was determined not to get into a discussion about whose point of view was more valid.

"I don't know," he sat back, crossed his legs and straightened his tunic. "If I do help you, it might mean I can't come back. I'd be stuck in the old world; that would be a big sacrifice."

"Oh, yeah, big sacrifice," she flicked her fingers at him. "Look, I'll double your salary. Or, if you want to change jobs I'll give you whatever reference you need. I'll do what I can to help you get what you want; as long as it is something back home."

"I get why you need to get back, but there are things you might like here. Well, not so much things as a person, I saw you react to Jode's attention."

"What?"

"You blush every time he looks in your direction." Simon laughed. "Hey, even I can tell he's hot. I get it."

"There's nothing to get." Madeline put down her wine mug with a thump of defiance. "You saw stress, nothing else."

"Okay, stress," Simon shrugged. "Look, no guarantees, we see how it goes. If I decide to support you, then you pay up when we get home." He put down his wine glass. "Heads up, here comes John, I guess it's show time."

4

John held open the door to a small room; there was a round table with five chairs in the center. Five candles augmented the light coming in through a series of long narrow windows cut into the wall.

Simon walked to the window and stared out, "it looks like there's a storm coming. Hard to tell in this light, but it's kind of a darker dark on the horizon, know what I mean?"

"Yes," Arabela answered as she flowed into the room dressed in layers of white lace. "You are right, there will be a storm. Please, do not worry. It will pass quickly." Behind her Jode held the door for a small person dressed in yellow robes, a heavy veil pulled down to its chest. "Please, let me introduce my priest Blu. He will help me tell you why you are here; But first he must protect the room from listeners."

The priest unveiled and revealed a smooth faced man with bright green eyes. He smiled broadly at the newcomers and rubbed his shaven head as though it itched. "I am honored to meet you. It was my scrying that found you in your world; to meet you face to face is something stupendous for me; you are to play a vital role in the coming days. I thank you for coming."

"You're welcome," Simon replied returning to the table.

"We didn't have a choice," Madeline muttered.

"No, indeed, we rarely have a choice in the important things," the priest answered Madeline while giving a nod to Simon. "Lady Arabela will tell you her story; I will help where I can. Ah, I believe the food has arrived, I hope you did not eat your fill while you talked."

"No," Madeline answered. "I can't believe how hungry I am."

Three servants with loaded trays in each hand stood in the doorway. They entered and started to place the contents of the trays on the table. One server, a teenage boy by appearance, moved clockwise around the table placing plates of patterned china. Another boy followed with cutlery; the third worked counterclockwise placing goblets and cloth napkins.

When the table was set, they picked up the contents of the other trays and placed bread, hot meat, and steaming roasted vegetables in the centre of the table, giving each platter a slight spin for effect. They bowed in unison, pointed to linen covered bowls they had put on a sideboard. "Sweets to follow your meal," one spoke and then they spun on their toes and trouped out through the door.

"They like to show off," Jode said as he fastened the door with a metal bar then pulled a curtain across it.

"It cannot hurt to let them play," Blu said. "Allow me to make some protections and we can start eating and talking."

He took a red ribbon from his robes and passed it over the table and sideboard, muttering quietly as he worked. Madeline opened her mouth to speak and Jode motioned her to keep quiet. Blu moved to the window, replacing the red ribbon with a black one. He started to sing, a high trilling that continued as he walked around the perimeter of the room, passing the ribbon in a complex pattern from top to bottom of the wall. When he completed the circle, he made three kissing sounds and put away the ribbon.

"You wished to ask a question?" He said to Madeline as he sat.

"I was interested in the prayer."

"Ah, that was not a prayer as such." He took a slice of bread and passed the platter to Madeline. "I checked the food for poisons because it is difficult to know who to trust these days." He poured a goblet of wine and passed the carafe to her. "The second spell was to protect us against listeners."

Madeline waited patiently while the food made the rounds of the table and they filled their plates and goblets, but she burned with curiosity for the story to start. She knew when she heard the details she would be able to find some loophole, some tiny detail that would convince them to send her home.

"The story begins many years ago." Arabela started abruptly, her voice quiet. "I will start with the most recent part and then let you know what led to it." She took a tiny bite of vegetable and a sip of wine.

"My husband was murdered; I'm sorry to say it so starkly but it is the truth. Three weeks ago, I came home from a visit to the village and found him lying in the centre of the courtyard curled into a ball. He had been dead for only a few minutes, his body was still cooling."

"Are you sure he didn't just die of a heart attack?" Madeline asked. "I'm sorry for your loss; I should have said that first."

"He showed signs of magical poison, his lips were blue, his fingers shriveled. It was not natural."

"I confirmed the cause was magical." Blu added. "The spell came from a distance. It targeted my Lord like an arrow to a deer. This is a difficult thing even for a master but it is a common way for the Scree to kill."

"What are the Scree?" Simon asked.

"Another race of our world, we humans are not alone here." Jode said.

"So you think one of these Scree killed your husband?" Madeline asked.

"One in particular, Sayer Goddard," Arabela spat out the name.

"Did you bring me here to prosecute him?"

"I don't understand that word," Arabela said. "What does prosecute mean?"

"It means to argue that someone is guilty of a crime in a court of law," Simon said. "Do you have courts where people who are accused of a crime go to be judged?"

"Yes, but they speak for themselves and witnesses speak against them, you come from an interesting world where someone has a job to speak against people."

"It's not quite like that, but if you didn't want me for my legal skills I have no idea what you want me to do?"

"It is to do with a prophecy." Arabela poured more wine. "First let me finish the story. When Blu confirmed it was magic, I knew it was Sayer. The blood feud will not end."

"Christ, a blood feud!" Madeline spat her mouthful of wine back into the goblet. "You dragged us into the middle of a fight to the death?"

"No, into the end of it, the feud started with my husband's grandfather and Sayer's father; Dayer. My husband's grandfather sent his daughter to be fostered with a kinsman two days away from this castle. She was but five years old and Sayer sent a unit of his armsmen to kidnap her. It did not go as planned; the child was killed and my husband's grandfather swore an oath that the bloodshed would continue until one bloodline was ended."

"Have you been at war since then?" Simon asked. "How on earth did your husband's line survive to marry you?"

"Both families employed priests and other magicians to cast protections. Accidents happened, and eventually the bloodlines came down to my husband and Sayer. If I am able to kill Sayer then the feud will die. He has broken the rules by attacking my husband in my home."

"I understand you want to protect your children, but could you not just try to broker peace with this Sayer?" Madeline asked, still trying to find a way to make her expertise the reason she was here.

"He will not discuss it; And, Scree are untrustworthy when it comes to negotiation." Blu waved the idea away.

"I have personal reasons for this and I admit one of those reasons is revenge." Arabela continued. "I loved my husband deeply and his loss has left me with no anchor, and our people with no leader."

"We saw children playing by the lake when we rode in. Were yours among them," Simon asked.

"No, my Lady does not have children to carry on the bloodline." Jode said. "It has been a great sadness in our realm that there was no heir. But, perhaps that is now a blessing. The blood feud has ended with the line of Summer Lands. When she has exacted revenge for my Lord's murder, the Goddard line will also end; such is often the way of blood feuds."

Arabela pushed her plate to the centre of the table and placed her hands on the cleared space. "I have not shared this news with anyone and I find I must bring myself to trust not only my friend but also two strangers. You must know, when Blu scryed for someone to assist me he searched both for someone who could complete the task and for someone who would not betray me. I will trust the scrying and share that I am with child; I carry the heir to the Summer Lands and will birth a boy in six months."

Madeline watched Jode's reaction, she found herself watching him more and more as events unfolded. He smiled, and heat rose through her body; then he realized the repercussions of the news. His face turned a sickly shade and he rubbed his temples.

"The feud continues," he said. "You must protect the child. I beg of you do not throw your life away on vengeance."

"Sir Jode, please believe me, I have no desire to sacrifice myself on my husband's funeral pyre. I cannot leave this child vulnerable to Sayer Goddard; this blood feud must end. Goddard has no heirs. If he dies then the feud is over and my child can live to rule the Summer Lands in peace."

"He can also live protected by spells. You do not have to embark on this dangerous folly." Jode stood and walked to the window, the darkness punctuated by lightning flashes. "Why have you decided to do this now?"

"Sir Jode, I know you speak from love of me and my people, as is proper, but it is not folly. Spells are not foolproof, if I do not do this, my child will not survive."

"We invoked a prophecy." Blu said, cutting across the building argument. "The prophet said it was time. There were conditions to be met, and if they could be met, we would succeed."

Madeline fought dizziness that had gripped her when Arabela said Jode loved her. What the hell did that mean? She knew she felt vibes coming from Jode, so what was going on?

"What were the conditions?" She heard Simon's voice through her dizziness. "Are you sure they have been met? In our world prophecies tend to be vague and easily misconstrued."

Blu shook his head, "Our prophecies are not a set of instructions but rarely are they misleading. Your prophets must not as talented as ours. Be that as it may, the prophecy called for the loyal armsman, Jode, I assume that is you, to lead a small retainer of fighting men. And two strangers would be brought to ensure success. It was clear that Lady Arabela must attempt the quest before the next full moon, we should start out in the next two days."

"What do Simon and I have to contribute that could not be served by someone else?" Madeline saw her opportunity to make them send her back. If Jode loved Arabela, why should she think of staying? Damn, where had that thought come from?

"Ah, the heart of the matter for you," Blu said. "I know you are impatient and do not wish to be here. I hope my explanation will help you to accept your role in saving our land. That is the purpose of the quest; to end the blood feud, of course, but also to prevent the Summer Lands from becoming part of a Scree holding. Sayer would urge his warriors to rape and enslave our women, to torture and kill our men and geld our children before making them the lowest of slaves."

"I get that this is important to you, I just don't see why it's important to me? I know how incredibly selfish that sounds but until today I had no idea this world existed. You ripped me from a familiar and comfortable existence to this medieval fantasy world where magic is a mundane tool. What on earth could I do to help you?"

"The prophecy said we would bring two people to this world; they would be the ones who made the quest a success. One would fight the deciding battle; the other would solve a problem. When I searched the known universes, the only people who rose in the glass were you and Sir Simon." Blu took a sip of the wine in front of him. "As you can see, our prophecy is clear about your importance. Only the details are not clear to us, yet."

"Oh, that's all. You got a lawyer and her executive assistant. I could sue him and Simon could refuse to give him an appointment. Woo hoo," Madeline slapped her hand on the table. "I know you think you got the right people but I haven't a clue what you need."

Jode spoke again from his place by the window. "I suspect you were brought here not because of your normal employment but because of a talent you may not think is important. I think that will be true for both of you. If we needed only a scribe and an adjunct, we could have found them here. And they would have been more willing."

Madeline felt the rebuke in his words and realized she was teetering on the edge of an explosion. She was tired, she was not in control of anything, and for some reason the fact that Jode loved Arabela just made it all worse. She looked at Simon, he was looking back at her expectantly and she recalled he wasn't at all in a hurry to return to the life they had left just that morning. She drew in another slow breath and spoke. "I need to sleep. I cannot make a decision under this pressure. Please, unseal the door and let me go back to my room."

5

"I think we can find our way to our rooms." Madeline snapped at Jode who had followed them to the hallway. "Why don't you go back to Arabela? I think she needs someone with her." She tried to make her words sound like she cared about Arabela's welfare, hoping the waspish bite in the tone was only audible to her.

"Very well, I bid you goodnight. I hope your sleep is restful and aids you in your way to a decision. Please remember the prophecy as you think about your choices; you are a vital component to the success of this." He nodded to Simon and returned to the dining room.

"Okay, let's find somewhere to talk." She grabbed Simon's elbow and started to drag him downstairs. "John and Elise will be in our rooms so we won't have privacy, but I need to talk."

"Hey, I can walk better if you don't drag me. I'm pretty sure me falling down stairs isn't what the prophecy meant about being an important part of the quest." He shrugged off her grip and walked beside her. The wall sconces gave enough light to ensure they didn't fall but not enough to clear the shadows in the hall below.

"Sit here on the bottom step, I'll do a quick check to see if anyone is lurking, then we can talk here if we keep our voices low." Simon waited until Madeline sat then walked the perimeter of the great hall. She watched as he reached into the shadowy corners to make sure no one was hiding there. There were no potential spies reacted to his reaching fingers. "All clear," he chuckled and rubbed his hands together. "I feel like a kid on an adventure."

"Yes, that's what we need to talk about." She reminded herself to be patient; Simon was technically still her employee but here she couldn't order him around. "I do feel for these people, but I want to go back. I don't understand what I can do to help them, and I don't want to be responsible for screwing this up."

"You should have faith in the prophecy. Whatever you need to do, you apparently have the skill to do it."

"What makes you the faithful believer?"

"Uh, they can do magic here. I think that brings a measure of credibility."

She changed tactics, knowing from experience arguments about belief were unwinnable. "Tell me what you think you can do, why staying here is more desirable than going home?"

"I don't think you'll like what I have to say."

"For god's sake, just say it." Madeline's fatigue overcame her resolve to be patient.

"I was going to quit today." He held up his hand to stop Madeline's reaction. "Look, surprisingly it's not about you. I kind of enjoyed watching you at work, you can rip someone a new one faster than anyone else I know. I just didn't sign up for life; I wanted to try something else."

"What else?"

"I didn't know. I had some savings to get me through. Life isn't always about knowing what comes next."

"It is for me. I've been working to get a partnership ever since I joined the firm. I've always known what I wanted and how to get it."

"I don't know if I envy you that or if I pity you. Isn't there something you love to do that isn't part of getting to be a partner?"

"I don't know, if I had to pick then, I like to teach, I guess. That course I taught in night school made me happy, but I did it to help make me a partner."

"Why did it make you happy?"

"When people got it, whatever I was teaching, I felt proud, of them, and of me. But that was all to get a partnership; the managing partner, suggested I do it."

"Yes, but maybe you just like to teach."

"So, let's get back to you." Madeline didn't want to go any further down this road. "What have you done that makes you happy? You can't possibly want to spend your life moving from job to job."

"Yeah, I guess I'm getting the itch to settle down into something and I knew it wasn't executive assistant. Like I said, what I always wanted to do was have a band, or maybe manage one."

"You can't do that here," Madeline leapt at the hook, if she could lure Simon back to the real world with a promise to support him in this she was in. "You don't know this but I handled a case for a record producer just before you started; I could make some calls when we get back."

"Slow down. I don't know if that's what I want to do. And, why can't I do it here?"

"There's no technology, how would you make albums and sell them?"

Simon laughed, "it's not always about making money. I would be happy with a band that played in small venues and didn't cut an album. Of course, I could find a way to do it here. That's the problem, isn't it? You can't imagine doing anything else. Even if you could, it would only be in a way that fits your worldview. I do pity you Madeline."

"Fuck off," her temper boiled up. "Just because I'm not an adventurer doesn't mean I have no imagination. You have no right to judge me."

"Okay, okay; chill, and cut the volume. You are way too stressed to talk right now." Simon recognized a losing battle. "You need to sleep and let your brain digest what's happened. I think Jode had it right. Just let your subconscious mull it over."

Madeline groaned and stood up, and groaned again, this time because of the stiffness in her body from the ride; apparently, the spell wasn't completely effective and she would feel some effects of her exercise. "I do need sleep. I don't know about anything else."

Madeline allowed Elise to undress her hair and then sent her to bed. Standing by the large window, she watched the fat raindrops fall straight to the stones on the patio and bounce back like dancing fairies. The lightning had stopped but the storm had not passed. She wondered if Jode was comforting Arabela, if they were alone. She sighed and pushed the jealousy aside, she was leaving and it didn't matter who Jode loved.

Eventually, the sound and sight of the rain calmed her stressed mind. She relaxed in the moment before slipping out of the evening clothes into the white cotton nightshirt that lay over the bed. It was warm; Elise kept it by the fire. Pulling back the bed linens, Madeline crawled inside, closed her eyes and tried to follow Simon's advice. A gentle snore came from the corner behind the curtain, Madeline felt oddly comforted that she wasn't alone.

6

"Wake up," Elise's voice broke into Madeline's dream of flying monkeys. "I will go and get your breakfast while you wash and take care of other things. The convenience is two doors down the hall. You won't run into anyone, they are all either in the dining hall or about their work."

"Am I so late getting up? Why didn't you wake me?" Madeline slipped her feet into a pair of grass green slippers that were sitting beside the bed; they fit like gloves.

"You had a long day; we thought it better to let you sleep. Now hurry along and I'll be back in five minutes." Elise slipped out of the door.

Madeline felt the chill of living in a stone building creep across her shoulders. Pulling on a robe she found in the armoire, she looked out into the corridor. She crossed her fingers, hoping the bathroom was better than the small closet she'd been shown to yesterday.

The second door down was decorated with a carving of a woman pouring water out into a wide river; it opened into a room tiled from floor to ceiling in pale green and white tiles. A real toilet stood in an alcove, a pile of soft paper sheets to the side. In the opposite corner was a sink with a jug of clean water on the counter. Madeline smiled; it was a beautiful retreat.

When she finished her morning routine and returned to the room, she found Elise placing a tray loaded with bread, honey and something that looked like yogurt on the stool. A jug of steaming liquid smelling faintly of herbs completed the breakfast. "Ah, normally this would be enough food to take me through to dinner. The ride and all the other stresses yesterday have done something to my appetite. Today this is barely enough to tide me over until a real breakfast."

"I'm glad you are enjoying it. I have some clothes for you here. Would you like to dress or eat first?"

"Eat, please." She went to the jug of liquid. "What's this?"

"Caf, we drink it in the morning it helps to shake the sleep off."

As she sipped the tea, Madeline felt a tingle of caffeine through her veins. "Mmm," she looked out the window and saw the yard was full of people, and some not so people-like beings. "What's going on?"

"Lady Arabela will explain. When you are dressed and have eaten I'll take you to her."

"Okay, let's dress and eat at the same time," Madeline spread honey and yogurt on a thick slice of bread and started to strip off the outer garment as she chewed.

"Would you prefer to wear trousers or a dress?"

"Trousers," she said, thinking it would be easier to get about in pants than a fancy dress. "If there is any horse riding on the agenda I want to be able to sit on the damn thing the right way."

Elise handed her a pair of woolen pants in a shade of pine-needle green that Madeline decided was her new favorite color, then a white shirt. She pointed to a pair of boots on the floor beside the bed. Madeline waited for a moment but Elise just stood with her hand out for the nightshirt Madeline was wearing.

Madeline looked around and didn't see what she was looking for. "Where's the underwear?"

"What would that be?"

"The clothes you wear under the clothes people see."

"Oh, is that what the tiny things were. They were very pretty but we didn't know their purpose."

"You don't wear underwear," Madeline squeaked. "How do you stop your boobs dropping to your waist?"

"They do eventually, when you have children, when you are old. Why would you want to prevent that?"

"Don't your men prefer firm high breasts?"

"Well, yes, but are you saying that those strips of cloth stop it from happening?"

"No, but it looks like it when you're dressed." What was wrong with this world? "And, it's a lot more comfortable to not have your breasts bouncing up and down as you move and ride."

"Oh, but what happens when …" Elise blushed. "Oh, I shouldn't ask such personal questions. I'll see what the seamstress can make now I know what it is for."

Madeline shook her head and pulled the pants and shirt on. The shirt hung over the top of the drawstring pants that hung at a point half way between her knees and ankles. The boots overlapped the hems and everything came together like the best designer outfit she could have bought at home.

"These seamstresses of yours do fabulous work," she said smoothing the shirt over her hips.

"Not seamstresses, the seamstress. Only one person does this and she does do wonderful work; I'll be sure to pass along your thanks."

Madeline nodded and hurried out the door to find Arabela. A servant cleaning with a mop sent her back to the side door they'd used the day before. Outside Madeline saw Arabela's curly black hair flying in the wind as she stood on a pedestal directing groups of people to different areas of the garden. Four small groups were setting up camp in the garden. Six men in black clothes were erecting a black tent in the far left corner of the yard. Five or six, it was hard to tell they moved so quickly, large headed scrawny fellows were running around a fire pit, their tents low domes of grey green rags. Three tall creatures with white skin and green hair, she couldn't tell if they were male or female, were strolling the perimeter, long rolls of material held between them.

Arabela finished speaking to six beings with wings. Reaching out for Jode's arm, she stepped down and came towards Madeline.

"Good morning," Jode bowed. "Have you eaten yet? We have a full day ahead and you will need your energy."

"Yes, but not much. Who are those people?" Madeline refused to be distracted.

"They are the team for the journey. We set out today if possible," Arabela said.

"Are you going without me? Great, send me back now if you don't need me."

"We are assembling in preparation for your decision." Arabela said. "Yes, we will go without you and hope we can be successful. If you agree to come, we do not need to hope for success, we will be successful."

"I haven't made up my mind." Madeline didn't know what to feel, the sudden hope she could go home was dampened by the realization she would never see these people again, never learn who or what these beings were.

Arabela shrugged, "I must still prepare for the quest. I cannot simply wait on your answer."

"No pressure then," Madeline mumbled.

"I beg your pardon?"

"I said it is difficult to make decisions that important on an empty stomach." Madeline tried not to start a fight with her hostess.

Arabela nodded seemingly willing to accept the response. "Please, have something to eat. I need your answer tonight." She walked away leaving Madeline and Jode standing in a shaft of sunlight.

It was unusual for Madeline to be on the receiving end of such a curt demand. She looked up at Jode trying to think what she should say. Arabela was serious, that tone carried no ambivalence. Madeline wasn't sure what her fate would be if she didn't jump on the quest bandwagon. Would Arabela send her home? Would she be stuck here without a job, without a means of support? If she was in Arabela's position what would happen? Probably send her back; it wouldn't help to have someone constantly harping while she was off on a quest. Madeline tried not to think about alternatives involving dungeons and rats.

"Come; let us break our fast together. I have not eaten and you have not eaten enough; I would enjoy your company." Jode held out his elbow for Madeline to take and she looped her arm around it without thinking.

"Would you really?" She asked, wondering what he was expecting from her.

"You bring sunshine into every room."

"Oh my god," Madeline rolled her eyes but her smile took the sting from her words. "Where is Simon? I didn't see him this morning."

"He is in the kitchen, I'm sure he is entertaining the serving women while they feed him."

"Entertaining, or annoying, who can tell the difference," she laughed and walked with Jode into the shadows of the great hall.

As they approached the kitchen doorway, Madeline smelled bread, bacon, and something rich, and sweet, and tomatoey; her stomach gave an audible confirmation that she was still hungry. As they entered the kitchen she saw Simon sitting at a long table, plates of half-eaten food pushed to the centre and a steaming mug of caf in his hand. The serving girls were laughing so he must be entertaining not annoying.

"And, that's why you need to check the door is locked even though you know the kids are at school," he finished to gales of laughter from the women working at the sink and fire.

"What are you up to?" Madeline said pouring some caf into a clean mug. "Don't cause trouble here. When we go you might have to bring a girlfriend back."

"That will not be possible," Jode said. "We cannot live in your world."

"What? You came over to get us and you are fine," Simon said.

"Yes, a short stay and in an enclosed environment, if I had stepped outside I would be dying now. There are too many things in your air."

"We know that, but how come you do? How many times have people moved between worlds?" Madeline filled her plate with what looked like roasted tomatoes and bread while she spoke.

"We haven't sent anyone else. Blu showed us possible fates so we could decide on a plan to contact you. One such plan was to speak to you after you left work. The result would have left me crippled with burns over half my body three days after we returned."

"I'm glad you didn't follow that one." Madeline shuddered. "How did you avoid the atmosphere inside the building, it's not that well filtered."

"I had a spell of protection; it cost the priest who cast it five years of her life to give me ten minutes of protection." Jode pushed his empty plate away. "She felt it worthwhile, I am grateful that we were successful; without her sacrifice I would never have met you."

"Oh, god," Simon rolled his eyes. "Are you going to get mushy on us? You should know she's not going to swoon into your arms, she's going to be a big bag of trouble."

"Simon, shut up." Madeline didn't want to get into a big discussion about feelings. "Look, I'm glad you didn't get poisoned or burned or anything, but why are we able to live here, why don't we infect your people with some germs we carry?"

"You ask excellent questions. There is a spell of containment on both of you. It will lift after another two days; by then you will have been here long enough for anything harmful to die. The priest saw it in a vision."

"You place a lot of stock in visions here." Simon said. "Where we come from visions are usually part of a con game."

"Con game?"

"Where people try to fool you for their own gain," Madeline snapped tired of this chatter. "Who are those people out there?"

"They are allies. Races who assist us against our enemies," Jode said.

"We know what allies are. What exactly are the races, the white beings or the ones with wings, for instance?"

"The Fay are winged; they are able to hear words at long distance and make excellent scouts. The Sylph are the white skinned beings, they spin webs of confusion on their enemies. The other people you saw were goblins. They can place glamour spells, but only on themselves. They are crafty people and it seems as though they are full of magic.

The men and women dressed in black are the Eldmen; they are remnants of a race that used to rule the lands we now inhabit.

Their numbers were severely reduced in a massive war, they are loyal to Arabela and will fight to the death for her."

"What, no elves?" Madeline pushed the plate aside; her irritation had driven away her appetite.

"No, the elves have chosen to wait and see, often that is the case. When they choose a side, they fight blindly and are difficult to stop. It is better that they wait until they are certain."

"Give me a break." Madeline pushed herself up from the table. "This isn't helping. Is there any reason I can't go for a walk?"

"No, please take a guard with you if you leave the grounds, it is not safe outside our protection for someone not used to our ways."

"Fine, see you later." It was hard to stomp out when she was wearing the soft boots, four-inch stilettos made much more of a statement. Jode watched her leave, a smile on his face.

"Simon, do you have any questions, it seems Madeline is always the one to speak."

"I've learned it's better that way, and she usually asks the right questions." Simon winked at a serving girl as she cleared the dirty plates. "I do have a question, though. Why do you like Madeline, she's a pain in the ass."

"Please, don't speak that way, she is spirited and passionate. And, the heart isn't always the most sensible guide." He smiled again. "Tell me, how a man woos a woman in your world."

"Why would you want to, man, you know she's going home as soon as she can make someone send her?"

"It is not certain. I believe she will stay if she is given the right reasons."

"Maybe," Simon considered for a moment. "Okay, I guess you could take two approaches; listen, and then do as she says. Or, you can fight back. She's not always right and it's possible someone who doesn't just follow orders'll intrigue her. I recommend you try the second option." Simon smiled; it would be the most entertaining, anyway.

"Thank you for that advice," Jode stood, "I must meet Lady Arabela. Please enjoy the day we will feast tonight if we can leave tomorrow."

"Take care, Jode and keep your fingers crossed that Madeline will make up her mind quickly."

Madeline stalked around the inside of the wall surrounding the grounds, acknowledging the two sentries inside the gate with a nod and a grunt. As she rounded the building, she came across the temporary bivouac. The buzz of conversation flowed over her, distracting her from the annoyance that had ruled her mind since leaving Arabela.

"Madam, can I assist you in some way," a small goblin spoke from her elbow. "Are you lost?"

"No, not lost, just wondering why you are all gathering here?" She waved her arm around to encompass the camp.

"We come to assist Lady Arabela in the defeat of the evil Scree, Sayer Goddard." The gravelly sound seemed to come from the tips of the goblin's toes. "I'm honored to serve her."

"Does she pay you? Are you forced to fight for her?" Madeline needed to hear the story from someone other than Arabela, someone less emotionally invested.

"Not at all, she protected us, well her husband did. We were living in the caves by the great river Iris when Goddard's tribe started to raid. He killed many of my friends and relatives, then one day, the Lord of the Summer Lands rode to our assistance. Sayer left us alone after that."

"Was there a battle?" Madeline had images of a great war like in Lord of The Rings.

"No, the priests cast spells of invisibility and protection. Sayer's mob could not find us," the goblin grinned, a horrible sharp-toothed grimace. "Most of his men couldn't see the edge of the cliff, either, and they fell over it. Too bad Sayer wasn't one of them." He stopped suddenly, "Apologies, I did not introduce myself, Prince Jugg, at your service."

"Madeline Higginbottom," she acknowledged his bow with a quick curtsy, "a pleasure."

"Prince Jugg, well met." Arabela spoke from behind Madeline. "May I steal our guest for a private word?"

"Of course, my Lady, I must return to the camp in any case. I hope we will have a chance to meet on the road." He turned and ran back to the closest ragged tent.

"We need to discuss your decision." Arabela pointed to a rose covered bower, "come, let us sit for a while."

"Yes, I want to ask you about that." Madeline said as she followed. "What would have happened if you hadn't found me? I mean how are you planning to do this if I don't agree?"

"I live in hope that you will not refuse. The prophecy said you would be the one who brings us success. I mean, you and Simon will somehow bring us success on our quest."

"So, without me and Simon you won't be successful?"

"The prophecy does not say we will fail without you, only that you will make us successful." She flicked her hands out in frustration, "I don't know why you don't understand this. These things we know as we know how to speak."

"And you are willing to put all these people at risk if I don't agree. You are still going to take them into a dangerous situation on the chance you will win."

Arabela's eyes sparkled with anger, or regret, Madeline couldn't tell. "If we don't go, Sayer will lead his tribe into the Summer Lands and destroy everything in his path. He will leave our fields burned to the ground and salted to barrenness. Then he will move on to destroy our allies. These people are doomed because a child died generations ago; I must go on this quest. If you choose not to come, you are the one turning certainty to chance, not me."

"Don't try to make me feel bad about this." Madeline felt guilt descend like a weight. "You kidnapped me and brought me here. I had no choice, no obligation, no clue this even existed." She waved her arm around the field. "You had no right to bring me here, and no right to make me feel guilty for not wanting to jump blindly into some violent confrontation."

Arabela stood and stamped her foot, tears of rage flowing down her cheeks. "I had every right to do what I had to do to save my people. I have to do this, how can you think I would close my eyes to the future."

"Your future, not mine," Madeline stood and threw up her hands. "Your people not mine. How do I know that I won't have to die to make your quest a success? How do you know I won't have to kill? I have no skills in combat. I hate physical violence. I don't know what you need me to do."

"Ladies," Jode's voice cut beneath the heated shouts from the two women. Madeline had not noticed him approaching as she surrendered to her temper. "This is not going to solve anything. You are disturbing the camp and causing fear in your allies."

Madeline looked around, her rage subsiding in the absence of confrontation. Every person in the field had stopped working. Goblin eyes were blinking at them; she could see Jugg start towards them, his face serious. The Eldmen were standing in a line holding their curved swords across their bodies; looking prepared for battle.

"It would be better for you to talk inside where Blu can keep the sound contained."

"I have no intention of hiding away and letting someone bully me into something I don't want to do." Madeline said forcing her voice to stay below a shout.

"I would not force you to do anything. I would think your own conscience would make you agree to help. If not, then I will ask Blu to send you home." Arabela spat the words, contempt obvious in her sneer.

"I'm done here," Madeline turned and walked away carefully managing her steps gently and avoiding a childish stamp.

She heard Arabela's voice behind her. "I will not be held up as wrong by that woman. I will be with Blu if she comes to her senses."

7

Madeline tried to walk off her anger and, she had to admit, fear. It didn't work. After walking back and forth for fifteen minutes, she realized that she would have to go outside the walls or substitute curiosity for space as a remedy for anger. Rather than ask for an escort outside, Madeline decided to explore the house.

The inside was warm and servants bustled back and forth arms full of linens, dishes and other items for the feast. She could hear musicians practicing somewhere in the back of the building. Wandering upstairs, she felt like she was walking through a movie set.

On the second floor, she turned left walking the length of the corridor, and back for five minutes. She followed the layout, a capital H, the bottom portion one large room, the sides corridors lined with small rooms.

It wasn't going to be easy to burn off this adrenaline or whatever was driving her brain in circles and making her feel like jumping up and down. She decided to do one more lap and try to get into the large mystery room.

The door, on the far side from her room, was unlocked and it led to a library. The walls were covered with shelves, bound books, scrolls, and stacks of paper with drawings and words filling the entire surface. Madeline felt peace start to descend on her mind. Reading may be the only way to cure this state she'd worked herself into. All she needed was a snack and drink, and she'd sit in that blood-red wingback chair near the window.

She returned to the library with a tray of fruit, cheese and a jug of wine, anticipating a lazy afternoon. Putting down the tray, she picked up one of the sheets of paper, pictures of flowers randomly drawn over the surface each had a few words marked down beside it. Words that made no sense to her, "No, oh, please no," she whispered feeling tears of disappointment rise. "Okay, maybe that's a scientific language. You can't read much Latin beyond legal phrases, that's probably this world's version."

She turned to the opposite wall and pulled down a book covered in a brown leathery material. She flipped it open to a random page. Words ran across from one side to another, apparently they hadn't invented margins here. The words were unreadable, "Damn it all to hell." She placed the book back on the shelf.

"Madeline," Jode's voice came from the doorway. "The kitchen maids told me where you were. Are you all right?"

"No, I wanted some peace and quiet and a good read for an hour. Is that too much to ask? I can't make life changing decisions on the turn of a moment."

"I understand. I think that is a good idea. Stepping away from the details will help you choose the right path. But you were not happy when I came in."

"Right, the translation spell doesn't work for reading. I can't make head or tail of any of the words." She flopped down into the chair. "How am I supposed to get away from the problem if I can't read any of these books?"

Jode chuckled and Madeline felt her pulse race, maybe with desire, but probably with annoyance. Her mood was delicately balanced between reasonable thought and mindless rage at the moment, and she felt it tipping onto the you will regret this side of the equation. "Why is that funny, damn you."

"Unless you are a scholar of ancient script you wouldn't be able to read the contents of this library. In fact, I'm sure even Blu can't read half of the books here."

"Oh," relief cut through her rage. "How was I supposed to know, the only library I could get into is a collection of learned books. It figures. So, where can I find something I can read?"

"What would you like? I can get you fictional stories, history books, travel books. What would help you with settling your mind?"

"Fictional, no, history, no…" she shrugged then curled into the corner of the chair's wing. "I don't have a clue. Look, instead of reading, maybe we can talk and you could tell me what you think I should do. I promise to keep my temper; I need some advice. Then definitely a book, one I can read later to help me sleep."

Jode pulled a second chair from the corner. "I cannot tell you what you should do. I am not unbiased in this situation. I can listen, perhaps that will help."

"Answer some questions, then. I have so many questions running around my brain it's hard to focus on a decision when I'm so ignorant about the situation."

"Of course, ask what you will and I will answer as truthfully as I know how." He settled back in the chair and crossed his legs.

Madeline tried not to lick her lips as she looked at him but it was hard, very hard. This man made her feel uncomfortable and supremely comfortable all at the same time. She wasn't ready to feel this way, she couldn't leave her heart here when she went home, and she was going home, either now, or at the end of this quest, but definitely she was going home.

"Let's start with Lady Arabela's husband. What was his name and what kind of man was he."

"His given name was Alric. He was strong in both body and will. Arabela married him to join the two lands, Summer Lands and Spring Valley. They loved each other deeply and this love flowed over the cup of their lives into the lives of their people. When Alric was killed, the people wanted to leave immediately to punish Sayer Goddard. Arabela cautioned them to patience; to wait until a plan could be made, a plan that would have a more auspicious fate than simple attack."

"And Simon and I are the auspicious fate," Madeline said. "How can that be? We don't know anything about your world. Neither of us are warriors, we're better at words than fists."

"Perhaps words are what are needed?"

"Oh, yeah, we'll shout this Sayer Goddard to death. Great plan."

"Perhaps you will cut him to death with your sharp wit?" Jode smiled to soften the words.

Madeline giggled again, "won't be the first time for me. Anyway, what do you really think we can do? The prophecy can't just be that we will make the difference, there must be something else."

"That is a question I have no answer for, Madeline. I was with Lady Arabela during the ritual, but all I heard was Blu say two people from another world would bring about a successful end to the feud."

"How did you know it was us?"

"I didn't," he sat forward in the chair, suddenly intent. "The spell found you; I was the tool of the spell when I came to your world. Blu sent a disruption spell through with me; I think that's why you were on the stairs when I found you."

"Hang on," Madeline frowned. "You mean you didn't come to get me and Simon? I thought we rose in the mists of the prophesy or something."

"No, I reached out my hand, or rather the spell did, at the right moment and I held Simon's hand."

"This gets weirder the more you tell me." She pulled herself upright and drew her legs into the lotus position, hoping it would draw her mind into a clearer state. "I am afraid I will do more damage than help. What if I can't do what is needed?"

"You will."

"What do you think might be needed?"

"That is one of the questions I cannot answer, I don't know what you will bring to the quest that cannot already be there." He touched her knee, fire ran up her thigh, and pulled back his hand quickly. "You have already made a difference in many small ways."

"So, maybe my role is to come here, learn what the problem is, and then go back and find the right person to help you."

"I doubt it. Lady Arabela's blood found you. The spell found the right person, or people. Remember, Simon has a role."

"Maybe I was brought here to support Simon? He tells me he wants to stay here in your world." Madeline felt the pain of frustration rise from her chest. "I don't know what to do. I want to do the right thing," tears slid down her cheeks; "I don't like not knowing. What should I do?"

"I can't tell you what to decide." He passed her a linen handkerchief. "I can advise you to listen to your feelings. Something is causing these tears. Is it fear? Are you afraid to fail, or afraid to commit to something you don't fully understand?"

She wiped her cheeks and her nose; damn she wasn't a pretty crier. "Yes, and I don't know. It's fear, I can feel my stomach tense every time I try to commit to a decision. I don't know what it is I'm afraid of."

Jode reached up and tucked a stray curl behind her ear. "You need time. I advise you to talk to Blu, or Lady Arabela, that is if you can stop yourself from shouting."

"I'm not sure I can stop fighting her until I decide. I look at her confidence and feel weak. I see the disappointment and hurt in her eyes when she thinks I will refuse."

"You see the truth in her then." Jode shrugged and changed the subject. "Perhaps you need some fresh air, would it help to walk in a less busy environment? I will happily walk with you by the lake, or through parts of the woods."

She shook her head, "No, I feel quiet here. I need to think for a while. Thank you for talking to me, I'm sorry about the tears."

"Never apologize for your passion. Think for a while," he bowed. "Please talk to Lady Arabela. Tell her how frightened you are. She isn't as blind on revenge as you think; she may be able to help you."

"Maybe," Madeline sighed. "I will try, I promise."

"I would like to ask something of you," Jode looked down at his hands.

"Ask away, I can hardly refuse to listen since you were kind enough to tell me so much."

"I do not wish to add to your confusion, but I must tell you that I have come to admire you."

"Wait," Madeline put her hands out to stop Jode.

"Please," he held her hands in his own. "I would like to court you. I know that you have many difficult things to worry over. This is not to add to your worries but to help alleviate them."

"How can this not add to the pressure?"

"You are not obligated to anything. If you agree to be courted, I will be able to help you with your decisions. I will at least be an ally; you need someone to talk to."

Madeline felt her emotions run through the full range from anger to relief. She felt angry that Jode would ask, and relieved that someone wanted to be an ally. It was not that anyone was acting like an enemy exactly but she did feel like she was pushing against everyone's expectations. "It would not be fair to you." Her voice was low.

"When I first saw you I felt my world change. I am already half in love with you; it would only be fair to allow me to explore the other half." Jode pulled her hands closer.

"No," Madeline felt something harden in her chest. "I will not make any commitments until I have decided what I need to do."

Jode released her hands, “I will not beg. You need to have time to clear your thoughts; I understand that. I will leave you to your decision.”

He left, closing the door quietly behind him, cutting off the gentle sounds from the musicians, sounds that seemed familiar to Madeline.

8

Jode walked toward the sound of stringed instruments rising and falling in an unfamiliar tune. He smiled; new music for the feast was a good omen for the journey. The sweet sound of the gutier played notes slowly then quickly and a sudden drum repeated bang, bang, bang, bang. A voice sang in a harsh tone, I see a red door… and the music collapsed into noise. Jode thought, if that is an example of the new music, I wonder if it will be a good omen.

He found the musicians practicing in a small room at the end of the ballroom. Pushing aside the curtain, he saw Simon leaning over a sheet of music with goblins grouped around muttering together.

"What is going on in here? That noise is the least musical sound I have ever heard."

Simon looked up and answered, "you aren't kidding, these guys have the music down, in fact they are very good at new sounds, but Christ that voice. Man, we need a lead singer."

"Was that supposed to be singing?" Jode covered his ears in mock pain. "Even I can sing better than that. Was it a ballad?"

"I guess, if you can have a ballad to grief and pain," Simon said taking another paper and sharpening a pencil with a small knife. "I'm trying to help these guys with some music for the party. Do you know what kind of songs would be best? Is there dancing?"

"It would be best to provide the usual music," Jode glanced at the four goblins who looked crestfallen at his words. "What music do you have to offer?" He relented.

"Maybe it would be better to have something a bit more oldie first. We can bring the music up to date later." Simon drew some marks on a piece of paper and handed it to the musicians. "Try this, guys. I'll write out the words, Jode, if you can really sing I would love to hear it."

The musicians passed the paper around then one picked up a flute and trilled a few notes. Simon turned back to them and nodded. "Look, try these words out." He passed the second piece of paper to Jode.

Jode listened, and then told the flautist to start again. After a few notes he sang, "it's not the pale moon that excites me."

"Wow, you really can sing, that puts the chairman to shame." Simon leaned back against the wall of the small room. "So, can you join these guys tonight, or are we totally instrumental in their first gig?"

"I cannot join the musicians, it would not be seemly."

Simon shook his head. "Dude, we can't let that voice go to waste. I've got hundreds of songs in my head; you would be perfect for a Chris Isaac style, or Michael Buble, or, anyone, I can train you up to be the biggest rock star in this world. The chicks will be hanging all over you."

Jode put up his hand to stop the rush of words. "I do not know these people you mention. I have no idea why a flock of baby chickens attached to me would be desirable, and I don't know what a dude is. I have duties that require me to be with Lady Arabela and have no time to practice with this group of musicians."

"No time, or no desire?"

"My desire is not important, I have duties."

Simon grinned, "You can't let that voice go to waste. Hey, if it's about the rock and roll thing, I can put the scores of some serious music on paper. I have a kind of musical photographic memory; I guess it's a phonographic memory."

"What the future will offer me as choices I do not know. For now, I need to talk to you about helping Lady Arabela destroy this enemy." Jode took one more look at the group huddled around sheets of music and sighed. "Will you come and sit with me over a cup of wine? I am looking for your advice."

"Sure." Simon waved goodbye to the band. No one noticed, they were watching as one assembled something from a set of wires, tiles, and sounding boxes. "I'm totally in heaven here. Look at them assembling that keyboard."

Jode stopped at the kitchen to pick up a jug of wine and two pottery cups, and then they walked outside where the grounds were still bustling with people. They sat on a stone bench against the wall of the building and Jode poured two mugs of red wine. "These people are willing to throw their lives at certain death for Lady Arabela's command." Jode pointed to the groups, now working together to build fires in the empty areas between camps. "Are you willing to come?"

Simon nodded, "I don't know what I can do to contribute but I'm in; I'm in need of an adventure before I settle down. If that involves saving the beautiful princess from the evil usurper, sign me up."

"It could mean your death, are you not concerned?"

Simon drained the wine and refilled both mugs. "The way I look at it, I'll die someday. I can live a long time if I am careful, or a short time if I'm stupid. I don't want to look back on a long life with a list of regrets." He nodded up to the second floor of the building. "Madeline is having a hard time, but she's not the same as me. I'm willing get involved in what is happening; she's worried about committing to something that might happen."

"Do you know how I can, or how anyone can, help her with this decision? I must confess I wish I could take away her fears, but I don't know how."

"Yeah, I'd noticed you watching her. Man, you picked a hard one to fall for."

"I don't think I picked her, I think she was picked for me." Jode laughed. "What a fate. I have found my match in a woman who wishes only to go somewhere I cannot follow." He slapped Simon on the shoulder; Simon grunted. "Ah well, fate will have its way. How well do you know her? Is there something I can say that will help her? At this moment, I care not whether she chooses to help or to return to your world. I care only that her pain be eased."

"You are going to need to let her work it through. I know her well enough that she won't take well to you taking charge. If she needs anything, she'll ask for it."

"Ah, she asked me questions about the history of the Summer Lands." He leaned back against the sun-warmed wall. "Perhaps I have already provided her with something that will help her."

"Maybe, but I wouldn't count on her being satisfied with it. I know that she likes a fight, usually not a physical one true, but part of her problem is that she does want to help. If she decides to stay, no matter what conditions she applies, she will be all in. She'll be a giant pain in the ass, but she will give the quest her heart and her soul."

"Then we must wait for her decision." Jode took a long drink of the wine. "Now, Simon, tell me about this music. I confess, like the musicians, I find myself drawn by the thought of new songs."

"I was part of a group of musicians; we call them bands, when I was younger. I always wanted to go back to that when I had the money and time. Now, maybe, I'll have the time." Simon paused and the sound of a piano floated out. "It seems your instruments have a similar sound, even if they look completely different from ours."

"That is another new tune. What is it called?"

"Didn't I blow your mind this time," Simon answered. "It's a great last song at a party, nice and slow. Lets you get close and cuddly."

"It is a sad song I think. Give me the words, and then we will see what the song sounds like. It will be something to help pass the time on the journey." Jode rose and picked up the empty mugs and the jug. "I must return to Lady Arabela. She will need my assistance in planning the journey."

9

Waking up after her all-afternoon nap, Madeline stretched all the kinks out of her body, and picked up the still full jug and plate and took them to her room. There was a dress of forest green fabric laid across the bed, white embroidered slippers on the floor waiting for her feet. She ran her fingertips across the cloth; it was like fine velvet, smooth under her fingers. "I love this," she said then ran to the convenience to freshen up, returning quickly to change.

Elise was in the room when she came back. "Madeline, I hope you enjoyed your day," she said while putting the dress away.

"I slept most of it away in the library," Madeline watched Elise change the beautiful green dress for a plain beige and green set. The white embroidered slippers had disappeared too, in their place a pair of unadorned brown ones. "Why are you putting the clothes away?"

"They were for the feast. It has been postponed until tomorrow. The Lady decided to wait one more day before starting out. That will give the seamstress time to make you a more suitable dress for the party."

"Why can't I wear the other dress?" Madeline looked at the soft fabric of the dress hanging in the closet.

"It is not appropriate for this evening."

"But, it's beautiful."

"Yes," Elise shut the wardrobe door. "But too pretty for tonight."

"Will I get to wear it sometime?"

"If you are staying," Elise smiled and raised her eyebrows, "there will be plenty of opportunities."

"Do you know where Arabela is?" Madeline hid her disappointment in the plainness of the clothes and started to dress. "I need to talk to her."

"She will be with the priest now, you'll find her in the dining room soon," Elise tied the strings of the overdress behind Madeline's back. "I think she will be talking to the servants in preparation for tomorrow."

Madeline patted her loose curls and tucked a strand behind her ear. The dress and slippers fit her perfectly and despite the plain cut, she liked the look.

"I'll go in search of her, then," she said and turned to the door with a quick goodbye to Elise.

As Madeline walked down the stairs, she heard the music again this time she knew the song, Jammin by someone who had never heard of Bob Marley or reggae music. The voice was not bad; it added a gravelly Tragically Hip quality to the song. "Simon, you're having too much fun," Madeline muttered as she headed towards the sound. When she opened the curtain screening the small room, laughter bubbled out of her.

Simon was trying to sing the original beat while three goblins were playing their own version of the song. Somehow, they had found a way to turn their hair into dreadlocks. A fourth goblin was reading a stack of papers. He looked up at her when she disturbed them and cocked his head on the side.

"Is the music not pleasing? Simon tells us we are not doing it properly but it is good." He stepped forward. "I am Dox; I play on the drums."

"Madeline," she shook hands. "I think the music is great. How did you change your hair so quickly? It looks very much like the original singer in my world."

"Ah, you do not know goblins." He grinned widely, uneven teeth showing from side to side. "Watch," he closed his eyes and Madeline saw the long dreadlocks untwist and somehow shorten until the goblin had only a few inches of curly black hair all over his head.

"Oh, that's wonderful," She didn't know what else to say.

"Yes, I sketched a picture of Bob Marley for them and they changed their hair in honor of the master. I'm not sure if it will be amusing for anyone else but I liked it, too." Simon walked over as the song ended. "I think we've invented a new song genre. What would you call it?"

"Reggae lounge. It sounded like Frank Sinatra crossed with Michael Stipe and blended in a tropical drink."

"We do need a new lead singer; these guys could murder every song I know," Simon turned and gave the band a thumbs up sign as they started to play some version of Wild Night; one neither

Van Morrison or John Mellencamp would have recognized very easily.

"I hope you aren't getting started on something that you won't be able to finish. You shouldn't make plans you can't follow through on."

"Not a problem. It's like the old rock and roll on our world. Now it's started it can't be stopped. I plan to be a part of this as long as I can."

Madeline didn't want to discuss Simon's future, on this world or otherwise. Putting aside her frustration, she wished them luck and turned to walk back across the room to the kitchens. Arabela might be with her priest for a while so Madeline decided she had time grab a pre-dinner snack to keep her blood sugar up, and maybe her temper down.

She was determined not to lose it; it was important to have a calm conversation with Arabela. If not, Madeline didn't think she would be able to get to the point where she could make the right decision. A decision based on facts and information not stubbornness or guilt. She knew that if she stayed she would have to do so without reservations.

The kitchen was busy; large cauldrons of soup boiled on the fire; small animal carcasses turned on a spit over another. As Madeline crossed to the table, one of the women took a tray of bread from one of the vast ovens on either side of the fire. On shelves along the left wall stood what looked like cakes and pies.

"May I have some bread and cheese," she asked a passing woman, "and some caf, please."

The food and drink appeared in front of her and she filled her stomach while she watched the preparations. It looked like the meal tonight would be a light one, probably in preparation for tomorrow. "Are you feeding the people in the yard?" She asked two women sitting opposite her having a break while the pots simmered.

"The soup will be offered to add to their provisions. But, no, they feed themselves from the game in the woods and the supplies they carry." A blond woman answered, wiping her shining face in her apron.

"We will serve the household and the remainder will feed the overnight workers."

Madeline glanced down at her plate, "I'm sorry, it's my fault you had to do this extra work." She knew that her indecision had consequences; she didn't like facing them.

"Not at all, now that the feast has been postponed, we can prepare special food. Food that is as important as the event the feast is celebrating. I didn't care for the haste of making a feast for tonight," a redhead in braids said.

"Yes, head cook was in a fine temper this morning trying to work out how to create a meal for so many different tastes in such a short period of time. He was a lot happier when the Lady came and changed the night," said the blonde.

"And the musicians will have more time to practice this new style of song. I heard them earlier and it's very interesting. I could feel my feet starting to tap without my mind driving them. It's a very exciting beat." She moved her head to the faint sound of LA Woman.

"Yes, it's certainly interesting," Madeline felt a pang of jealousy at how easily Simon had become part of this world. Then she smiled imagining the goblins with a Billy Idol platinum spike look. "I'm sure it will become more and more interesting over the next few days."

"Elga, Jossa, back to work." A large bull of a man called from the far side of the room.

"Head cook," the blonde acknowledge him with a nod. "I see his normal humor is back."

The two women returned to the vats of soup and stirred before using a spoon to taste the contents. One added some red powder from a jar on the mantle of the vast hearth.

"I was worried about you," Arabela's said sitting down beside Madeline. "I hope you enjoyed your walk."

"I found the library and passed the day there," Madeline poured caf into a mug for Arabela. "Unfortunately, I slept the afternoon away rather than reading."

Arabela laughed. "I have slept a few afternoons away there too. If you like reading I'll have Blu find some lighter fare for you; I don't think you will be able to decipher the books in there."

"I appreciate it but, Jode promised to bring me a book or two. I miss having one on my night table." Madeline reminded herself to stay calm and not get angry as she moved to a more difficult topic. "I was wondering if we could talk."

"Of course, we can take our food to the large dining room if you like. It is set for dinner with some of our allies." She picked up the jug and motioned Madeline to follow her. "I have an urge to listen more closely to this music before dinner."

Madeline rolled her eyes, "I think the dining room is a good idea. I'm sure the musicians will be happy to have you listen."

The two women sat at a table next to a wall of French doors.

"I've been thinking this over and over and I have not been able to come to a decision," Madeline started. "I know how important you think it is that I stay. I don't know what I can contribute."

"The prophecy said you were the one who would make the difference. Simon will help, but it said you were our success. I don't understand why you cannot just believe."

"I'm not a person who just believes; I'm sorry." Madeline sighed and listened to the strains of the Eagles, Peaceful Easy Feeling come from behind the curtain. "Why do you think I am important? What could you possibly have missing in your company that I will provide?"

"Can you fight with a sword or bow?"

"No, well not really, I fence for a hobby and I can ride a horse, at least at a trot and when I'm properly outfitted." She lifted the green dress. "Not in this."

The voice that came from behind the curtain was warm and fully in harmony with the music, and with the intent of the words. It wasn't Simon, his voice was fine but this one was top quality.

"It is good then, that we have no need for sword fighting." Arabela seemed to be thinking, her fingers were tracing circles on the tablecloth. "If it was so simple we would not have had to endanger Sir Jode."

"There are many people on my world who would fight this battle for you. There are mercenaries that will take the contract if you can pay."

"What are you suggesting?" Arabela looked up sharply. "My warriors are the best in the land. They do not need someone to fight for them."

"Okay, let's not get all worked up again. That's not going to get us anywhere." Madeline heard the twang of a guitar come from the curtain. Then Simon's voice started the lyrics to Colin James' Why'd You Lie, one of her favorites. "I was suggesting maybe I could find someone who would be better than me. I could go back and send them here. Or, could you ask for another prophecy?"

"No, this one was clear, and we don't have time. I must complete the quest before the next moon, or I will be showing my pregnancy and not be able to journey." Arabela firmed her lips. "Why are you afraid? I find it hard to believe the prophecy called for a coward to help us defeat Sayer Goddard."

"I'm not a coward. I'm just trying to make sense of why it chose me." Madeline could hear the whine in her voice.

"If you were one of my subjects I could just order you to come."

"You would dictate someone to go to a possible death?"

"If it would save many more than died, yes," Arabela said. "But, my subjects do not need to be ordered to do their duty."

"And you know what is best," Madeline kept her voice low but the words were being forced through her lips. "Where I come from you would be called a dictator and would be condemned for oppressing the people."

"Oppressing, I don't care for this word, nor do I care for dictator." Arabela's voice was calm but her eyes focused on Madeline's, her force of will pinning Madeline in her seat, demanding a response.

"I don't care if you like it or not, you are one," Madeline answered.

"Why? Would you allow people to choose their ruler?" Arabela started to laugh, and then stifled it as she realized Madeline was serious. "People would choose the person who promised them the most. Madeline, I've been trained to rule all my life. My every thought is focused on the wellbeing of my people and this is the least I can do. Did you not understand when we told you what would happen if Goddard is not stopped? The future of my subjects is only possible if we succeed. How can you not help?"

"The question is how can I help? That's what I keep asking myself. If I say yes to you and I can't do what is needed then I will have caused more trouble for you and the people you claim to love," she stood.

"Please," Arabela reached out her hand. "We need to know your answer. The company leaves the morning after tomorrow. You must answer by then or we go to uncertain fates."

"I will give you an answer; will you accept it, even if it is not what you want?"

"I will not force you." Arabela stood and walked away.

Madeline watched her go, knowing her decision was probably made, but unwilling to commit until there was no choice. The new singer was attempting A kiss from a Rose, the sound was right but the soul was missing.

10

An hour of walking around the camp didn't help Madeline come to a decision she felt comfortable with. She returned to the dining room in time to see Simon coming through the curtain as she stepped into the brighter light of the dining room. The room itself was empty of everyone except staff clearing the bowls and cups from the tables.

"Hey," Simon called across the room. "You missed our debut."

"Sorry, how did it go?"

"Mixed reactions, some of it was a hit and some of it not so great. Mellow Wind, that's the name of the band, needs to find a style." Simon waved goodnight to the four goblins who wandered out into the garden talking together excitedly, their crazy hair slicked back like some big band act. "You look like crap."

"Thanks that helps so much," Madeline slapped his arm. "I can't get my head around this problem. I feel like I've been worrying about the same issue for weeks. It's only been two days, but it feels like my entire existence has been changed and I'm supposed to hit the ground running in this new paradigm."

"Duh, your whole world has been changed. Look, you know you can't worry this for any longer. It's not fair to anyone, you included." Simon winked at a passing server, the blonde girl from the kitchen, and she smiled back.

"If I'm interrupting anything, please let me know, I would hate for my identity crisis to interfere with your sex life."

"No sex life, yet," he sighed. "I'm not ready to catch a disease, or get a girl in trouble, until I know more about this world and what's going to happen in the next few weeks."

"How noble of you, I need to talk this through with someone who might understand. Can you spare some time?"

"Happy to," he took her arm. "John leaves in the evening. Sneak out on Elise and come to my room. We can talk undisturbed for as long as you need."

"I would rather not try to sneak out, it isn't fair to her. I don't know what punishment she might get if she is supposed to keep track of me. I'll wait in the library, you come there."

"Give me half an hour," he looked her over, noticing the paleness of her skin and the slight frown lines between her eyebrows. "Should I bring food? You look like you are about to pass out."

"I don't think I could eat, at least not until I make this decision. If you need to eat bring food for yourself."

She stood at the window of the library watching the shadows of people passing between the bright campfires until the door opened behind her, turning the window to a mirror for a second.

Her reflection was ghostly; she understood what Simon meant when he said she looked like crap.

"I grabbed a sandwich before I came up." He placed two mugs and two jugs on the stool she'd used as a table. "I brought caf and wine. I think you should start with the wine, you need loosening up."

"That's a fast road to alcoholism," she said, pouring a mug of wine. "What the hell."

"I may have worked out a way to help."

"What, you found the spell to send me home?"

"Nice, if you aren't interested in working this out let me know. I can find something easier to do with my evening."

"Sorry," she sipped the wine. "What's your plan?"

"I think you are trying too hard to incorporate everything into your decision. When you need to cross examine a witness you focus on only the really important questions, right?"

"That's true, what do you think I should ignore?"

"Not so fast." Simon leaned against a wall of books and sipped his wine. "Forget what you should ignore; focus on what is important to your decision. It's not about what I think; it's about what you think. To be honest, I don't remember you ever thinking about what other people wanted or thought when you were working."

"Am I really that self centered?" Madeline felt her defensiveness rise and mentally calmed it to a manageable level.

"No, well yes, but not the way you mean. You have this ability to put aside all inconsequential details and find the points that matter and will help you win the case or argument. What is it you say?" Simon paused, and then nodded. "It doesn't matter who the politician is sleeping with; it only matters if they are honest with the tax money."

"The key pieces are less clear in this situation, though. It's not a win or lose situation. Stay or go I will always feel I've given something important up."

"That's the difference between us. I have no problem giving up the past, I see the possibility in the future and it excites me. Madeline, I will stay if I can, but if you decide to go and I have to go to make that happen I will."

"Why?"

"I can find a new possibility there or here. I'm not tied to a place, and it turns out, I'm not tied to a world for my identity. You aren't that way; I couldn't live with myself if I forced you to stay."

"Crap, that doesn't make my choice easier. I thought we were trying to help make the decision not remind me how complicated it was."

"There's the difference. My decision is mine to make, and I've made it. You don't have to make me happy, it's not your responsibility here anymore than it was in our world."

"So, my decision should be based on things I can control, right?" She was starting to feel as though she had direction, the past few hours had been like walking through a dense cloud looking for a way out. "Okay, I can control what I decide, but I need Arabela if my decision is to go home. I need a lot more if the decision is to stay."

"Like what?"

"Information about this world, training and some fucking clue as to what I'm supposed to do."

"Do you need that now?"

"Yes," she frowned at his raised eyebrow. "No? I guess if I stay, I have time to figure out what I'm supposed to do. So, that shouldn't form part of my decision. But what if Arabela won't send me home?"

"My take, is that she won't make you stay. I don't think she would be so loved by her people, and she is if you haven't caught that yet, if she didn't stand by her word."

"I guess, well I can control that. If I decide to stay I can have her make a written agreement to send me home after the quest is over."

"Good idea," He yawned. "Sorry, it's been a long day."

"What are you going to do here?" She waved her hands to stop him speaking. "Not that I will need it to make my decision, I'm just curious."

"I'm going to build an entertainment business. You heard that group of goblins. It took them about an hour to figure out how to play almost every genre I know. It's not perfect but it's not about copying the originals, it's about them finding their own rock and roll." His eyes sparkled as he spoke. "Imagine what they could do with symphonies if they pick up popular music that fast."

“I’ll tick worrying about you off my list of things that get in the way of my decision then. What did their music sound like before you got to them?”

“A cross between Japanese and Apala,” Simon saw the question on her face. “It’s drum music from Nigeria. And, I’m not planning to bury that style, just open them up to a more varied songbook.”

“I had no idea you were a musical scholar.”

“I’ve done some research. Stop running away from your problem, it’s not about me, remember.” Simon raised a finger and shook it at her.

“Yeah, yeah, okay, let’s say I go home. I need to know what that offers, if I follow your reasoning. What I’m going home to is a key piece of information. Regardless of how much time has passed there I could go back to a legal practice and become a partner, or open my own firm.” She wasn’t looking at Simon anymore; she was staring into the fire. “I’ve worked so hard to get there I don’t know if I have any other choices.”

“You always have choices; you just need to have the guts to change.”

“Thanks, that’s twice today I’ve been called a coward.” She waved off his protest. “Okay, I could change careers. I could open a bookstore, or a cooking school. Or, better yet, a cooking school with a bookstore attached.”

“Really?”

“Yes, I’m not just a one track mind, despite appearances.”

“So what stopped you?”

"Everyone else's expectations," she sighed. "It takes a lot to turn your back on everyone who helped you get where they thought you wanted to go."

"What if you stayed? After the quest was over you could do that here, not that they need help with cooking. You could introduce a few different cuisines; as good as it is, I'm getting a bit tired of meat and potatoes."

"What if the quest is only successful if I die?"

"So, can you control that?"

"I could go home."

"That's not control, that's avoid."

"Fine," Madeline knew he was right. "So, what would make staying the right choice for me, I guess is the real question."

Simon yawned again. "Sorry, sorry. I do need to get to bed soon. If we both fall asleep here there will be scandal."

"Go to bed, I can figure this out myself," Madeline rose. "I guess I should head to my bedroom, too, Elise might send out a search party."

Elise was napping in the chair by the fire when Madeline came in. The bath was set up, a kettle of hot water sitting on the hearth. A long soak before bed was probably the best idea.

Elise woke as Madeline tried to pick up the kettle and groaned at the weight. "Wait, let me." She fit a metal arm into a hinge on the side of the hearth. The hook on the end of the arm went through a chain and then onto the handle of the kettle. Elise worked a crank attached to the hinge and the kettle rose and swung over to the bath. The hot water steamed and she tipped the kettle to empty the contents into the bath.

"You look tired," Elise said. "I'll put some lavender in your bath it will help you sleep."

As she closed her eyes and lay back, Madeline tried to ignore the little voice that whispered there's one other thing to think about if you go home, one person.

Elise woke her out of the doze before the water was cold and helped her into the nightdress. Madeline fell asleep to the sound of a crackling wood fire.

11

Madeline woke the next morning to find a tray of breakfast food on the table and a steaming mug of caf on the hearth. The light coming through the window was pale and weak; she hoped it was just past dawn because if it was later this light probably meant a shitty day. She ran to the convenience before eating even though her stomach seemed to be crawling out of her throat to get at the food.

Standing at the window, she munched on toasted bread spread with honey, and sipped from a large mug of caf between bites. She watched people in the yard get ready to leave. A line of packed wagons lined up at the near end where the passage between the wall and the house was widest. The tents were still up and the fires still tended but it was clear to her that this camp was preparing to up stakes and move. Probably tomorrow morning, since tonight is the feast, she thought. "No more delay, I guess I'd better dress and go find Arabela. It's time to strike a deal."

The trousers she wore yesterday lay on the chair with a pale yellow shirt on top. The boots were set near the fire. On top of the shirt were two garments that seemed familiar but not quite right.

She picked them up and realized the first was underwear; thank god. Madeline was not comfortable going commando. The second looked like a set of straps sewn together at right angles. The ends of the straps hung loose, obviously meant to be tied. "I guess it's a bra," she muttered. She wrapped one set of straps around her body, twisted and turned to try to figure out how to deal with the other straps. She looked up at the sound of a hearty laugh from the doorway, Elise stood there, hand over her mouth.

"I'm sorry," she said pushing the door shut quickly. "I don't think anyone saw you."

"Stop laughing at me and come show me how this is supposed to work." Madeline held out the bra hanging it from her fingertips.

"I'm sorry, that was not polite, but you did look funny. I suppose you wouldn't realize the seamstress wouldn't make something too complicated to use." She took the straps. "I want to thank you for inventing this. I have one on," she pointed to her breasts, sitting much higher and firmer than yesterday. "The seamstress is busy turning them out in different sizes; she can't keep up with the demand. I can run around and up and down stairs without bouncing around all over the place."

"That's the point, although some women in my world refuse to use them." Madeline watched as Elise arranged the straps into a pair of shoulder straps and two cup like arrangements. She slipped it over her shoulder then Elise passed the longer straps around the back, then around the front again.

"Take these and give them a tug until you are comfortable," she instructed. "The size should adapt to you and then you just tie them and let the ends hang down the front. I'll trim them when you are set so you don't have to worry about tucking them in."

"There, God that feels great." She stretched and the bra moved with her and resettled comfortably. "If I go back I'm taking this with me. It will be the next best invention in women's lingerie." She picked up the yellow shirt and buttoned it closed then pulled on the boots. "You said that I would have enough clothes to take with me on the quest if I wanted to," Elise nodded. "Are they ready?"

"Yes, the clothes are packed in a traveling case for you and will be taken in the service wagons. There will be three other sets of trousers and shirts, a dress, just in case, two pairs of boots and slippers. On a journey people usually sleep in their day clothes so they can leave quickly if needed."

"Good," Madeline looked around the bedroom. "I'll miss this, will you be coming too?"

"No, my duty is here. There will be women in the camp who can tend you if need be. Then you have decided to go with the Lady?"

"I'll let you know," Madeline said, not ready to broadcast her decision. "Do you know where I'll find Arabela right now?"

"Downstairs, in the large dining room, she is meeting with the leaders of the allies to plan the route. If you wish to speak with her I'm sure she will allow the interruption."

The room was undergoing a transformation; servants moved around preparing for the departure feast. The tables were covered in brightly colored cloths, with contrasting napkins folded like swans at each place. New candles sat the wall sconces, and two young boys filled vases with huge bouquets.

Arabela sat at a table in next to the open French doors. Five others stood with her looking over what seemed to be a pile of maps. Jugg was standing on a chair to get enough height to lean over the paper. A feathered winged creature standing next to the goblin and an Eldman next to him or her, Madeline couldn't remember which sex was feathered and which was scaled. On Arabela's other side one of the tall white-skinned green-haired people was speaking and pointing out a path to the others. Jode's blond head turned from the group as Madeline walked into the room. He smiled at her and said something to Arabela who nodded and excused herself from the group.

"Good morning," she said approaching Madeline and gesturing to a table in the corner. "Have you come to your decision?"

"I have," Madeline said, sitting next to Arabela. Both women sat with their backs to the room, which gave Madeline a sense of privacy. "I will come but I need some assurances before I start out with you."

"I cannot give you assurances that you will be safe, I will try to keep you so but we are embarking on a dangerous quest, Madeline. There will probably be fatalities."

"That's not what I'm looking for; I want a contract that guarantees you will send me back after the quest is complete if I want to go."

"I'm not sure the spell translated that word, what is a contract?" Arabela's shook her head in confusion.

"It is a written agreement. A contract lays out all the actions we will each take and the terms that will define completion." Madeline started to tense up at having to explain the word. What if Arabela said no? What if she'd insulted her? Damn Simon, she should not have listened to him.

"I see. Why would you need such a document? Does my word not carry sufficient weight? Do you lack trust in my word?" Arabela straightened her back as she spoke.

"By writing it down we can make sure we both understand what we mean. I think we could easily misunderstand the intention if we just speak; we come from different worlds and words carry meanings that are not apparent. When things are written down it gives people an opportunity to make sure the right words are chosen." If she didn't agree, Madeline had no plan B.

"I have not found it to be so confusing. When people agree to something they agree." Arabela turned and pointed to the people, Madeline could only think of them as people, standing around the other table. "These others are here only on my word, we have no written agreement, and we don't need one."

"I do." Madeline stood firm despite the babbling fears fluttering between her stomach and head. "It is the way of my world. We have many years of examples why writing agreements down is important."

"I still do not agree," Arabela stood. "But, you may ask Blu to prepare this document if it is so important to you."

"Wait," Madeline said as Arabela started towards the planning table. "Do you want to be there when we write it?"

"No," Arabela looked surprised. "Our agreement is that you will come and do the best in your ability to help us succeed. I will do my best to train you and protect you during the time you are here. When we are successful, and I will not entertain the idea we will not be, I will send you back to your world if that is still your wish. What else would you write?"

"Can Simon stay if he wants?"

"Of course," Arabela looked puzzled for a moment. "I see you are worried about how your decision will affect him. No, the spell will not require him to return with you. You can both stay without causing great damage to your world. There you are not important in the grand scheme; here you are vital to our well being." She looked at the other table. "I think you are vital to more than that. I am glad you are staying. Thank you."

"You are very welcome," Madeline said to the receding back of the Lady of the Summer Lands.

Jode looked up and nodded, Madeline hoped it was to her but it could have been to Arabela. That thought brought a sour taste in her throat. Damn, she had no reason to be jealous. She was here to do a job then she was going home.

~~~

The priest was standing in the great doorway to the house. The sun shone on him and he raised his arms to the side and then above his head. Madeline was reminded of the pope giving a blessing. She waited until Blu turned and then walked towards him.

"I would be happy to help you," he said after Madeline had explained what she needed. "Come to the library, we will get it done right away." He took her arm and they walked up the staircase together.

"Why aren't you telling me I should just take her word? Arabela seemed put out that I needed a written document."

"Ah, written agreements are not unknown in this world. They are only used, though, when the two people do not trust each other, usually in settlement of a long and bloody war."
~~~

"It's not that I don't trust her."

Blu patted her arm, "no, it is that Arabela expects too much from you; you barely know each other and perhaps Arabela did not understand that you need to know someone before you trust them."

"Ah," Madeline smiled. "So, you know just what we need to do. Let's get it done then."

12

Blu carefully placed a sheet of blotting paper over the final signature on the document. "I will store this in the archives." He said. "It will become a part of our history. When we look back in future time, it will remind us of the woman who saved our land."

"I like your confidence in my abilities." Madeline said.

"Not so much your abilities, I am confident in the prophecy." Blu rolled the sheet and tied it with a pink ribbon.

"Now we must prepare you for the journey." Arabela stood and beckoned Madeline to the door. "Elise tells me your clothing is ready. We should meet with Simon and Jode to show you how to wear your weapons and riding clothes. We may be traveling through some poor weather and it is important for the two of you to know how to get at your sword even when you are bundled up in a cloak."

"I won't have to use a sword, will I?" Madeline asked. "I can ride well enough, but I have no idea how to ride and fight."

"Let us hope not, but it is best to be prepared."

Madeline felt like she was being pulled along by a powerful undertow. She was as helpless to stop, as she would be to save herself from drowning.

"Ah, John," Arabela said as he came from Simon's room. "Will you send Simon and Sir Jode to the fighting barn? We need to get these two ready for the journey. Please have someone take the riding gear and their swords there as well."

"Of course, my Lady," he bowed. "Should I bring Elise to show the proper way to put on the gear?"

"No, neither of you will be joining us. I don't want them to get dependent on your help." She smiled and steered Madeline to the staircase.

"You know, I don't like being talked about as if I'm not here." Madeline said.

"What do you mean?" Arabela seemed genuinely surprised. "Did you have something to contribute to the conversation? If so, please in future feel free to speak."

"No, I didn't have anything to say," Madeline struggled to explain. "I am not used to being referred to as 'they' when I'm standing right there. In my world it would be polite to use my name."

"How interesting, I will try to remember that."

They reached the ground floor and Arabela led Madeline through the front door and past the sentries at the front gate. The sudden opening of her world made Madeline feel dizzy. For two days, she had lived enclosed in the wall of the castle. Her mind had been so focused on her decision that she'd forgotten what the world outside looked like.

About a half kilometer from the gate, the lake spread out in front of her the other shore so far distant she could only see it as a line of trees at the base of a hill; the woods they had arrived through on the left. Arabela steered her right, a quarter of the way around the outside of the wall. Along the way, Madeline watched people clearing the weeds from the lawn, or walking towards the lake, fishing poles in hand. There were soldiers taking a break from training, and a few people who had set up camp along the wall.

"This is where my soldiers train," Arabela explained as they approached a spacious stone building. "We will be taking only a small contingent of them. When we go we wish to appear as though we are traveling the land on a tour, not as though we are going to war."

"It makes sense. You're planning to sneak up on this Sayer Goddard and not give him a chance to form up an army."

"Goddard would not need a chance; he has a standing army ready to fight on an hour's notice. We wish not to alarm him; if we approach quietly we will have a better probability of success." Arabela pointed to a long wooden bench. "We can sit here while we wait for the others."

"Where are the horses?" Madeline didn't want to get into a talk about strategy, plenty of time for that on the road. "Will I choose my own?"

"The stables are further around the wall," Arabela pointed in the general direction of the back of the wall. "You can have the choice of horses if you wish. I will ask the stable master to pick five. You will then pick two, your primary and secondary mount. Would that suffice?"

"I think so," Madeline tried to push away the creeping feeling that Arabela was being too nice, too accommodating. It was suspicious.

"Ah, here is your equipment. Why don't we get started since the men have not yet arrived?"

"Sure," Madeline answered staring at the sword that a young boy had placed on top of the stack of leather straps and belts. "Um, is that supposed to be for me?"

"Yes," Arabela said. "It has been made for your height and sex. "You can practice with it and the sword master will make the adjustments." A large man wearing a leather apron and a lot of soot wandered up to the two women.

Arabela handed the sword, hilt first, to Madeline. It was not as heavy as it looked and Madeline worked through a few moves from fencing class; she would need to strengthen her wrists for this instrument.

Simon and Jode joined the group; Simon carried a much larger sword with him. "I expected some kind of elven carving and spells, it's just plain metal." He said showing Madeline the blade.

"I guess you can't have everything. Hey, maybe you could add pretty swords to your list of things to change here." She laughed.

"To make an instrument of painful death beautiful would be a new idea, indeed," Jode said. "I am glad to see you here, Madeline."

Before Madeline could respond, Arabela ordered Jode to show them how to attach the harnesses and sheaths for the swords. He turned to Simon and demonstrated the proper method of winding the belt around the waist and turning the belt harness into a back harness for riding. They made Madeline and Simon repeat the process each time faster than the last.

"You seem to be comfortable in the back harness," he finally said to Madeline. "And you, Simon, seem more able to quickly use the waist harness. I suggest you stay with that." While he spoke, he kept his eyes on Madeline, whose face glowed with the exercise.

"Before they choose," Arabela interrupted, "they should try drawing the sword. It would not do for Madeline to cut off an ear just because she was comfortable with the harness."

"It would truly be a pity to lose any part of Madeline." Jode blushed, "I mean we might need her whole to complete the task."

"Yes," Simon said, winking at Arabela behind Jode's back. "That might be the case."

Arabela laughed, "draw your weapons in the harness as it stands."

Both obeyed quickly; Simon pulled his weapon out awkwardly, not cutting anything off but in no position to use the blade. Madeline pulled her sword smoothly over her head with her right hand, the left rising to meet it mid- chest and support the sword, which now faced blade out perpendicular to her body. She felt the muscle memory take over and her reasoning mind step back as she moved.

"Perfect," Jode said quietly. "You are perfect."

"Yes, Madeline," Arabela added, "very good technique. We will give you opportunity to practice combat on the road with some of our better fighters, I think. You need a challenge and endurance practice. Now, Simon." She tapped her chin. "I think we need to give you basic training. Jode, will you take him on as a student?"

Jode turned his gaze from Madeline who was practicing sheathing and unsheathing the sword and not paying attention to anything else. "Of course, it would be my honor to share my knowledge."

"Good," Arabela clapped him on the shoulder. "Then let's show them how to wrap in a cloak and still be able to draw blade. After that we should find them mounts."

They spent the next hour practicing the cloak wrap that allowed for ease of drawing the sword. Madeline helped Jode to instruct Simon in the basics and by the end of the time, he was able to draw his sword and end in a defensive stance.

"You are going to have to practice with someone," Madeline told Simon. "It's fine to be able to stand there in perfect pose, what happens if someone rushes at you with a pointy stick?"

"I'd probably be dead," Simon admitted. "Jode says I'll have time to learn the basics while we ride. That is if I can move my shoulders tomorrow."

"It will get easier." She rubbed his arm in sympathy.

They handed the swords to the sword master who promised to make the adjustments and have them ready tomorrow morning. Arabela and Jode led the other two around the curve of the wall to the stables. It was time to pick their horses.

"Come, Simon, ah, we really must find you a title, it seems odd to just call you Simon, anyway let me help you choose your mounts." Arabela pulled him to the end of a line of stalls and started to confer with a stableman.

"Do you have a preference," Jode asked. "Spirited? Reliable?"

"In a horse," Madeline teased.

"What else?" Jode smiled as he spoke.

"Do you think it's a good idea to have different preferences for different things?"

"That depends," Jode coughed, "on your answer."

"Ah, well, if I'm going to be riding for any length of time all I ask is a smooth gait and even temperament."

"A wise choice," he called over another stableman and asked for two horses to be brought to the paddock outside the building. "Try these two and we can find others until you have the right pair."

The stableman led a white horse with black mane and tail to the paddock first. The horse tossed his mane and pranced as they led him around the paddock before holding him still for Madeline to mount. Jode bent and offered his linked hands to boost her up; Madeline shook her head and grasped the reins and the base of the horse's mane with her left hand; turned the stirrup with her right and put her left foot in. Grabbing the saddle with her right hand, she bounced on the ball of her right foot. She launched herself onto the saddle swinging her right leg over to catch the stirrup with her toe.

"Well done." Jode said. "You have a good seat."

"I wasn't sure I could pull it off but hey, thanks." Madeline listened as the groom explained the hand signals and then practiced as he led the horse around the paddock.

The horse responded to her signals and carried her comfortably. When they returned to where Jode stood waiting. The stableman told her to circle again without him. The horse refused to move. Madeline sat quietly for a moment and then squeezed her knees and shook the rein. The horse moved and circled the paddock under her control. When she returned to where Jode and the stableman waited, Madeline asked, "What is his name?"

"Fortune," the stableman answered. "He's a good brave horse."

"He's perfect. May I have him?"

Jode laughed, "that is why we are here. Bring Glory out and see if she makes a good second." He instructed the stableman.

Glory turned out to be a roan and Madeline quickly decided to take her as well as Fortune. Simon had chosen a black stallion and a chestnut mare for his mounts, "Witch and valor," Simon announced when she asked what their names were.

For the next half hour, Jode instructed Simon and Madeline on the leg and hand signals that would guide the horses. Then Arabela declared the visit a success and led them back. She walked arm in arm with Madeline ahead of the men.

"Sir Jode admires you." She said without any preamble. "He would be a good mate."

"I'm not looking for a mate." Madeline had no intention of making any more entanglements than she absolutely had to.

"Everyone has a mate somewhere." Arabela pulled back her face showing surprise at Madeline's statement. "Why would you not wish to find one?"

"I don't know if I'm staying it would not be fair to him."

"It is not fair to leave him hanging on this string." Arabela shook her head. "He is obviously aware that you might choose to return to your world. Why not be wooed while you are here?"

Madeline pulled her arm away from Arabela's, "I think I have enough sense to decide what is best. I won't be dictated to when it comes to love."

"As you wish, I thought it would be amusing for both of you. I see it is more serious than I thought."

"It's not serious at all," Madeline snapped.

They walked the rest of the way back to the castle in silence.

13

Madeline was packing her new wardrobe into the travel trunk at Elise's direction when someone knocked on the door. "Ignore it," she said when Elise moved to answer it. "I don't feel like entertaining anyone right now. Show me how to open that compartment again, please."

Elise reached towards the box to show Madeline, "remember the rose."

"The rose," Madeline said, looking at the interlace pattern of roses and vines carved around the box. "Do you think these books will be safe?" Madeline had chosen two books to take on her journey.

The knock came again, sharper and repeated several times.

Elise pressed the centre of a carved rose and the drawer sprung open. "Remember, it is the rose to the left of centre. If you press the others more than three times in a row, the drawer will lock itself and will have to be cut open. Your books will be safe. When you finish writing make sure you reheat the wax and let it seal tight."

The knock came again. Elise looked at the door and then back at Madeline. "I think they will keep knocking."

"I guess you're right. Let me get it." Madeline stalked over to the door and wrenched it open. "What." She snapped at Simon.

"The leaders of the allies are gathering in the dining room and Arabela wants to formally introduce us. Will you come and just get it over with?"

"Okay, I'll be down in ten minutes."

Simon nodded and headed back down the hallway. Madeline watched him go and sighed. She really didn't want a fuss, and particularly didn't want to see Jode right now. Arabela's comments had not helped her ignore the attraction she felt towards him. "Focus on the quest and keep your mind off his muscles, and especially off his great smile that made her heart skip a beat and her breath catch." She told herself. "You don't need any more complications when it comes time to leave." She knew herself well enough to know that if she fell in love and stayed to be with Jode she would come to resent him.

Turning towards the trunk, she pulled a strap that held her toiletries in the lid and extracted a brush. She tugged the bristles through her curls getting stuck half way down the length. "Let me," Elise said taking the brush from her hands. "Whatever is bothering you will work itself out. Don't worry. Before you know it this will all be over and we can get back to normal."

Madeline swallowed her sudden tears. "Elise, that's the problem. No matter what happens on this quest I will have to find a new definition of normal. I can't go back to what I used to be or have."

Elise brushed the last tangle out of Madeline's auburn curls and twisted the shining mass into a loose braid tying it off with a ribbon that matched the pants. "Some would think that is a good thing, a new opportunity. Was your life before this so wonderful that you would wish to have it back?"

"It wasn't perfect, but I knew where I stood and I was in charge of what went on," Madeline admitted.

"If it is the life you were meant to live then it will be," Elise said. "Worrying about what will happen will only make you old. Now, you look presentable. Go be introduced. And then come back so we can start to prepare you for the feast."

"I don't want you to fuss over that. I can wear that same dress from the other night."

"This is my last opportunity to show off my skills before you go. Please, let me make you look as though you were raised as a princess." Elise looked at her, bottom lip protruding slightly eyes, blinking back fake tears.

Madeline laughed; apparently, this was a common expression for 'pretty-please' across worlds. She agreed and hurried out.

At the door of the dining room, a man at arms was waiting to escort Madeline in. He snapped a bow and preceded her through the door.

"The Lady Madeline, from beyond the world," he announced to the waiting group.

Madeline felt her cheeks burn with embarrassment, and a sudden excitement. There were representatives of every race standing around, wine mugs in their hand, all looking at her. She saw Simon and Arabela standing with a small group of goblins by the hearth. Arabela waved to her and held out her arm as if to pull her into the group.

As she walked towards them, Madeline scanned the room. Jode was not there, he wasn't with Arabela, and he wasn't watching her as she walked across the room. Madeline tried to ignore the slight dampening of her excitement because of his absence.

"Madeline," Arabela started as she approached. "Please assist us in a decision."

"Whatever I can do to help," Madeline was a little taken aback by Arabela's playful tone, perhaps there were no bad feelings about the way she reacted this morning.

"Sir Simon has requested that the musicians be allowed to introduce some new music into the playlist tonight."

"Sir Simon?"

"I have given him the title of Sir Simon of the Blue Mountain. It is a small estate and will not require his constant presence," she answered. "Now, tell me, do you think we should allow him to lead our court musicians onto a new path?"

"I thought it would be good to add some new songs in honor of our addition to the quest."

"That depends," Madeline considered. "What has he suggested be added?"

"He named more than one person, but one of royal blood, a Duke of Ellington, do you know this music?"

"Yes, I think it would be very appropriate." She winked at Simon. "This is old music from our world and very appropriate to a large company."

"Then, Sir Simon, I agree. I look forward to hearing your music." Arabela nodded her head as Simon led the musicians to the curtained room.

"Now, let me introduce you to our companions on the quest." She took Madeline's arm and started towards a group of goblins. "Not, all of course, you will meet the entire company on the road. It's fitting the leaders meet you first."

Prince Jugg looked up as they approached, ending his conversation with a dark stocky man to greet Arabela and Madeline. "My lady," he nodded to each. "Well met again. I am please that you will join us Lady Madeline."

"I hope that remains true, but please, I am not Lady Madeline, just Madeline will be fine."

"Oh, please forgive my lapse of memory. I completely forgot to tell you that I also gave you a small estate." She patted Madeline's arm. "You are Lady Madeline of the Far Lake."

"You didn't need to do that." Madeline felt another tiny hook dig into her skin, another tie to this place. "What will happen if I go?"

"Oh, Sir Jode will take the land back into his estate, don't concern yourself." She excused them from the group and walked to the next, patting Madeline's arm again.

"Here are two more people you must be introduced to," she said approaching a couple standing near the windows. "Madam Ethard, and Sir AaLa," she pointed with her open hand at the solemn looking woman and the brightly colored winged man. At least since Arabela called him Sir, Madeline assumed he was the Fay equivalent of a man.

The two bowed and reached to shake Madeline's hand. "My honor," she said to each of them in turn.

AaLa touched her hand to his forehead in greeting. "It is my honor, you are the chosen," he said.

"Oh," Madeline said, taken aback. "Chosen?"

"Don't worry about that, dear." Ethard said. "The Fay tend to be formal in their speech. You are going to be a welcome diversion on a long day of travel. I look forward to speaking to you when we have time."

"There will be time on the road, as you say," Arabela said. "Please excuse us. I see Light is waiting patiently by the door."

They turned and walked across to the doorway, threading between the tables and dodging the servants who were putting the final touches on the room for the feast. Light was one of the white-skinned green-haired people, and the last of the races to be introduced.

"Light," Arabela smiled as she spoke. "This is the Lady Madeline, who I spoke of earlier. Will you allow me to introduce her?"

"I feel as though I have been waiting my entire life for this moment." The voice was whispery and baritone. "My people predicted this day a thousand years past. It is my great joy to be the one to meet you." He bowed, full out court bow.

"Tell him you are similarly honored," Arabela whispered, as Madeline stood with her mouth open.

"I…" she paused and gathered her wits, "it is a great pleasure to meet you. I only hope I can fulfill whatever it is you need of me." She matched his bow with a low curtsy, which would have looked better if she was wearing a dress.

"I must take my leave. My companions and I still have much to do to prepare for this evening." He bowed again and then strode out to the front door.

"Okay," Madeline said. "Please tell me I won't have to be that formal every time we meet."

Arabela laughed again, she seemed to be in a very good mood; Madeline tried not to be suspicious. "No, now that he has made formal greeting you will find Light and his companions to be very informal. In fact, you will see the Sylph dancing tonight. They are rehearsing, that's why he had to leave. Sylph dances are joyous and exciting. You will see."

Jode walked through the doorway and nodded to Arabela, "I think it is time," He said.

"Hello, Jode," Madeline said. She felt her body warm to his presence and suppressed the feeling; now was not the time to let her libido loose.

"Lady Madeline," he gave a short bow of his head.

"Thank you for providing the land that goes with the estate." Madeline felt hurt at his formal manner, and then annoyed at herself for feeling it. Arabela must have told him about their conversation.

"It was given freely," he thawed enough to add, "I think you will like it. The lake touches on the small hunting lodge; you will have many visitors if you choose to stay."

Arabela let go of Madeline's arm and walked to the fire. She stepped up on the hearth, which sat a foot off the floor.

"Companions," she said loudly enough to get the attention of everyone in the room. The small groups turned to look at her; a few people raised their glasses in her direction. The servants stopped running around and stood watching her. "We are gathered to bring an end to a threat to all our lands and all our people."

A few voices called out, hear hear, and damn right. She raised her arms as if to encompass them all in her protection.

"When Sayer Goddard reached through the protections of this castle to strike down Alric of the Summer Lands, he changed the rules of the feud. That fight was between his family and my husband's family. It was to be waged outside and not invade the homes of others. You know that is why we lived here, in the castle of Summer Lands, my home."

More encouraging words came from the audience, this time louder. Madeline could feel her own emotions rise despite knowing that Arabela was purposefully rousing the passions of her companions. It was the pep talk and it was good.

"Yesterday we agreed to the plan. Today Lady Madeline joined us. Tomorrow we set out. We will be victorious." The crowd responded with cheers.

"It will not be easy," she said when the noise died down. "We may lose friends to the battle, we may be lost ourselves."

The response was more muted as people agreed that it would be dangerous.

"Tonight, we feast. If it will be our last feast, it will be our best." She threw back her head and laughed long and loud. "Tonight we will celebrate the life we fight to defend. My companions, no my friends, go prepare for the celebration. We will meet here again when the torches are lit."

The applause seemed too loud for just these few people; she realized a drum pounding behind the curtain was augmenting the clapping. A flute note floated out riding on top of the wave and then the raspy tone of a bassoon wove in and out of the other sounds. It was odd but it resonated with the emotions in the room.

Madeline's hands smarted from clapping; she rubbed them against her side Madeline looked around and saw the people leaving through the door and French windows. The room was almost empty. Arabela stepped off the hearth and came towards her.

"You should go to Elise," she said. "It will take some time to prepare you for tonight and she will need to school you in a few dances too. You must enjoy yourself. We consider it a good omen if the first day of a journey is difficult because of the effect from events of the night before."

"Nice speech," Madeline responded. "You have them eating out of the palm of your hand."

"I do not understand."

"She means you got everyone excited and ready to fight for you." Simon said as he approached them. "It is a good thing."

"Then, thank you." Arabela said. "Now I must go. My servant will be very upset if she doesn't have time to dress and redress me three times before the night starts."

14

When Madeline returned to her room, Elise ordered her out of her clothes and into a steaming bath scented with roses. "Ten minutes," Elise said. A waste of good hot water, Madeline thought.

Elise brushed Madeline's hair until it was dry, then passed her a jug of violet scented oil. "This will make your skin soft and keep away the small insects that will come into the light and heat of the dining room later."

While Madeline rubbed it into her skin, Elise moved around the room cleaning up the thrown clothes and placing items on the bed. Madeline saw shiny forest green fabric and bright white filmy material. Then Elise passed her new underwear, both were silky, the bra was of a black material.

"Sit here, please." Elise pointed to a stool. "No, face the fire I need to dress your hair. You can watch in the mirror on the mantle."

"Will you be at the party?" Madeline asked as Elise separated her now dry and almost straight hair into wide sections.

"We will be outside," Elise said through a mouthful of pearl studded hairpins. "The servants who are not assigned to the party have their own celebration."

"Do you have someone you will be meeting?"

"I have a husband, Lady Madeline." Elise slid the hairpins in as she wrapped the sections around Madeline's head, the ends left to hang down in the back. "When you are ready I will be going to him, after I change into my best dress, of course."

"You sleep here every night when you have a husband?"

"Of course, you must have a married woman to chaperone you. An unmarried one will not know what she is protecting you from."

"Wow," Madeline refrained from letting Elise know that it was too late to protect her virginity. "I guess you'll be going back to your husband tomorrow night, then."

"No," Elise twisted the hanging strands into loops intertwined with white ribbons. "Tonight, don't worry. What happens on a feast night is forgotten in the morning."

"Like Vegas," Madeline muttered.

"What is Vegas?"

"A place where you can act like it's feast night until you leave."

"Ah," Elise didn't add anything else. She tucked the end of the last ribbon in and held it with a final pin. This one topped with a brilliant green stone in a star shaped setting.

"I look like a princess," Madeline turned her head left and right. "You're very talented."

"You are too kind," Elise said, blushing. She handed Madeline a pair of earrings that were composed of a stack of the same green stones on a silver rod. "Lady Arabela sent these jewels for you to wear. They are her favorite."

Madeline looked at the necklace Elise held out. This time the green stone featured as a centre ball of smooth polished stone, and smaller stones alternating with milky white stones cut square. "I can't wear that, I might lose it."

"How will you lose it? The clasp is spelled to remain closed until you say the release spell." She placed the centre stone on Madeline's chest and drew the ends of the chain around to the back of her neck. Madeline felt Elise touch the clasp together and heard her say, "seal." The necklace shifted slightly and the clasp clicked.

"How do I unseal it?" The necklace had adjusted to sit an inch below the ends of her collarbones. It would not be possible for her to pull it over her head to remove it.

"You touch the clasp and say, "unseal. If you are not touching the clasp then it will not open. See, you can't lose it."

Madeline stood to see the necklace in the mirror. The glow of the stones brought out the creamy tone in her pale skin. The pearls in her hair gleamed against the red that was highlighted by the color of the green stone.

"Wow, I guess if I don't have to worry about losing it I'll be okay." she looked toward the bed. "Let's get the rest of this outfit on so I can get used to moving in it."

"Not yet, you don't want to arrive at the party with a wrinkled dress. First let me teach you one dance, it will be the first one and you must be able to manage the steps. After the first dance you should be able to learn from watching, the first one sets the omen for the evening."

Madeline looked from the dress on the bed to Elise who stood with her arms held out as though she was holding hands with someone on each side.

"This is the starting position." Elise said. "Take my hand."

Madeline did and then mimicked Elise's stance as though she held another dancer's hand.

"You turn clockwise a quarter turn," she demonstrated. "And bow to the person you are facing, it should be a man."

Madeline followed the actions knowing if she walked through the steps it would be easier to remember.

"You turn back then turn a quarter turn the other way and curtsy to that person, it will be a woman."

They curtseyed to each other. "Then you move around the woman clockwise, changing partners."

"That's not too hard," Madeline said, "what's next?"

"The men have changed places in a similar fashion. The dance is around a circle, when you face a man you bow and go counter clockwise, a woman curtsey and clockwise."

"When is it complete?"

"Arrive back with your original partner. Remember, the first movement is to bow to your partner; you don't change with them. You bow and turn, curtsey and turn until you face your partner at the end, then you bow and turn and you end where you started."

"No offence, but that doesn't seem so hard."

"Ah, well are you ready to try it at the right speed?"

"Yes, sure," Madeline sensed that she was about to find out the problem.

Elise placed the stool and a night table at intervals around the room. "Pretend the furniture is men; ignore the fact they don't move it will work. Stand to the left of the stool, he is your partner."

Madeline got into place and Elise stood beside the bath across the room. She pulled a pipe from her apron pocket and blew one note. "Are you ready? Good, the dance starts on my next note."

Elise blew one short note and the moved; then she blew the tune, at double time to what they'd been practicing. Madeline found herself spinning out of control between the bed and the end table. She doubled over in laughter.

"Okay, I get it. Let's try again. Can you play slower for a turn, then speed up?"

"Good idea." Elise giggled and ran back to the start place.

They practiced the moves until Madeline was able to complete two full circles at the right speed. She stopped and then checked her hair in the mirror, "hey, not a strand out of place."

"Of course not, it will stay in place until first light." Elise was not so kempt; her hair was flying out of the braids and there was a fine film of sweat on her face and chest.

"Why don't I sweat?" Madeline asked, passing a towel to Elise.

"The oil will stop you from getting more than a glow. You will be very thirsty tomorrow but you will be beautiful tonight. You'll need it too. I understand the men have decided you are fortunate. Each one will want to dance with you so they can get a bit of your good fortune by association."

"Oh, it will be a fun night then," Madeline grinned. "I love to dance. And, I think Simon and I will have a few new moves to teach them."

"Let's get you dressed. The sun has gone down and the party will start very soon."

Elise picked up the white confection and stood on the stool to drop it over Madeline's shoulders. When she finished adjusting the layers, Madeline stood in a cloud of white that fell from an empire waist to the floor, the black bra showing at the top of the very low neckline. "Is it supposed to show?"

"Yes, but it will look different when the green is covering it." Elise held out the shiny green over-dress. It had short sleeves that covered the straps of the white dress and when it was fastened to hooks on the empire waistline. The bra only showed in a small vee in the center.

"Perfect." Madeline was impressed with the way the bra was incorporated into the dress.

"Yes, that bra invention has brought a lot of possibilities to the seamstress; she sends her thanks in the form of this dress."

Elise handed Madeline a pair of white and green striped slip on sandals. "She also used your shoes as a model for these. I like the height; I think there will be a fashion for all women next season.

As she walked down the stairs, Madeline heard a buzz of conversation. The quiet music that flowed around the voices sounded more fitting than the earlier sounds. The bassoon and flute softened by the velvety sounds of talking and the roll of laughter played a counter tempo to the drum. She drifted through the hall towards the crowd in the dining room, hungry for company and the food that was generating a delicious aroma.

"You look delicious," Simon said, a little too loudly, as he walked towards her. "Have a glass of wine, it's way nicer than the stuff we've been drinking up to now."

She accepted the glass he held out admiring the pattern cut into the bowl and stem, stars and balls. This must be the equivalent of the good china coming out. "Maybe you should slow down a bit. You know, pace yourself," she said. "You don't want to pass out before the party is over, do you?"

"Don't fret," he placed his hand under her elbow. "I know how to make a drink last. And, I aim to be one of the last out of here tonight."

He led her to a table in the centre of the room. The cloth was layered in sheets of silver, white, and blood red. The glasses and china were delicate and beautifully decorated, Madeline reached to touch a plate and felt the fine raised pattern of stars around the rim.

"This is our table. For the next hour we'll be mixing and meeting. If you want a drink hold up your glass and someone will fill it. If you are hungry there's a buffet of appies in the corner." He glowed with enjoyment and turned around to point out the small groups standing chatting in the corner. "Let me take you around the room until you find a group to talk to. I have to check on my band, we have a surprise or two for after dinner.

Did you get your dancing lesson? Talk about line dancing, it took me nearly an hour to get the steps right."

"Did you want to take a moment to breathe?"

"Hah, don't be a wet blanket, have fun tonight tomorrow we may die, or something like that."

"I understand that's the idea," she took his offered arm. "Just introduce me to that group of Eldmen and then you can leave me to my own devices."

Simon introduced her to two of the Eldmen and then asked to be introduced to the others. He slipped away as soon as Madeline was involved in a conversation about wines. She watched him head towards the curtained room where the band sat.

"In your world, Lady Madeline," the Eldman named Whill asked, "are there other intoxicating spirits?"

"Many," she said. "We have distilled, brewed, and fermented just about everything that we could. Not all of it was a good idea though. Is wine your only drink?"

"Most of the peoples here have some type of wine that they produce, but as you say, not all of it is a good idea." His companions laughed. "We enjoy wine on special occasions, but we also brew a concoction from grains and flavor it with honey. You might enjoy a sip with us one night on the road."

Madeline recognized the face of a hustler when she saw it. There was going to be a drinking game involved here; oh well, it couldn't be any worse than tequila. "I would certainly enjoy that. We must arrange it. Please, I see someone trying to get my attention. Let's talk later."

"Most certainly, I will be standing in line to dance with you." He made a slight bow and watched her leave.

Madeline worked her way around the room until she arrived at the musician's alcove. Curiosity pulled her to the source of the music; she was dying to know how they amplified the sound so it carried across the room.

"When you sing it you have to think about the words and how you would feel if they were true." Simon was saying to Jode. "You are hurt and sad… Oh, hello Madeline."

"I wondered where you were, Jode." She also wondered what he was supposed to sing but though it better not to ask. "Are you coming out soon?"

"Yes," he slid a sheet of paper inside his white shirt. "I should not ignore my duty as a host. Please, allow me to walk with you around the room, or if it is too warm, perhaps we can find a place to sit on the terrace."

"That sounds better," she took his arm and steered him out of the room, pleased that he seemed to have relaxed.

She hadn't intended to find him, but when she saw Jode standing there she realized that she wanted to talk to someone familiar and not another group of strangers. They had their glasses refilled before stepping out to the mostly deserted terrace. In the corner, almost in the shadows, a bench and small table sat empty. They sat silently for a few moments, Madeline enjoyed the cool and relative quiet.

"Is there something you wish to talk about?" Jode asked.

"Yes, I've been so tied up in trying to figure out what I'm supposed to do that I haven't asked many questions about your people, your history, anything." She said.

"There are hours of conversation in those topics. We can discuss them while we journey."

"I suppose," Madeline felt like she always did on a first date, she wanted to be brilliant but couldn't think of anything to say. "Tell me instead about the future. What will happen when we have fulfilled the quest? It feels like we have all kinds of plans to get there but nothing afterwards."

"That is true." Jode stared off over the campground. "It will be up to Lady Arabela."

"What do you mean? She will come back and rule her lands, won't she? This can't just be about revenge, she seems too invested in the people here for that."

"It is what her people would like," he sighed. "It is what her allies would like, too."

"So what about her? What does she want?"

"You should ask her that question," he turned his gaze back to her. "I can only tell you what she has told me."

"And?"

"Lady Arabela has said that she wants to retire from public life, to live a life of study and contemplation. Of course, that will need to wait until the child has grown."

"Is this the same Lady Arabela I know?" Madeline laughed. "Can you really see her shut away from people for more than five minutes?"

"She is quite determined that she is not fit to rule." Jode smiled at Madeline's words. "I am in agreement with you, though. I cannot believe she will have this child and allow someone else to be regent."

"Maybe she can't see beyond the current crisis," Madeline felt sympathy for that. "It is sometimes hard to understand that other people might know what's best for you."

"That sounds like a confession," he raised an eyebrow.

"I wasn't talking about me." Madeline liked this less serious version of Jode, perhaps too much for her heart's safety.

"Are you sure?" Jode frowned. "May I ask how you will decide what your future holds?"

"That's a long way from now." Madeline squirmed under his gaze.

"Has no one told you how long this will take?" He sat forward she felt the heat from his body on her face.

She shook her head trying to bring her senses back, realizing that she had very little knowledge of what she was about to undertake. "I assume a few months."

"What makes you assume that?" He spoke quietly, intimately.

"Well," she thought for a moment, trying to find those reasons for herself. "If Simon and I need training it will take time. I don't know why."

"Madeline, this quest will be complete within two weeks."

She stood and stared at him. Two weeks? They were supposed to be trained to fight or something in two weeks?

"That's not going to work! Simon and I can't possibly be ready in such a short time." Madeline could feel her heart racing; it was panic.

"Please," Jode stood and reached for her arm. "Do not be alarmed. I am truly sorry no one told you, but the prophecy said we must complete our tasks within the moon and that is two weeks."

"What's the rush? Is this Goddard guy getting ready to attack?" She tried to ignore the feeling of his hand on her arm.

"Not that the Fay have seen with their magic." He slid his fingers down her arm; it stirred emotions in her that were far from comforting.

"Jode, I can't… does Simon know…?" She found it difficult to complete a statement between the panic and the passion rising from her gut. "What has he said?"

"Sir Simon knows; he is not concerned about it. It may be because he is anxious to start working with the musicians here to bring new music to us. I confess I am interested." Jode removed his hand from her skin and touched his shirt where the sheet of paper lay.

Madeline sat back down and reached for her wine glass. She swallowed the contents and looked around for someone to refill it. "I need another drink." She looked at Jode. He nodded and took their glasses and stepped inside the dining room. A minute later he returned with two full glasses and a plate of pastries.

"Please, eat something; I don't want you to miss the dancing or the rest of the party because I have upset you." He picked a shiny puff pastry off the plate and handed it to her. She bit into it and smiled as the soft custardy center touched her tongue.

"Good." Jode nodded. "The attendant tells me we will be called to dine in the next fifteen minutes but I know from experience it will be almost another half hour before you will find a plate of food in front of you. People like to make speeches before dinner so they can enjoy the party afterwards."

She drank half the first glass of wine and swallowed another pastry before speaking again. "I don't know what to do."

"Why should you do anything?"

"I'm supposed to save your world and I have less than fourteen days to figure it out." She finished the first glass and reached for the second as she spoke. Jode took it out of her reach. "Hey, why did you bring me two glasses if I can't drink them?"

"You may, but not so quickly." He held the glass away. "If you drink this glass the same way you drank that one you will not make it to the dinner table. Wine is made to sip not guzzle."

"But."

Jode placed the wine glass on the table behind him and sat next to her. He placed his arm on her shoulder and patted it, rekindling the tingly feeling where their flesh touched. "But nothing, Madeline, what can you do to solve it now? If you are meant to learn something within this quest you will find it in the right time."

Madeline heard the wisdom in his voice, his lovely calm, rich voice. She breathed deeply to clear her head. "Okay, I'll take your word for it. It's not what I'm used to. I'm used to knowing everything and solving crises. I haven't had to rely on luck since I was five years old."

"You are sure you will trust me?" He removed his hand; she fought the urge to pull it back. "You will enjoy tonight? You will dance and stay to the end?"

"Yes," she reached out for the glass of wine. Jode passed it to her. "I guess I should ask how late the end is likely to be?"

"Hah, you have learned something already." He laughed. "The official end will be well before sunrise, to give those who must prepare for tomorrow time to do so. The actual end is usually just as the sun rises."

"Now, that's a party." She sipped her wine and held up the glass in salute. "I promise to try to stay to the official end. Anything past that is up to luck."

The music suddenly ended with a crash of drums and then the flute gave three piping notes.

"We are called to dine," Jode stood and offered his elbow to escort her to the table.

As the last of the pre-dinner speeches finally ran out, Madeline turned to Simon who sat on her left, "that was merciful. I'd been warned people might talk all night."

"I have a feeling people are itching to get to the food. You know it's going to be twenty courses, right?"

"You only need to taste them," Jode said, handing her a platter covered with pieces of thinly sliced green vegetables in a dark red sauce. "Here is the first, take care it is highly spiced."

After an hour and a half and twelve dishes of meat, fish, vegetables, and other things Madeline didn't recognize, she saw Simon take the last of the honey covered sliced fruit from the plate. The servants cleared the tables and a few plaintive notes drifted out of the back of the room.

"It is time for the first dance," Arabela stood and beckoned the three of them towards the center of the room. "I will partner Sir Simon. Jode, you take Madeline,"

She survived the first dance; Jode had reminded her of the steps as they approached their assigned circle on the terrace. During the dance, the servants cleared the dining room of the leftover food, removed the large tables and replaced them with small ones. This left half the room available as a dance floor. The glasses were kept full and plates of dessert pastries were constantly replenished as everyone enjoyed the freedom of the dance.

Madeline was exhausted after demonstrating the waltz with Simon and then being swept into a lively reel by the Eldman Whill. She watched as the others swayed to a slightly twisted version of The Tennessee Waltz. She sat alone at one of the small corner tables, taking a break to get her breath back after the dance, when Arabela floated into the chair next to her.

"Here," she placed a glass of clear liquid in front of Madeline who sniffed it suspiciously. "It is water. You will need to drink water as well as wine if you don't want to feel ill tomorrow." She laughed.

"Thank you." Madeline raised her glass. "This is a great party."

"Yes, it bodes well for our journey." Arabela sipped her own glass of water. "We believe that a successful feast will lead to a successful journey."

"So, what is the plan?" Madeline leaned towards Arabela. "I don't know what to expect, especially since it will take so little time to complete the quest."

"Sir Jode mentioned that you didn't know it would only take two weeks." Arabela looked away. "He was quite angry that I hadn't told you. He cares for you a great deal."

"Yes, we've been down that path. Let's put that behind us. What's the plan?" She swallowed the last of the water and leaned back in her chair waiting for an answer.

"We will travel towards the Scree, keep as though we were embarking on a royal tour. Sayer Goddard will not be on guard and we should be able to approach without causing him any suspicion."

"Wouldn't it be better to get there as fast as possible? Be in and out before he can figure it out?"

"We cannot get to him fast enough for that. If he suspects we are coming we will face an army."

"Why wouldn't he just ask for his own prophecy?" Madeline had suddenly envisioned Sayer Goddard as a tall scrawny being in a grey robe bending over a stone bowl. "He could know our plans already."

"He could, but he would not ask what we are doing? It is not in his nature to imagine a woman would exact revenge. When you raise prophecy, you must ask a specific question. Unless he asked if I was planning to attack him he would not know."

Madeline shrugged; it made sense in a weird way. "What exactly did you ask for your prophecy?"

"It does not matter," Arabela looked out over the dancers. "The prophecy said we must act quickly and with surprise. We must complete the task before the next moon. That is in two weeks."

A tall servant standing in the doorway to the house caught Arabela's attention and he gave one deep nod. "Ah, the next song signals the official end of the party." Arabela said. "If you wish you may stay but I will be leaving. I need my rest for tomorrow. We will depart three hours after sunrise." She stood and said goodnight.

Madeline decided it was time to go up to her room; she was tired and worried that she would not be able to stay on the horse tomorrow. She stood and tucked her chair under the table in preparation for leaving.

"Wait," Simon's words came from across the table. "You can't leave yet. I'm making my singing debut."

"What?"

"The last dance is coming up in ten minutes, can't you stay that long?"

"You're singing?" Madeline wasn't sure she was hearing correctly. "What are you singing?"

"Aw, come on, stay." He said. "I want your opinion. The rest of these guys won't know if it's good. You know what it's supposed to sound like."

She couldn't think of an argument that would sound reasonable. Simon had been willing to listen to her complain and he'd said he would go back with her if needed. The least she could do is stay awake for his big singing debut. "Fine, I'll stay. Don't make a fool of yourself. God, please tell me you aren't doing an Elvis."

"No, they aren't ready for the king, baby." He twisted his hips and shoulders in the signature Elvis move. "Did you have fun tonight? You look like you had fun."

"Yes," she sighed. "I guess I forgot my problems. I took dancing lessons with my last boyfriend; he was a bastard but I learned to dance. Thanks, by the way, knowing some of the music helped."

"It's all part of the job," he waved as he turned back to the room.

"Hey, how do they get the sound to carry? They don't have amps."

"Magic."

She laughed and then realized he wasn't kidding. Pulling out the chair, she settled in to enjoy the remainder of the evening. The current song was from this world; Simon had created a playlist that threw the new sounds in every few songs. The people on the dance floor were swaying around each other in a complex rhythm to what sounded to Madeline like a snake charmer song.

"Would you honor me with the next dance," Jode stepped in front of her with a bow.

She considered declining then changed her mind; her feet were just fine, not how they would feel after a night dancing at home. She could listen to Simon's singing while she danced.

She stood, took Jode's hand and walked with him to the centre of the floor. The rest of the dancers drifted away as the song started and Jode swept her into the waltz position. Simon's voice came from the corner of the room.

"You can dance every dance with the guy who gives you the eye, let him hold you tight."

His voice was warm and on the low side of the range, she smiled as she realized it was a set up. Jode spun her gently around and dipped her in the process.

"You've been taking lessons." She said.

"Yes," Jode smiled down at her. "Sir Simon provided me with this skill in exchange for the first dance steps. I must admit I enjoy your style of dance, it is more intimate."

They owned the dance floor for the duration of the song. It ended with applause, for Simon and for the dancers.

Servants moved in and started clearing tables away, and the guests drifted through the French doors into the night. A few returned to the tables and wine glasses.

Jode led Madeline to the foot of the stairs and bowed over her hand, placing a light kiss on the back. "I have duties to attend before I retire. Good night, Lady Madeline, sleep well."

Madeline had crawled into the bed after leaving Jode to his duties. She expected the usual after party buzz to keep her awake for a while, but there was no buzzing, and no need to put a foot on the floor to keep the room from spinning. She sank into the mattress, tunneled under the covers, falling asleep on her exhale.

15

In the morning, Elise woke her and placed a tray with a warm bread roll spread with honey and a cup of caf on her bed. "You need to be ready to ride in an hour." She said.

Madeline ran to the convenience and returned to find a set of black pants a white sweater and a black cloak laid out for her. The dress from last night had been removed and so had the travel trunk that had been packed yesterday. She dressed quickly and slid her feet into a pair of stiff black riding boots.

"This cloak can go over the back of your saddle until you need it." Elise rolled it and tied straps around it. "The day is beautiful, a good omen."

"We probably need all the good omens we can get." Madeline felt like she was about to jump up and down with the sudden excitement that flooded her. She swallowed the last of the sweet roll and walked to the window. The grounds were empty. "Everyone has already gone." She turned to face Elise, "When did they go?"

"They started to move out just before sunrise. A group that large moves very slowly. You and the mounted men will leave soon and will catch up by noon. Don't worry, you aren't holding anyone up." She laughed. "You have certainly changed in the last day. Your decision to stay has agreed with you."

"Maybe," she turned from the sight of the broken camp. "I don't know if the decision itself, or just making a decision has agreed with me. I hate not knowing what I should do; it feels good to be out of the fog."

She tucked the rolled cloak under her arm and gave Elise a hug goodbye before running down the staircase, across the courtyard and through the gates; the two sentries wished her a good journey and she thanked them over her shoulder as she turned right to follow the wall. When she approached the practice barn, she saw it was full of men, some were listlessly tapping swords, it was clear they were waiting for something.

"Lady Madeline," one called out, she thought she recognized him from last night as one of the many men she danced with. "Will you be leaving soon?"

"I don't know," she replied, it wasn't up to her to tell him if Arabela had not chosen to. "Why?"

"We are not allowed to come on the campaign. The least we can do is give a formal farewell."

"Oh," she understood why there were so many of the men here, and why they were so formally dressed. "I don't know but it probably won't be long."

"Thank you." He bowed at the waist and started to button his jacket. "Men, form up."

She hurried around the curve of the wall. If she could hurry the start of the journey, she would. The thought that the soldiers would stand at attention for hours while they prepared to set out made her feel uncomfortable. At the stables, she saw a small group of people standing around saddled and waiting horses. Jode stood next to a large chestnut stallion, Arabela a white mare, and Simon his chestnut mare. The other horses were solid looking mounts with well-used gear. A stableman stood just off to the side with Fortune on a tight rein.

"Good morning," Arabela walked towards her. "Are you ready?"

"I guess, there's nothing I need, according to Elise everything is on its way and I just have to get going."

"You don't have quite everything." Jode handed her the sword she had practiced with yesterday. The new belt and sheath were made of green dyed leather and decorated with white stones that seemed to glow. "Please accept this as a gift from me."

"It's beautiful," she wrapped the belt and straps so the sword hung across her back. "Thank you, it's a perfect gift." Great, now she was going to have to find him a gift before she left.

The stableman took her cloak and tied it behind her saddle. She tested her bounce before vaulting perfectly into the saddle. "Shall we go?"

Everyone else laughed and jumped on their own mounts the column aligned in two rows, Arabela and Jode in the lead, Simon and Madeline next, the other four pairs lined up behind. Arabela put pressure on her horse's flanks and they started at a trot. They were headed out towards the woods where Simon and Madeline had entered this world.

As they rounded the wall, the soldiers were standing in two rows, facing each other at attention, backs straight, red-jacketed chests out. They stood far enough apart that the pairs of riders could pass. As Arabela and Jode entered this human passageway, the soldiers hit their chest and bowed their heads. Each said something as the horses passed, "luck."

When the entire company had passed through Arabela stood in her stirrups and turned to the waiting soldiers. "Guard my people well, I entrust them to you until we return."

The soldiers raised a cheer that had the horses dancing. Madeline held her seat and hoped it wasn't apparent that it was precariously. Arabela turned and sat in the saddle, let out a blood-freezing howl, "Summer Lands," and kicked her horse into a full gallop. The others followed leaving behind the sound of the soldiers' roar of approval.

They slowed to a walk as they entered the forest. Madeline was glad of the change of pace; the gallop had blown some of her hair out of the careful braid. "Was that really necessary?" she asked, pushing hair back out of her eyes.

"Yes," Arabela looked at her quizzically. "We needed to show confidence for my men. If they thought I had doubts, they would not have slept until I returned. It was hard enough for them to accept they had to stay. Would you have me worry them over-much?"

"No, I suppose not," Madeline sighed. "I would have liked a bit of warning. I almost fell off. What would they have thought if the chosen one had landed on her ass during the first five minutes of the quest?"

"I assumed you would be capable. I saw you ride yesterday. You have good posture and control of your mount."

"You know what, never mind. It's not worth arguing about. In future let me know if the ride is about to get exciting and I'll do my best not to embarrass anyone."

"What happens if someone other than I causes the excitement?"

"I don't freaking know. Look, I am trying my best."

"To do what?" Arabela smiled. Madeline couldn't help seeing it as a smirk. "To ride? Then your best seems adequate."

"It is more than adequate," Jode said from the other side of Simon. "Not many would have been able to control their mounts during that farewell. You did well, I'm sure some of the others were also in danger of falling."

"Really?" Arabela asked. "Who, I was assured we traveled with the best riders of the camp."

Madeline refused to let Jode step between her and Arabela, if they were headed for a fight then that's where they would go. "It is kind of you to say so, Sir Jode. I am sure it was just kindness and that the rest of our party is exactly as Arabela has described them."

"It is a pity that I cannot visit your world." Arabela said, looking straight ahead. "It must be a peaceful place if you are so startled by a loud noise."

"Yes," Madeline said. "It is a pity. I would love to see you try to cross the road during rush hour with no assistance or warning."

Both women smiled icily at each other. Madeline tried to control her growing irritation; she could feel the tension transferring to Fortune in the way he stepped nervously. It didn't make sense; she had started the day in such good spirits. If she was going to get pissed off every time something unusual happened how the hell was she going to fight this coming battle, whatever fighting it meant.

"When will we catch up with the others?" She tried for small talk. "I understand they left hours ago."

"The main body will reach the river in a few hours; we should catch up with them after they ford it." Arabela said, apparently trying the same tactic.

"Then what?" Simon asked.

"We will pass them," Jode said. "They travel slowly because they have the baggage and the supplies. When we reach them we will stop for food and water to take with us."

"Aren't we camping with them?" Madeline was confused. If they were not camping with the rest of the party why was their baggage with the slow group?

"Have you forgotten that we are supposed to be on a grand tour of the land?" Arabela sounded irritated.

"No, but what does that have to do with it?"

"We must visit some of the towns to keep that story realistic." She shook her head.

"So are we staying in a town or something?"

"We will visit the village of Whitetree and eat our evening meal with the mayor." Arabela said. "After that we will ride to join the camp. They will have set up for the evening we will have an hour or two before retiring to talk and train."

"Thank you," Madeline bit back the word bitch. Arabela seemed to have a bug up her ass about something. "I appreciate knowing what is coming. Am I expected to talk to the villagers? Or, should I pretend to be mute?"

"You two need to cut it out." Simon snapped. "If you are going to snipe all day we'll be exhausted before we meet the main camp."

"I'm just asking for information." Madeline said.

"I am only answering questions." Arabela said.

"Look," Simon continued. "Lady Arabela, we need a lot of information until we're comfortable here. And, Madeline, you are perfectly capable of conducting an evening of small talk without being prepped for every fact and rumor."

"Ladies, please, if you cannot actually be pleasant it would be better if we didn't ride together." Jode said. "I am happy to drop back with Lady Madeline if it means keeping the peace."

"I'm sure you would," Arabela said with a laugh. "Riding with Lady Madeline would be such a trial for you. I appreciate the sacrifice."

Madeline laughed too, "Okay, I'll behave. Arabela, perhaps it would help if you gave me some information, or at least told my why you won't."

"It must be nerves," she admitted. "Until we set out I could imagine us attacking Sayer Goddard and leaving him dead. Now we have set out it's too real."

"Okay, so let's gossip, that always takes my mind off anything that is bugging me."

"What shall we gossip about?"

"Tell me about your family, or about the village we are headed to, or about friends, anything."

"I could tell you about Sir Jode." She looked at Madeline out of the corner of her eyes, a small Mona Lisa smile on her lips.

"If you must," Madeline rolled her eyes. "I'm not going to fall for him, you know. At least not until I know what I am going to do."

16

Whitetree consisted of ten small stone houses clustered close to a central green; a large inn occupied one side, the blacksmith the other, and a substantial house for the mayor at the east side. The center of the square was set up with tables and chairs for an afternoon of games and drinking.

The mayor and his wife invited Arabela to sit at the head table with their six children and four dogs. They heard the villager's disputes and helped to reach a settlement. Madeline sat with Jode and Simon across from them and watched the proceedings.

"So, I thought you didn't have lawyers," Madeline said to Jode. "This looks very much like a court of law."

"You must be patient." He answered and patted her hand. "Watch before you judge."

She sighed and moved her hand away. "Okay, I'll hold back."

The first group to approach the head table seemed to be a family trying to make a man take responsibility for his bastard child.

"Hmm," Simon muttered, "let's hope the punishment isn't death."

Madeline smacked his arm, "idiot. I hope you aren't using this as a way to assess the risk. Getting a girl pregnant here may mean a lot more than just punishment."

The man and the pregnant girl's family each told their story. He was married; the family had a different husband in mind for the girl.

"Not what I expected, shouldn't he be trying to deny he's the father?" Simon asked Jode.

"Why," Jode looked surprised. "The priest would confirm the girl's story."

"But won't his wife want to leave him?"

"No, they have a good sized farm, if they left each other the farm would be split and it would not be as productive. Besides, they have their own son to provide for."

Madeline tuned out the questions, concentrating on the two groups at the head table. She was turning over solutions in her mind when the mayor and Arabela turned from a short conversation and gave the judgment. They suggested that the man put up the dowry for the girl and provide the new couple with a cow and a bull to start their new life with. Both families agreed and shook hands.

"Will he really do what they agreed?" Madeline asked, thinking that the agreement could not be resolved so easily.

"Of course," Jode answered. "The man's wife will ensure it is done."

"Why? It takes something away from her family."

"Ah, but it isn't as much as it could be. If there were no husband for the girl then she would move in with them. They would be responsible for her health and would take the child as their own."

"And, the other man, the new husband, won't he mind that his first born is another man's?" Simon asked.

"The child will be his in all but blood. If it's a boy he will work the farm, if it's a girl then she will help to keep the home."

"Okay," Madeline tried to end the discussion. "There are definitely different customs here. Now, please be quiet and let me hear the next case."

The next case was about a land dispute. Madeline expected she would see some representation for each side. Even if both people told the truth, they would have a different interpretation. She smiled and prepared to point out Jode's error, and that they would need her legal skills.

One farmer claimed his land ran to the river, the other claimed it ran to a fence. The amount of land in dispute was extensive. Arabela and the mayor heard both sides and then asked three questions. Madeline looked around for the lawyers, or whatever they called them here.

It turned out the river used to flow next to the fence; the fence was originally built along the riverbank. The previous winter a landslide upstream caused the river to shift; this had exposed a large tract of land as the river narrowed and ran faster. The ownership of the new land was under dispute.

To Madeline's dismay, she watched as Arabela and the mayor suggested two solutions. One, each farmer take half the new land, moving the fence to mark the new boundary. The second choice, one of the farmers would raise a crop and give half the proceeds to the other farmer. The second solution worked for the men. It meant they didn't have to move the fence.

"So, they really have no use for lawyers," Simon said, his shock showed in the awed tone of his voice. "Maybe they need your charm and diplomacy."

"Very funny," Madeline slapped his arm again. "Seriously, do you see this happening back home? It relies on a lot of trust and decency, both of which are in short supply."

"I'm sorry," Simon rubbed his arm. "I know you were counting on it being something you knew. It looks like you are back to guessing."

"Can you not simply trust the prophecy?" Jode asked. "It brought you, and that cannot be simply to break my heart."

"You aren't helping," Madeline snapped. It was bad enough that Jode insisted on trying to court her, even though she wasn't encouraging him, it broke her heart when he sounded so disappointed in her lack of trust.

"I just have to ask," Simon pushed on ignoring the other conversation. "Why go back? Why not stay and explore a different approach to life?"

"Don't push it," she snapped, turning back to the proceedings. When that was finished, they mounted up and rode out to join the main camp.

They arrived at twilight; fires burned giving a warm welcoming feeling to the camp. Tents stood in concentric circles around two main tents. Those were large, square and had canopied doorways. One door curtain was made of layers of green and silver fabric, the other layers of black and crimson.

"We will share a tent," Arabela said to Madeline. "The green and silver stand for your house and mine, the black and crimson for Sirs Simon and Jode."

Arabela led the way into their tent and Madeline saw it was divided into three chambers; one in the center looked like it was for visitors. Arabela showed Madeline to the right hand chamber, and then walked through a break in the fabric to hers. "I feel the need for meditation with Blu. Please, make yourself comfortable. The camp will settle in for dinner in about an hour. I'll join you here."

Madeline walked, slightly bowlegged, to the other room and lay on the low mattress. Her body was starting to stiffen from a day in the saddle and she needed to stretch so her muscles could cool down without becoming immobile.

~~~

In the other tent, Jode and Simon went to their separate rooms and met in the center one five minutes later, wearing more comfortable clothing for the evening.

"Come on, Jode," Simon said holding open the door curtains. "They'll be waiting for us."

They walked to the eastern portion of the camp and met four of the goblins, there were two other people sitting with them. "Hi, guys," Simon waved. "Jode, I'm not sure you know all the band members by name." He pointed to the four goblins, "You know Yorr and Buck, but this is Urr and Dass. I guess you probably know Jode, but maybe you don't know he sings."

Jode nodded a bow to the four goblins.
~~~

“Sir Simon,” Yorr said. “I have the pleasure of introducing to you two people who wish to join our company; the Eldman Zora, who is proficient on the long flute, and the Fay lady Asla, whose voice is a joy to hear.”

“The more the merrier,” Simon said. “I look forward to hearing you play and sing.”

“Ah,” Jode said, “You have someone to sing. I will sit here and listen.”

“Oh, no you don’t.” Simon pulled him back into the group. “A band needs more than one voice.”

“No, it is not important. I will be happy to listen as you practice for your performance.”

“Sir Jode,” said Asla, “I cannot be the only voice, you must sing with me. If there is only one note there is no music.”

“I would not want to intrude on your performance. My voice is not trained, well not anymore.” He tried to move away towards some barrels beside a tent. “I’ll sit here.”

The goblins ran between Jode and the barrels, “Sir Jode, please. We heard you singing in the hallway and your voice is perfectly trained. Will you honor us by singing while we rehearse? If you wish to step out after that, we will not stand in your way.”

Jode looked at the four faces staring up at him, the goblin’s grins and wide eyes imploring him to agree. “If everyone wishes, of course I will. Sir Zora, are you agreeable to this notion?”

“Sir Jode, I see in your heart a great desire to sing, yet in your mind a great reluctance to try.” He thought for a moment. “We need a male voice to complete the band. I imagine you would not want that to be me, or one of our goblin friends."

"I have seen the result of Eldmen singing, it is not conducive to a pleasant evening." He looked at Simon whose face was surprised. "The Eldmen chant their magic, when they sing they raise powerful, and often destructive, magic."

"And, the goblins?" Simon asked.

"You have already heard a sample. When goblins sing, strong men cry from the pain in their ears," Buck answered for Jode.

"I see," Simon nodded. "Well, you may be pleasantly surprised at the joining of their voices and the new music."

"Then we are settled," Dass declared, her voice reminiscent of gravel in a cement mixer. "Simon, let us dispense with all the sirs and ladys, what is it we need to start with?"

For the next hour, the seven musicians listened and practiced songs that Simon sang, or wrote out for them. The rehearsal ended when a gong sounded and Dass, said, "finally, dinner. I could eat a morge."

"What's a morge," Simon looked at the horror on Dass's face. "I guess I don't want to know. Let's practice again tomorrow at camp," Simon said as the band quickly broke up. "I want us to be able to play the following night. A little Dylan and a little Springsteen should do it for our first concert. Hey, and don't forget to think up a name for the band."

17

"Wake up." Arabela threw a cloth at Madeline's bed. "It's time for training."

"Okay," muttered Madeline, turning over in the bed and pulling the blanket over her head.

"No," Arabela shouted. "Get up." She pulled the blanket off and rolled Madeline on to the ground with it.

"Can't we just do this later? I'm tired."

"No, you need to train and we will have no time later. We have another village to visit and by the time we set up camp it will be too dark to train."

Madeline pushed herself up from the ground. The ride yesterday had taken its toll on her, the pain in her thighs only outdone by the stiffness of her back. She groaned and pulled herself up right. "Oh, dear god, how am I supposed to train when I can barely move?"

"Wash and prepare yourself. I'll wait for you with a trainer in the front of our tent. You have five minutes." She looked at Madeline and softened. "You will feel better after the training. I promise, you'll warm up and tomorrow will be easier. Now five minutes."

Madeline got ready, missing the luxury of the castle facilities as she used the jakes at the edge of the camp. Running to make the five-minute deadline warmed up her muscles and she felt less pain by the time she picked up her sword and exited the tent again.

Jode stood in the space in front of the tent. He was dressed for practice, a loose white shirt open at the throat, dark pants and flat boots. He was walking through a warm up exercise and Madeline swallowed as he thrust the sword forward and then moved back into a stance, sword held point out over his head. His back straight, legs apart, chest out, torso turned to minimize the target area.

She exhaled in one long controlled breath, trying to send the passion out with the air. It would not be easy training with Jode.

"Ah," Arabela said, "on time, well done. We have about half an hour. Jode will walk you through some basic exercises this morning so he can gauge your expertise. Tomorrow, and every morning going forward, he will push you to become capable of defending yourself with the weapons on that table."

Madeline walked over to the table. Laid out were another sword, a bow and quiver of arrows, and a set of knives with no handles. "Wouldn't it be simpler to make sure I can attack? I don't think defense is what the prophecy meant."

"No," Jode said. "You must defend yourself first. We do not have time to teach you the skills to defend and attack. We would need months, not days. Defense can result in attack if you are proficient. Today, we will work through the sword positions because you have some training."

"But if it's about defense, why is there a throwing knife?" Madeline stepped into the center of the space as she spoke. Jode walked around and prodded her to better posture, his touch leaving tingles in her body. "What kind of defense weapon is that?"

"Put your sword on at the waist, please," Jode said. "If we are engaged in battle, it may be that we will not be, but we must prepare, you may have to defend yourself as you flee. A throwing knife is an excellent way to stop your attackers as you do that. Good, now draw your sword and we will run through the movements."

She drew her sword, stepped back and placed her left hand on her hip as she turned her body to the side.

"Good, contra parry, sixte. Excellent, tierce. Good, carte, perfect. You have excellent posture. Now, I will attack and you must parry. I wish to see how well you respond with a blade coming at you."

"Wait," Madeline felt her body flush with heat and stepped back. "These are real blades. Shouldn't we be using practice blades?"

"Mine is a practice blade. I don't think you can do harm to me with yours. Please get back in stance."

"No," Madeline felt fear close over her soul. "I will not practice with a sharp blade. Do you have a practice blade, or can you wrap this one?"

"Are you so certain of your skill?"

"Yes," Madeline could feel the certainty in her bones. She knew, for no logical reason, that she would hurt Jode if she used this blade. "A practice blade, please, I promise I will fight as though it was real."

Jode motioned to a man standing behind the weapons table and he brought a thin metal sheath that slid over her weapon blunting the edge. She would still hurt her opponent, but it would leave a bruise rather than a gaping wound.

Jode stepped forward to face her and waited while she tested the weight and balance of her sword with the sheath.

"Ok," Madeline said, nodding at him.

He lunged, sword out aimed at her stomach. She twisted her wrist in a counterclockwise motion that pushed his blade away. She instinctively thrust further as Jode's blade moved and aimed for his heart. Her blade made contact before she realized what she was doing.

"Well done," Jode rubbed his chest where the blunted point had struck hard. "I appreciate your insistence on practice weapons. It seems you will have no problem turning defense into attack with a sword. I think we shall spend the rest of our time honing defense. Tomorrow we'll spend time with the throwing knife."

Madeline felt herself relax as she saw he was not badly hurt. "I will pay attention to my instincts more often, I could have killed you."

"Now that I have the measure of you, let's see if you can touch me again. En Garde."

Jode stood in the position and when Madeline mirrored him, he lunged towards her. She deflected him, and tried to attack, her instincts taking over her mind. He countered and attacked again.

They chased each other back and forth, alternating between grunts of effort and laughs of victory until Arabela called an end to the session. They raised their swords and bowed to each other.

"You will want to wash and change before breakfast, both of you," Arabela said. "Ten minutes then back here."

Madeline could feel the endorphin high as she ran back into the tent. There was a woman in her room holding out a towel and some soap as she entered. "There's water there, get out of those clothes. We'll launder them, and you can have them back tonight."

Madeline saw at there was a full set of riding clothes on the back of a chair that held a large bowl of steaming water. She stripped out of the sweat soaked outfit and washed quickly. The woman emptied the bowl and waited until Madeline had dried herself before piling the clothes and towel in the bowl and carrying it out. "We'll be packing your tent while you eat. Take anything you need with you, or it will end up in the baggage wagon."

"Thank you," Madeline called after the efficient woman. She took her cloak, still rolled, and her sword and sheath with her as she dashed back outside, stomach growling.

Breakfast sat on a table in front of the tents; they ate standing and took mugs of caf with them to the enclosure where their horses waited. The horses had been curried and fed, but the saddles sat on the ground waiting to be put on.

"We saddle our own mounts on the road." Jode explained. "It is important that you know how well the horse is equipped if you face bandits or some other enemy."

"Kind of like packing your own parachute," Simon lifted his gear as he spoke, heading towards his mount. Arabela followed, her horse was tied close to the chestnut mare Simon was riding today, Witch.

"Sir Simon," she said. "What is a parashoo...?"

"Parachute," he laughed and put his saddle on Witch's back. "It is a large cloth that catches the wind as you float to earth from a great height."

"And, you pack it yourself because you must be sure it will work?"

"Yes," he tightened the girth strap.

"Is this falling from a great height something that people do often in your world?"

"No," Simon decided not to get into explaining the concepts involved in flight. "They are emergency equipment and some people use them for sport. Do you require assistance?"

"Thank you, but no." She slapped her mount on the butt. "He doesn't like the girth tight so he takes a deep breath when I try to tighten it. He just needs a little reminder that I don't want to fall off on the road. That's all."

They finished the routine actions required to get the horses ready for the road. Arabela allowed Simon to assist her into the saddle before he launched himself into position.

"You must teach me this method of mounting. It is sometimes not convenient to require assistance," she said.

"It's harder for you because of your height, but it is still possible as long as you can reach the back of the horse without having to stretch to your limit." He turned his horse to join the others of their party. "It's all about bounce and balance. I'd be happy to show you next time we stop."

"Lady Madeline is not so much taller than I. If she can do it, then I should be able to master the technique." She rode closer. "You are close to her, are you not?"

"I worked for her, yes," Simon pulled his horse into line and realized Arabela had maneuvered him to the middle, away from Madeline and Jode. "Is there something you want to know?"

"I find it difficult to persuade her to follow my wishes."

"Yes, she's not good at following orders. She likes to be in control."

"Can you suggest how I might be able to persuade her to be more amenable to guidance? It is wearing to fight with her over every decision."

Simon shrugged and shook his head, Witch side stepped in impatience to get on the road.

"If I might be honest?" He waited for Arabela to nod. "It seems to me that you are also someone who likes to be in control. If you had been pulled into an unknown world and told you must participate in a quest, but no one knew what you were to do, how would you react?"

"I think I would listen and then help." Arabela answered immediately.

"Then we have different opinions," Simon laughed. "I beg your pardon, but from what I've seen of the way you work, Madeline is only a shadow of what you'd be like."

"It is to be hoped we do not find ourselves in the position to test your theory," Arabela said. "So, you were her employee in your world?"

"Yes," he nudged Witch into motion as the horses ahead started to walk away from the camp. "My job was to keep her organized. I had to get her to meetings on time, and to court in time for a case."

"How did you manage to do that if she would not follow your suggestions?"

"That's the difference," Simon said. "She hired me to do that job, so when I said she had to get somewhere she went."

"So she argues with me because I am not an employee?"

"Sort of," Simon considered for a few minutes as their party passed through the first few trees of the forest. "It's not like she doesn't want to help. She can be a team player, but in this circumstance she doesn't know the rules of the game. I think she's too afraid to do the wrong thing."

Arabela sighed. "What do you suggest then? I don't think it will be good for anyone if we continue to argue about everything."

"I don't know how to tell you to resolve it. But, you won't solve it asking me for help. Madeline is a reasonable woman; you need to talk to her."

Arabela rode forward in the column until she reached Jode and Madeline. They were deep in conversation about the next village.

"This village is very different from yesterday's visit. They are merchants in Lanewall. The day will be shorter so that the business of trading is not interrupted for too long. The disputes are often solved between the parties and the meeting will be more about the tax rate and the condition of the roads," Jode was saying.

"Yes," Arabela added. "The people of Lanewall rarely have disputes. They say it interferes with trade."

"Hah, sometimes I think the merchants in my world trade in disputes," Madeline said. "The bulk of my work is based on interpreting and trying to enforce agreements between companies."

"You come from a very interesting world," Arabela said, as though trying to build a level of camaraderie. "I would enjoy hearing about it as we ride."

Jode dropped back as they approached a narrow part of the road. The two women rode side by side for a few minutes without speaking. Arabela broke the silence.

"Sir Simon tells me that you are a powerful woman in your world."

"Well, not powerful, but I do know how to do my job. What else does he say?"

"That you prefer to be in a position of control. I think perhaps that is why we argue."

"Perhaps," Madeline tried to keep her voice level, but could tell the pleasantness was draining out. "Did Sir Simon provide you any other insights?"

"You sound angry," Arabela said. "Have I done something wrong? I am trying to find a way to work with you. I spoke to Sir Simon with the aim to learn more about you."

"Did he suggest you try to be my friend? To disarm me with your kindness so, I would be more compliant."

"Please, control your anger," Arabela said. "He told me I would be more successful if I simply talked to you."

"Good."

"That is what I am trying."

"Are you surprised that you are not being successful." Madeline's anger was transferring to Glory, who started twitching and sidestepping in nervousness. She reached forward and patted the horse's neck. "There, there, Glory. Don't fret. I don't like being handled, Arabela."

"The spell translates that to being treated like a horse or other beast. I am not doing that."

"You may not think so, but you're trying to impose your wishes on me. I've agreed to go along but I am not going to lie down and roll over just because you say so."

"That is not what I want," Arabela's frustration boiling over into the words. "Why are you so determined to be difficult? Is this situation not hard enough already?"

"Difficult for you?" Madeline was shocked. "Look, you get to exact your revenge on your husband's killer, and then rule in his place. What's difficult for you?"

"Many things," Arabela's voice dropped to a whisper. "I loved my husband and when his life was taken my own became of no worth to me. I waited for the pain and sorrow to take me to join him."

"It doesn't look like that to me." Madeline was not going to be taken in by a story of grief; this woman was far from the grieving widow.

"When Blu told me I was… you know what he told me, I put aside my grief. I could not indulge my emotions in this condition. The person you see today is not just Arabela; it is the future of my people."

"Yes, you get to rule an entire land when we're done, I don't know what will happen to me." Madeline heard the resentment in her voice. "I hate sounding so pathetic, but you have no idea what I feel about not knowing if I will survive."

"What do you mean?"

"What if the prophecy needs me to die to make your revenge successful?" Tears pushed at Madeline's eyes. She felt an overwhelming regret at all the things she hadn't done in her life. "I don't want to. I'm not ready to die."

"No one is," Arabela said, a frown on her face. "Do you think my Alric was ready to die when the lightning bolt hit?"

"I know. I'm not stupid," Madeline said. "Look, I need to have a plan; even if I die doing this, it will be okay if I have a plan."

"What plan, the plan of how to defeat Sayer? That is not for you to make, it is my responsibility. When the time comes, you will know what to do. Do not waste your time worrying about that."

"No, a plan of what to do when we are done," Madeline snapped. "I know I can't control what happens up to whatever I was brought here to do. I need to have something to look forward to."

"You think that I do not understand your need to plan your future?" Arabela snapped back. "I too am a creature of fate. I do not wish to rule the Summer Lands. Like you, I have to do something I am not sure I want to do. You are not the only one who feels a need to control the future."

"If you understand, why don't you help me? Why are you always telling me what to do instead of asking me?"

"Because I know my duty. It is apparent that in your world duty means nothing in the face of your desires for your own comfort and pleasure." Arabela's face was flushed with her anger.

"Don't tell me I don't know my duty. I spent my life so far meeting expectations from my parents, my friends and my employers. Life is not just about duty." She kicked her horse into a canter. "I do not wish to talk anymore."

18

She could hear another horse catching up. "Leave me alone," she shouted over her shoulder.

"I cannot," Jode's voice came back. "I will not speak if you wish peace but it is dangerous to ride alone in the forest. I will stay with you."

She slowed to a walk and looked back over her shoulder. She and Jode were the only riders visible. She regretted her words, and her tone.

"I'm sorry. I thought Arabela had followed me."

"No," Jode pulled alongside. "I asked her to stay with the others. I did not want to listen to you argue any longer."

"I don't know why I can't keep my temper. She just seems to push me over the edge all the time," Madeline sighed. "I know it's not her fault, I am as much to blame as she."

"It must be difficult for you to be here," Jode said. "Are you missing your friends, your life?"

"I didn't have many friends." It hurt to acknowledge that.

"You know that she did not look for you, just for an answer to her question," Jode said. "If she had known that she had to pull you here, she may not have asked for the prophecy."

"But she did."

"What would you have done in her place?"

"I don't know." Madeline was silent for a while. If she were honest, she would have done the same as Arabela. She couldn't explain why she was so quick to anger. She'd always been able to be reasonable even with the most difficult client.

She finally said. "Jode, I am not used to just waiting for something to happen. I just keep trying to make things go faster; it's like a compulsion."

"So you can go home?" Jode looked away as he said the words.

Madeline could see his disappointment in the straightness of his back and his refusal to meet her eyes. The thought of going home didn't settle her feelings. In fact, the thought of leaving him made her sad, and the thought of leaving this beautiful world made her feel depressed. The fact that she couldn't find an acceptable option made her frustrated.

"I don't know," She admitted. "When I first got here I would have said yes. When I made my decision to stay and help it seemed to change things."

"In what way," riding closer, he glanced at her before focusing on the forest edges that now ran right up to the road. "Have you made friends here?"

"Maybe," she thought of Elise who helped her to get through the first two days without totally embarrassing herself and realized she had made a friend. "Yes, I supposed there are a few people I would miss if I left."

"What is it that draws you back? Is there a lover waiting?" He looked down at his hands.

Madeline shook her head, Jode's ability to display his love in every action was endearing. Back home, she might have found it borderline creepy, here it was charming. "If there was, would he have given up by now?"

"If he loved you, he would never give up. It has only been a few days. What a poor love that would be."

"How do you know it hasn't been years in my world?" Madeline was surprised. She had assumed that time passed faster on her world, it was a pretty standard plot device in movies.

"Blu tells us we are parallel to your world. Each minute you spend here is equal to a minute in your world." Jode shrugged. "Even so, if necessary Blu may be able to send you back in time to your world. No one need miss you."

"Oh, well, someone will be looking for us now, I suppose." She thought someone in the firm would eventually phone the police when she didn't come to work.

"I hope someone would care enough about you there to try to find you. If you disappeared from here, I would never stop looking."

"Oh, Jode, I am sorry." She felt her heart turn at the thought of him wasting his life searching and waiting for a lost love. "I don't know why you feel this way. I can't say what I feel for you. There is too much rolling around my brain."

"You are not responsible for my feelings. If fate has meant me to love someone who does not love me back, then so be it. I will say this only once," he turned to look at her. "I would lay my life down for you, Lady Madeline. Whether or not you stay here, please consider my heart yours to hold."

"You don't make it easier for me to figure out what to do," She smiled at him. "I do feel attraction to you. I don't know if it is anything more than that."

"Let us leave this topic." He turned his gaze back to the forest. "Is there some way we can find that will allow you and Arabela to work civilly together? I ask because it will have an effect on the whole company if you bicker all the time."

"I try," Madeline laughed, "God knows I do, I can try harder. I understand why she talked to Simon; I can be a pain if I don't know what is going on."

"Can I answer any more questions for you to help you learn what is…going on?"

"Yes," Madeline brightened. "If you can tell me about the world you live in. I can figure out how to use the knowledge. I just don't have any understanding of where I am, or how to survive this world. I feel like I keep asking the same questions, I'm sorry."

"Do not be sorry, ask questions and I will answer to my best ability." He rode closer again. "Please, though, let us wait here where it is clear until the others catch up. There are bandits who would happily take us for ransom."

Madeline looked around; the trees were well away from the side of the road. The left side of the road bordered a fast running river and the other was clear of anything but low growing ground cover for about half a kilometer. "Yes, it you think this is the best place to wait. I don't want you to worry; I want you to talk. And, I swear to you I will find a way to work with Arabela."

They sat on their horses and talked while they waited for the rest of the company to catch up.

~~~

Later, in Lanewall as she watched the proceedings Madeline realized she had no desire to help Arabela and the mayor, Mr. Timwell, as they settled disagreements and listened to complaints about quality of goods, delivery times, and breakage allowance. This type of thing had been her bread and butter back in her old life. Now, she was happy to sit on the sidelines, sipping a local beer and munching on spiced nuts with the other members of the company.

"You look bored." Simon said, passing her a new mug of beer. "Is it better to be involved?"

She pushed her empty mug to the end of the table so the server could clear it more easily. "I'm not bored, I'm watching. I think the problem is that here there's no problem. This is more like a managed forum for discussion. There's no intricacy of interpretation, no shade of precedent. And, have you noticed, everyone seems to want to find a solution. Where's the challenge in that?"

"So, it sounds like you might have come to one decision."

"What decision?" Madeline took a long drink of her beer.

"If you stay you won't want to be a scribe, mayor, or anything that looks like a legal profession." He tilted his head in question.
~~~

"Okay, I'll take it. Like I said, I need a decision." As she spoke, Madeline felt the fog in her brain thinning. "I still have to figure out whether to stay or go, and what to do either way, but let's call this progress."

"You forgot one decision." Simon said.

"I forgot a lot of little decisions, which one in particular?"

"Jode," Simon looked over his shoulder where the man in question was sitting talking to a group of small children, telling stories, if their rapt stares were anything to go by.

"He's not a decision," she sighed in resignation. "At least not the way you are thinking. You know he loves me."

"Yes, I'm not blind, or deaf, or stupid," Simon laughed.

"Well, the problem is that he does really love me." She watched Jode pretend to have a sword fight. "I've heard the words too often from men who wanted something from me and thought that was the way to get it. The guy loves me with all his heart."

"So why is that a problem?"

"I don't know what I feel for him," She took a long swallow of the beer. "I think what I feel might be love. It's hard to tell under all the confusion and stress, but what if I can't stay? What if I have to leave? Or, what if this quest kills me?"

"What difference would any of that make? If you love him, you love him. What's the saying," he wrinkled his forehead. "Oh, yeah, what the heart wants the heart wants."

"So, what do you think I should do?" She laughed at his surprised expression. "This is me being less controlling, get used to it."

"I think you should go for it, whatever IT is in this culture. If you let him court you according to his rules, then you can call it off if it gets too much for you. You just need to leave the baggage back home on the other side of the tree we came through."

"It won't make my final stay or go decision any easier." She watched Jode reach the climax of the story and the children all scream then laugh so hard they rolled on the ground.

"It won't make it harder, I promise. If you don't love him, then no harm no foul. If you do, then why would it make it harder?"

"I wouldn't want to resent him for making me stay. My mother stayed with my dad because she got pregnant with me. She wanted to be a dancer and I think she regretted it forever." Madeline blurted out the information like a confession.

"I'm sorry. Just remember this; if you do love him, and want to spend your life with him, there will always be something about him you'll resent. Shit, you can't expect to live together for more than a week without something annoying one of you, probably you. If you are together, you will always have the opportunity to resolve it. If you go back, you might regret leaving and would have no way of fixing it."

"I didn't realize you were so wise in the ways of love and life," she raised her eyebrow.

"I have hidden depths," he grinned, "and I watched a lot of Oprah and Doctor Phil."

The group rode out of the village with bags of trail food and a couple of barrels of beer on the horses, walking slowly to avoid jostling the beer on the short journey to the main camp. The ride took them through a small warehouse district just outside of town, the guards waved as the horses past. The fields that surrounded the village were full of flowers and bordered with herbaceous hedges.

"This is pretty, like a painting of a forgotten pastoral time in my world," Madeline said as she moved in beside Arabela. "The scent of these fields is almost overwhelming."

"They are for the perfume factories closer to the ocean. The merchants here provide the dried and fresh ingredients for the scent makers."

"Industry is not so pretty in my world." Madeline cleared her throat, "I want to apologize for my mood earlier."

"I think we both acted badly. I forget how much you have had to accept in such a short time. I am accustomed to solving problems for the people who I consider friends, not letting then solve their own problems."

"And, I am used to the same thing." Madeline looked over at Arabela. "If we stopped fighting we could probably solve any problem put in front of us."

"Ah, and then where would the world be," Arabela asked chuckling. "It may be that between us we do not know everything."

"That may be true, but would anything we didn't know be worth the bother?" She reached out her hand to Arabela. "As one control freak to the other, maybe we should call a peace."

"I like that term," Arabela said. "It describes you perfectly."

"Hey, lady," Madeline said. "We're supposed to be getting along, don't start a fight."

"I was simply making an observation." Arabela blushed, "I suppose I see how that would be offensive. Perhaps I am forgetting to look in the mirror before speaking."

"We have an expression for that," Madeline said, "the pot calling the kettle black."

"Are you saying I'm the pot?" Arabela said looking at her flat stomach, "I don't show yet."

Madeline laughed and held out her hand again, "peace?"

Arabela leaned across and shook the hand. "Fate help Sayer Goddard," she said.

Madeline rode in silence for a few minutes, thinking over what they should do next.

"I think it would be a good idea if you met with me and Blu this evening." Arabela said, before Madeline could think of anything concrete.

"I'm not a religious person," Madeline said. "I don't know what good meeting with Blu would do."

"Blu is a priest," Arabela said as though that would help.

"Yes, and I still don't understand what religion has to do with it." Madeline reminded herself that they had just agreed to peace and thought a moment. "What function does Blu have beyond religion?"

"The priest is also a secular advisor here. Are they not in your world?"

"No," Madeline said as understanding dawned, "or, rather not in my country. We have had many ugly situations happen when religion is involved in the day to day running of a country."

"It would not be possible to run the country without the priests."

"How many religions do you have?"

"One, how can there be more than one true path?"

"If my world is any example, you can't peacefully have more than one. We have hundreds of paths and many of our wars, past and present, have been about how people worship and what name they give to god."

"And, yet you wish to go back?" Arabela sounded astonished.

"Sometimes the familiar is better than the unknown, even if the familiar is imperfect."

"We have a saying," Arabela said. "It is better to serve a bad lord than a good Scree."

"Hah," Madeline laughed. "We say better the devil you know than the devil you don't. I guess should meet with you and Blu tonight."

19

They trotted into the main camp in the late afternoon. After helping to stable her horse, Madeline went back to her tent to wash the dust off her face and brush out her hair.

"Come back to the central room within ten minutes," Arabela said before slipping through the curtain to her room.

Madeline looked longingly at the clean clothes laid out on her bed. She weighed her choice, really clean clothes tomorrow and stay in the road soiled ones she was already wearing, or clean clothes now with no bath.

She heard quiet noises on the other side of her room wall, quickly braiding her hair she joined the two people sitting around a stone bowl of water. She would appreciate the change of clothes tomorrow.

"Welcome, Lady Madeline," Blu said beckoning her to sit on the vacant stool. "Thank you for agreeing to join us."

Madeline sat and peered at the still surface of the water; it was dark as ink. She couldn't see through the liquid to the bottom of the shallow bowl.

"Do not touch the surface," Arabela said quickly as Madeline leaned further over. "It is dangerous."

Madeline drew back and looked around the tent. The doorway was closed, and the light from outside was seeping through the thin fabric walls; the light was so diffused there were no shadows in the room.

Blu laid a thin indigo cloth over the bowl, not touching the surface. "We will scry for our enemy first, before the shadows come. I have place protections over the tent but they will only last a short while. We cannot risk stronger magic."

"Isn't scrying strong magic?" Madeline asked, thinking of the few fantasy novels she had read.

"The magic is minimal," Blu said, passing a burning stick of incense over the cloth. "It is a matter of focus more than magic."

"Will I be able to see what is happening?"

Blu muttered a few words she couldn't hear over the smoke. "I see now why Lady Arabela has such difficulty with you. Please, keep your questions until we are finished here. Now, you must concentrate your thoughts on the bowl. I will direct the vision, but you need to drive all thoughts and questions from your mind."

"Okay," Madeline had learned how to meditate a few months ago at the suggestion of her mentor, something about stress relief.

"You may see things here you do not wish to see. I ask that you school your reactions until the vision is over. Too violent a reaction may draw the attention of Goddard to our work."

"Got it," Madeline said. "I need a minute to find my center and then I'll be ready."

"One minute, then," Blu agreed, his face calm and neutral as he waited, fingers pinching the center of the cloth waiting to remove it.

Madeline looked at Arabela, her face was also calm her eyes looking towards the cloth covered bowl. Focusing on the center of the cloth Madeline closed her eyes. Slowly breathing in and out, she emptied her mind of questions and thoughts, visualizing them as snowflakes melting on the ground. When she was ready, she opened her eyes and nodded. Blu muttered two more words as he drew the cloth straight up and dropped it on the floor behind him.

Madeline had expected to see misty clouds or something in the water, but it was more like the changing of a channel on a television. The surface of the liquid was dark, and then it was not. On the still liquid, she could see a picture of a room in a castle somewhere. The stone walls were draped in tapestries and the floor covered with straw and fur pelts.

She watched a man sitting at a table eating. He was tall and broad shouldered. His long, red-blonde hair was braided into thin ropes with bones woven in to them. His face was clean-shaven. She could see the detail of the scars on his arms and chest, they looked like badly healed slashes, she thought they were likely sword cuts. She almost cried out when he seemed to look up at her, his deep blue eyes moved past her, landing on a black haired woman sitting on the floor.

He said something to her but Madeline heard nothing. The woman scurried away on her knees, bent over facing the floor.

The man threw the contents of his plate at her and stood up. Madeline realized his proportions were not right for a human; his upper body was too long, his legs shorter in the thigh than the calf.

She could see he was shouting now, his face contorted in rage. Even though she couldn't hear his words, Madeline felt her stomach tighten in remembered fear of her father's temper. Her father had been an unforgiving man, a man with standards no one was ever able to meet.

A teenage girl ran into the scene, her hands thrown out in plea, she wore rags and a series of bruises on her arms, legs, and face. She moved between the man and the woman and knelt in a pose of fear. Madeline thought she was offering herself as a victim to spare the woman. The man grabbed the girl and picked her up, throwing her out of their line of sight. He grabbed the woman's black stringy hair and slapped her, hard, across the face. Madeline couldn't see her face because the woman's back was to her.

The man laughed and said something else. He reached down and grabbed the woman and lifted her, he ripped her dress, more a collection of rags, and buried his face in her large breasts. The woman's body went rigid and then seemed to melt against the man.

The edges of the vision started to waver and then the liquid turned back to the black opaque substance.

"Lady Madeline," Arabela's voice cut through the emptiness Madeline felt. "Madeline, are you all right? Madeline?"

She blinked and felt tears fall. Someone pressed a white cloth on her face and she felt a hand rubbing her back. "I'll be okay," she assured them. "I'll be fine. That was just a bit intense."

"I did not expect that you would react this way," Blu said. "I would not have included you if I had known your sensitivity. Please, tell me what you saw."

She wiped her tears, and accepted a mug of wine from Arabela. "A man, he was abusing two women, well, really a young girl and a woman."

"You saw Sayer Goddard," Arabela confirmed. "The two women were his current lovers."

"Is that the way these Scree treat their women? It was horrible, but the one woman seemed to willingly participate at the end."

"No," Blu answered. "Sayer Goddard treats his wives more respectfully, the way most Scree treat the women who carry on the bloodline. What you saw was how he takes his pleasure. Not all Scree are so vile unless they are in the middle of a battle. Most are harsh but fair masters to the women they capture as slaves. You must remember that being Scree is not evil, just as being a human is not good. The evil here is Sayer Goddard, not Scree."

"Well, I'm pretty sure if I have to, I can find the motivation to kill him. That's a good thing, I guess." She sat taller on the stool. "I won't let what I saw weaken me. I will do what it takes, don't worry."

Blu carefully poured the contents of the bowl into a flask and then rinsed the bowl with clean water before wiping it dry. "It is good to hear. You should know that I saw only Goddard. Lady Arabela, what did you see, exactly?"

"Goddard," she said, spitting out the name. "He was at table; he threw his plate at someone I couldn't see."

"I must think on why Lady Madeline saw so much more. It is possible she is touched with some power. If that is the case she will need a teacher."

"What do you mean?" Madeline watched the tiny man as he packed away all the equipment.

"You saw much more than we did, and the vision lasted longer for you, I think that if I had not broken your concentration you would still be watching the scene." He placed the bag with his equipment by the side of the door curtain. "It is curious that someone from a far world would possess any magical talent at all, and yet, if you do have talent, it is powerful."

"Great, now I'm a witch," she said rolling her eyes.

"We will see," Blu said not matching her sarcastic tone. "I must meditate on this. I will speak with you about it when I have an answer. In the meantime, please do not try any magic."

"I will try not to," She laughed. "It's not as if I will suddenly find a way to use it even if I have magical powers."

"True, but before this you did not know about your talent, if talent it is, knowing changes things," Blu said, pulling aside the curtain. "Until we know how you express your magic, please do not wish for anything."

"Well, it's not a wish, but I am starving, is it time for dinner?"

"Yes, we were in the vision for over an hour." Arabela said, "Or, rather you were, I've been trying to wake you for most of that time. And, I too am hungry. Let us join the rest of our party."

20

The rest of the party consisted of Jode, Simon and an Eldman. They were standing in a clearing at the edge of camp, snacking on food that sat on one end of a long wooden table. The other end held a black cloth on which lay seven knives of varying sizes; none of them had more than a cloth wrapped tang for a handle.

Jode stepped forward from the group as the two women entered. "Madeline, I hope your time with Blu was fruitful. I would be happy to hear the story later if you would be kind enough to tell me. For now, please allow me to introduce the Eldman knife master, Kapeni. He will train you today."

The Eldman bowed deeply, hands together in front of his chest. "It is indeed my honor Lady Madeline."

"I am please to meet you Sir Kapeni." She responded.

"Not sir, just Kapeni," he pointed to the row of knives. "If it is convenient we can spend the remaining daylight increasing your knowledge of the silent killer."

Madeline judged there was only about a half hour of light left and decided she would wait to eat rather than cut short her training. "Where are the targets?"

"We will aim first at the trees," he led her to the table. "Do you see the white tree standing alone?"

Madeline saw what looked like a birch tree, about ten feet away. "Yes, will I be throwing that far?"

"At first, it may seem close, but throwing accurately is the point of the exercise. When you have that distance perfected, you will be able to adjust your technique to up to four times that distance. It will be enough for this purpose that you are proficient at these short ranges."

The blades of the knives were unsharpened, only the point of had any edge. The weights ranged from a light knife around four ounces to a heavy knife of over half a pound. Madeline reached for the lightest knife. Kapeni lifted it out of her hand and replaced it with one that felt like it weighed around seven ounces.

"I don't know if I can throw this more than a couple of times," she said, lifting her hand up and down to test the weight.

"The lightest knives are the hardest to control, this one will serve you for training." He laid a rope on the ground to the side of the table, "this is where you will stand. You will throw from the back of the rope until you hit the tree. Then you will throw until you consistently hit it."

Madeline watched as he demonstrated how to hold the knife, sort of like a hammer. Then he raised the knife until his elbow was in line with his shoulder, the knife slightly behind him. He released the knife as he brought his arm down in a smooth motion; it rotated in the air and sank into the tree.

"I'm sure it's not that easy," she said as he motioned her to try. He nodded in agreement and corrected her grip; then he tsked and corrected her stance.

"Now do not release the knife yet, simply move your arm forward and down slowly."

Madeline did her best to mimic his earlier moves.

"You see where in that movement you are pointing at the target?"

Madeline raised her arm back to where she thought he meant, "here?"

Kapeni nodded, "take your arm back to the top. Release the knife at the right point. We will see how far you can throw and then correct your movements until you get it perfect."

Madeline released the knife and it went in the right direction but fell short of the target. "Damnation." She had hoped it would come naturally to her. It looked like she was in for some long training before she became proficient.

They walked to the tree together to retrieve the two knives. As they returned to the rope, Kapeni said, "you are aiming correctly, but you release the knife a little too late. You also absorb the strength of your throw into your body by leaning back."

"Really?" She didn't remember leaning back. "Okay let's try again."

Madeline followed his instructions through several more attempts until she finally made the throw to the tree.

"Well done. Now, do you know why that worked?"

"Not really, I just stopped thinking about it so much. I had the movement all down and I finally felt myself leaning back and forth while I threw, I stopped doing it. I guess I was trying too hard; I decided to just let it happen."

"Good," now there is still enough light for you to throw ten more times. Please use these knives and I would like the target to have ten knives in it when you are done." He stabbed the knives blade first into the grass at her feet.

Madeline was getting very hungry, "I might throw better if I had something to eat."

"You will throw better if you know you will eat after," Kapeni said. "Besides, the light will go soon.

Madeline accepted defeat and bent for the first blade. She stood holding it for a moment as she remembered the feeling of throwing the blade perfectly into the wood, the sound that it made, a hollow thunk, and the position of her body when she was done the throw. She raised the knife and swiftly brought her arm down releasing the knife at the right point and following through. Thunk. She picked up the next knife and repeated the movements. Thunk. Seven more times the knife went directly into the tree. The last knife clanged and bounced back because there was no more room for it to sink into the wood.

"Well done," Jode handed her a mug of wine. "Go and eat something; I will retrieve your blades."

Madeline thought of protesting but didn't, she was too hungry and her arm ached, not having to pull the knives out would be a blessing. She walked back to the table shrugging the pain out of her shoulder. Platters of meat and bread with a salad of bitter greens had replaced the snacks. She filled a plate and sat with the rest of the group.

"The knives you threw are now yours," Kapeni said. "Please practice each day until you can place each blade in the target. As you become proficient, move one foot length away from the target and extend your reach."

Madeline swallowed the mouthful of salad and said, "thank you, Kapeni. I am not familiar with your customs; do I need to give you a gift in return?"

"It is not necessary," he bowed again. "If you would honor me with a visit to my home after the quest is complete I would consider it gift enough in return."

"If it is possible, I will be happy to do so." She said, hoping it would be, even if she decided to go home. These grave Eldmen interested her and she wondered how they had come to be who they were.

Kapeni took his leave and Jode rolled the knives in the cloth giving them to a passing server to take them back to the tent. The camp torches were lit as the light finally faded; groups of people drifted to gather around the campfires.

"If you find you need a refresher on how to throw, I am a serviceable knife thrower," Arabela said. "It is sometimes difficult the second time one trains, particularly without a master."

"I think I remember," Madeline said. "I just hope my arm and shoulder are not too stiff to work out tomorrow."

"You should wake early and warm up with the sword before you start throwing," Arabela suggested.

Madeline noticed that Simon and Jode were watching the two women carefully. Probably waiting for us to start arguing, she thought. It was true Arabela's offers to help were grating on her nerves and it felt like orders, not like suggestions. She pushed the irritation aside and smiled her biggest sunniest smile.

"That's a great idea." She laughed when even Arabela expressed surprise. "I admit I need some help with this. I'm not sure I would be able to actually use a sword or a knife against another person, but I do need to know what to do in case it turns out I have to defend myself."

"I will have to excuse myself from you, ladies," Simon rose from his seat. "I have a meeting I need to attend with some friends."

"Good night," both women responded.

Jode excused himself and promised to meet Madeline at dawn for sword training. He followed Simon towards the left side of the camp.

"I think they expected us to disagree," Arabela laughed. "I think it frightened them when we did not."

"They'll get used to it," Madeline said, "well, I guess if we give them the chance to. I'm trying not to lose my temper. If it unsettles the men, then it's just more reason to be reasonable. Do you need to go anywhere or should we head back to the tent?"

"The tent sounds the best," Arabela handed her plate to the woman clearing the table. "Perhaps we can have a glass of wine and, if you wish, we can talk about the vision."

"I'd rather not dwell on it," Madeline said, trying to push aside the sudden memory of Goddard looking into her eyes.

"Then, you can tell me about the men in your world. It seems they are not so different there, if Sir Simon is any example."

They walked back to the center of the camp gossiping about inconsequential things, winding down so they could sleep. When they arrived, it became apparent that drifting off to sleep early was not going to be in the cards. Two Sylph males waited for Arabela, two armed men and Blu accompanied them. The Sylph prostrated themselves when she walked towards them.

"What is this," Arabela looked to Blu. "Why are Caver and Light here?"

"They presented themselves to your guardsmen," he answered. "I was summoned after they arrived, at their request apparently. I am as unenlightened as you, perhaps now they will tell us what has brought them here."

Arabela told the two Sylph to rise and they did, keeping their eyes on the ground. Madeline tried to excuse herself, but the two green-haired men asked her to stay.

"Please," Arabela said, her worry clear in her tone, "tell us why you have come."

Light spoke, "a grievous error, my lady, one that may have repercussions beyond this night. This inattentive Sylph has imbibed too many glasses of the strong brew of the Eldmen. He became melancholic for his lover; she stays in the home cave while we adventure with you."

The other Sylph was rocking slightly back and forth, muttering quietly. He suddenly dropped to his knees and raised his eyes to Arabela. "I do not know how to apologize or how to undo this thing."

"What thing, Caver?" Arabela's face drained of color, "tell me now, no more begging, no more delay. Only when you have spoken the words can we find a solution."

"I reached out to her mind," he responded in a hushed voice. "I did not think. It has been so long since we have had to guard our magic."

"Blu, what can you do?" Arabela ignored the Sylph, "what can we do?"

"We can only be on guard," Blu answered.

"What is the problem," Madeline asked. "You said Sayer will not notice us unless we do something to provoke his attention."

"It is not Sayer we must concern ourselves with," Arabela said. "There are creatures out in the forest who will only notice our passage if we announce it with the use of magic. Scrying is not that type of magic, it's a receiving of vision. What Caver did was to send magic out. Damn, this was going too well."

She turned to Caver and Light. "What is done is done; we will leave it at that. I thank you for coming forward with this; we can at least be on guard. Go back to your fellows and rest. Tomorrow the road will require us to be alert. As punishment, you will scout ahead and to the sides. Hope that no creature awoke."

The Sylph ran to their camp after thanking Arabela for her wise decision. The two guards returned to the small unit that had accompanied them. They were to report to Jode and then arrange for patrols of the camp throughout the night. Blu and Arabela spent a moment discussing the possibilities, then he left to scry the surrounding area for threats.

"Is there anything I can do?" Madeline asked.

"You should sleep if you can. I think it is important for you to rest and rise early for your training. I will be joining Blu in his tent for a few hours."

Madeline wasn't sure she could fall asleep with this unknown threat overhead, but she agreed. It was clear Arabela didn't need anything else to worry about.

~~~

Madeline washed her face and braided her hair back into tight ropes to minimize the morning tangles. As she prepared for sleep, the quiet seemed to roll a blanket of weariness over her shoulders. Riding all day and then throwing knives was taxing on her body, and this was only day two of the journey, how bad was it going to get.

"Maybe I'll get used to it," she said kicking off her boots and curling up under the blanket.

Five minutes later, she tossed herself onto the other side of the bed. "Crap," this was going to be one of those nights, one where she wasn't going to fall asleep. She decided to lay there waiting for sleep, trying not to toss and turn every few minutes. If she were at home, she'd turn on the light and read a book until her mind shut down. Here she had a book, but no bedside light.

The camp was silent; she knew that somewhere people were walking the perimeter, watching for threats. She was a long way from the edge of the camp in this tent. Madeline heard Simon and Jode come back about an hour after they had left. They were talking quietly about something. She felt comforted by the sound of Jode's voice, in another world she might invite him in and burn off some energy while waiting for sleep to come. "No," she told herself sternly, "he's off limits unless you commit."
~~~

She heard Simon say goodnight to Jode, and then Jode walked away from the tent. He must be on sentry duty, she thought. He'll be tired tomorrow.

She dozed off for what may have been anywhere from ten minutes to an hour, it definitely wasn't anywhere near morning. Her skin itched and burned. The camp was still quiet but she could hear whispering nearby.

"We can just cut it."

"No, they will see."

"What you think we should do?"

"Disappear and then walk in, take prize."

"Too dangerous."

Madeline thought the conversation was odd, what prize would someone be taking from the camp?

"Cut quick, grab prize, disappear."

"Quick, quick, you have potion?"

"Yes," a different voice answered.

Madeline watched as a slit appeared in the side of the tent. She opened her mouth to scream and felt a wet rag cover her mouth. It smelled sweet, and she struggled against the hands holding it, but other hands held her still. She couldn't see who the hands belonged to, not because it was dark, because they were invisible.

"Breathe, pretty," a dry voice whispered directly into her ear.

She arched her back trying to escape the hands, holding her breath and praying that someone would come in. But, the arms held her until she had no choice but to breathe. Sweetness entered her lungs and the world turned from dark, to grey, to nothing.

“Good, prize,” a voice said. “Pick up, quick quick.”

21

"Madeline, get up." Arabela called from the central room. "It is sunrise you need to train before we ride out." She walked out to the training area in front of the tents; Jode was waiting working through some warm up exercises. "I will give her a minute or two, but then I'm going in and pulling her out of bed."

"She needs her rest," Jode said. "We can train this afternoon while you meet the people of Wildfield."

"She agreed to train in the morning. You were up on duty all night and you are here."

"I am used to short sleep. She, apparently, is not."

"Well, she needs to be up anyway, we should be on the road early." Arabela stomped into the tent before Jode could comment. She threw back the curtain in the doorway to Madeline's room and saw the bed tossed all over the floor, no Madeline. Then she saw the gaping tear in the rear wall. "Jode, come in here."

He ran through the tent, sword held unsheathed pointing down.

"She's gone," Arabela pointed out the obvious. "Someone or something came last night."

"Get Blu," Jode ordered. "He will find our clues. Damn that Sylph, he will feel my sword in his gut if she is harmed."

"We will find her before anyone can do her harm," Arabela assured him and then ran to find someone to bring the priest to the tent.

She returned to the room. "He will be here as soon as they can bring him. I will look around. There is no one here to threaten me; go and tell Sir Simon, it is not right that he should not know."

"Don't touch anything," Jode said. "Blu will need everything as it is."

"I know, you oaf," Arabela pushed him out. "If you weren't so obviously in love with her I would take affront from your words. Go, Sir Simon will want to be here."

Jode ran and woke Simon; both of them crossed the space between the tents as Blu hurried towards them.

"Sir Jode," the tiny priest said a little breathlessly. "I am sorry that the consequences fell on Lady Madeline. I know your feelings for her are strong."

"Don't worry about me," Jode tried to keep his voice respectful; it was not sensible to annoy a priest. "We need to find her for the prophecy."

"Just so," Blu nodded. They entered the tent and found Arabela bent over the bedding, carefully not touching anything.

"There's a scent here." She pointed at the pillow. "She was drugged, I think."

"That explains why no one heard anything," Simon said. "If she'd had a chance to yell we'd still be trying to stop the ringing in our ears."

"Please," Blu said. "Stand where you are while I look at everything." He walked slowly around the bedding and then over the floor to the slit in the wall. "See here, the foot marks in the dust."

"Dray," Jode said. "Damn."

"What are Dray?" Simon asked. "What are they going to do to her?"

"Scavengers," Jode answered his face white. "I do not know what they will do to her. They are unpredictable, and Madeline is not the kind of person they are used to dealing with."

"Blu," Arabela said. "Can you find them?"

"Probably not, but it is worth a try." The priest cast out his arm and spun in a full circle. "We are protected here. Does anyone have anything that will reflect an image?"

Simon looked around the room and patted his pockets; Arabela shook her head, but Jode pulled out his sword.

"Here, the side of the blade should work." He handed it hilt first to Blu. "Hurry, we don't even know how long she has been gone."

"Be as calm as possible," Blu said, touching Jode's shoulder. "Everyone clear your mind, or leave."

Simon shook his head and stepped outside the tent. "Even if I knew how to, I don't think I could."

As soon as he stepped outside the other three moved close together over the surface of the sword. Blu had wrapped the ends in the edges of his robes and held it through the cloth. The gleam of metal suddenly flickered as though a light had been turned on inside the metal.

"Think of Madeline," he said in a steady quiet voice. "Ask the question what happened here and the sword will answer."

Three voices spoke the question in unison. The light within the blade flickered and came back dimly; the tent was dark. Madeline lay in the bedding apparently asleep. She moved suddenly, sitting up and looking to where the rip in the tent would be.

She struggled against unseen hands, and seemed to resist breathing until finally she took in a deep shuddering breath and closed her eyes, falling limply into invisible arms.

"Definitely Dray." Arabela said. "It looks like it happened in the darkest of night, when they entered through the hole there were no stars, or fires."

"She has been gone for four hours." Blu agreed. "If there were many of them she will be a long distance from here."

"That's only if there were ten or twenty of them," Jode said. "If there had been more than three or four we would have smelled them."

"True," Blu said. "We can extract one more question from the sword. What is it to be?"

"Is she still alive," Jode said. "It is vital to know that."

"Where is she is a better question." Arabela said.

"No," Jode whispered. "If we ask that it may show us the interior of a cave, of what use would that be?"

"And if we find she is alive, but do not know where, what good would that be?" Arabela snapped.

Blu placed the sword on the bedding and stepped back gesturing for the others to do the same. "You are asking questions and I do not wish the sword to answer the wrong one."

"What do you think we should ask?" Jode asked his voice tight with tension.

"I think we should ask ourselves what is the most important thing we cannot find out by other means."

"If she is alive," Jode said. "We cannot know that by any other means until we find her.

"And, what if she is?" Blu asked, "and, what if she is not."

"Do not say that," Jode stepped forward then checked himself. "I am sorry, but do not curse her."

"I am not," Blu waited for the answer.

"If she is alive we will move quickly to rescue her," Arabela answered for Jode. "If she is not, I pray that is not so, then we will move to recover her body. The prophecy was clear she needed to be there at the end of the quest, it did not specify she would need to be alive."

"I think we should ask, not where she is but for directions," Jode said. "Ask in what direction she was taken. We will still need to track them but we have people to do that, it would gain us time to know which way to set out."

"A good question," Blu said but did not reach for the sword.

"What if we ask how we can get her back?" Arabela blurted.

"These are Dray, we will need to negotiate," Jode said.

"Yes, but what with. Dray do not always respond to money. Sometimes they value things we do not understand," Arabela said then turned to Blu. "Is this a better question?"

"I think it is. It maybe we will not understand the question until we are with the Dray, but it is a good question." The priest bent and picked up the sword. "Focus your minds on that question. Jode, do not consider the other questions or we may have an answer to something else."

"I am ready," he answered.

The three heads bent again over the sword and muttered the same words. The light flared and encompassed them in a bright white ball, then faded away leaving only the metal.

"We must leave quickly," Jode said. "Sir Simon, come back in, we are done."

"What happened?" Simon pushed back through the curtain. "There was nothing going on. How come you are all ready to get going?"

Blu handed the sword back to Jode. "The protective spell stopped you hearing or seeing what occurred. We know that Lady Madeline was indeed taken by Dray. We will explain Dray as we ride. We also know that to get her back we will need to tell a secret."

"No, a lie," Arabela said.

"No, the truth," Jode said.

Simon threw up his arms in frustration. "Great, where do we start?"

"Call for the Sylph Caver and the Fay AaLa," Arabela said. "And get yourself ready to ride."

"That's it? No tracking animals, no broken twigs leading the way?"

"The Sylph will provide secrecy by muddling the minds of any person or creature that approaches, or notices us. The Fay will ride behind you while casting for Madeline." Arabela picked up the hairbrush and pulled at the bristles. "Give her this hair, and she will follow a trail to return it to its owner, Madeline."

"But isn't magic how we got here in the first place?" Simon asked before he turned to the curtain again.

"If there are Dray about there is no other creature for us to worry about. This is small magic, in any case," Jode started to leave. "Hurry yourself, I will collect the Sylph and Fay and meet you at the horses."

~~~

Madeline woke in a dingy tent. She was lying on a pile of rags that smelled of sour milk or something that smelled like sour milk. She closed her eyes again and waited for her vision to adjust. When she opened them, she could see more detail. The tent was a low rounded dome; she would not be able to stand. If
~~~

she were going to escape, it would be on her knees. She tried to sit up and found that her hands and legs were bound; a single rope moved between them just long enough that, with her hands low on her back, she was able to keep her legs straight. If she tried to pull up her arms, she yanked on her legs. This would require some thinking through, and her head was still foggy from the drug.

As she rested on her back waiting for the fog to clear, she became aware of voices outside the tent. They sounded like the voices from last night, raspy and harsh like a lifetime smoker. "Keep her," one said. "Good servant, no more need for us to work, she do for us."

"No! Trade," another one, she decided to call him Mo, argued. "Too skinny for servant, too weak, trade, buy good servant, maybe breeder too."

"Who get breeder?" A third voice asked. Madeline named him Curly. "Maybe get more breeders and no servant. I don't mind doing work for breeder." The three voices cackled in laughter.

"Where trade?"

"Pig Eye," Mo answered.

"Pig Eye want to know where we get her. Pig Eye want to know if trouble come with her."

"We tell truth," Curly said.

"Yes, truth, we hear call of magic, come take our prize."

"Good, truth," the first voice agreed; Madeline called him Larry. "If no prize why do magic?"

Madeline's mind cleared slowly as she listened to the conversation. Pig Eye didn't sound like her kind of company. "Okay, how to get out of here? Here being a tent where I've been tied up by invisible creatures." The sound of her voice calmed her. She kept talking, quietly.

"I could try the 'pull feet through arms' trick so I can get my hands in front of me. Running bent over will be a lot easier if it's forward instead of backward." Her mind remembered they were able to disappear. "Shit, is there someone here?" She asked.

No one answered. "Okay, that doesn't mean there's no one here but I have to work on the assumption it does, otherwise I might as well just wait for Pig Eye to trade me."

She rolled off the pile of rags onto the dirt floor, landing on her back. She thought about the three Pilates lessons she'd taken and drew a deep breath. Holding in her abs, she arched her back and rose up on her shoulders, sliding her arms as far down her body as she could; just under her butt. Then she curled her spine and tried to slide her arms down the back of her thighs while pulling her legs in. It worked, her arms were straining painfully but her wrists were at her ankles, she only had to find a few more inches of flexibility. Then her back spasmed and she arched it involuntarily, her arms sliding back down to the small of her back. The spasm relaxed and she breathed through the pain.

"Okay," she said on the exhale. "Calm down, rest for a moment and try again." Four long breaths later, she started the movement again, as she arched her back, a second spasm of pain ripped through her upper back. She collapsed on the floor. "Time for plan B, I guess."

"Food ready," Mo shouted. "You take to prisoner, she wake soon."

Madeline rolled onto her left side and closed her eyes. It seemed a good idea not to let them know she was awake.

"You awake?" Larry asked. He kicked her and Madeline felt his bare toes in the small of her back. "How you get down there?"

"What happen," Curly said, close to her ear. "Look she awake."

Hands roughly dragged her back to the heap of rags. She opened her eyes and stared right into the brown ones of a tiny person. His teeth were broken and jagged where they weren't missing, and his hair stood up like porcupine quills.

He pointed a dirty finger at her, the nails long and hooked. "You stay there, no bruises. You worth less if damaged."

She watched as the creature standing beside her slapped the first one. "You not kick, damage."

Larry pushed back at Curly, "no damage. Shut up."

The two small creatures tussled until the food bowl went spinning and dumped its contents over the far side of the tent. "Now she go hungry. Already too skinny," Curly smacked Larry and stomped out of the tent.

Madeline gave a small prayer of thanks that the food had spilled. It was grey and lumpy and seemed to be the source of the sour milk smell.

~~~

The Fay tapped Simon on his shoulder, "they are close now, in that direction." They were riding at the head of the small group; Simon stopped and waited until the rest caught up.
~~~

"Okay, what's the plan?" he asked.

"We don't really have one formed yet," Arabela said. "We are close enough that AaLa does not have to seek. I can smell the reek of Dray on the wind."

"So," Simon said, "we really need a plan."

"Dray are creatures of negotiation. They will keep any deal they agree to no matter what the consequences." Caver said, his head down.

"I don't know what we have to offer them," Jode said. "If it will free Madeline, I will give them my lands and income."

"That isn't the kind of deal they want. Land and income require work," Arabela said. "Dray do not like to take on more work than necessary."

"Then maybe they'll be ready to hand Madeline back. She's a lot of work," Simon said. Looking at Jode's expression, he added "sorry, I guess it's not a good time to joke."

"No," Jode said.

"Why can't we just go in and fight them off and take Madeline back?"

"They are able to become invisible, and cause anyone they are carrying to become invisible also." Arabela answered. "If we can convince them that they had no right to take her we can take her back. If we have something to exchange her for it would be better."

Caver slid off the back of Jode's horse. "I caused this, trade me."

"I cannot do that," Arabela said. "It would not be right."

"Then for a year's service. I go willingly, Lady." He bowed low again. "It will allow me to remove my foolish error from my conscience."

"Very well, if we have to," Arabela nodded. "First, I would like to find a way to win her without trading anything."

"It occurs to me that they would not have taken her from camp if they didn't think they had a right to." Jode said. "It might be good to start the negotiation by finding out why they thought that."

"Yes," Arabela said. "If they had no right to her then they will give her up."

"So," Simon said, "the plan is we go in and talk these guys around. They give us Madeline back and we just continue on with the quest."

"I don't know if it will be so simple," Arabela said, "but, yes, that is the plan."

Simon sighed and thought, sarcasm doesn't fly here.

"With one exception," Jode said dismounting. "Only Arabela and I will approach the Dray. The rest of you will stay with the horses."

"Wait," Simon said. "Why only you two, I don't want to stand here waiting and wondering."

"The Dray are masters at this," Jode said. "The fewer people involved the less likely it is we will find ourselves trapped in a complex and untenable deal. If we need someone, it will be you.

If Arabela, or anyone, waves this white scarf from the top of the hill, you come, only you."

Jode and Arabela walked in the direction AaLa had indicated.

"Dray, come bargain," Madeline heard Jode call out. Through a gap in the tent flap, she could see him walk towards small fire.

"Who calls," Larry answered. "Who thinks it is wise to bargain with the Dray?"

"Sir Jode Montgomery of the Lower Plains; I escort the Lady Arabela of the Summer Lands. It was her camp you entered last night."

She could see the three Dray huddle together, and hear them arguing in low voices.

"We will speak with the Lady of the Summer Lands. What is it you wish to bargain for?" Mo said.

"You took someone last night." Arabela said without introduction.

"We took our prize. We come when magic called and we took our prize. You know rules. Do magic without permission and pay a price."

"You took the wrong prize," Arabela stated.

Mo gestured to the other Dray. They hurried to the tent and came back with Madeline slung between them, Larry at her head Curly at her feet, her butt dragging in the dirt.

"Our prize," Curly pointed. "This is right prize."

"Why do you think so," Arabela asked, trying not to catch Madeline's gaze, to keep her focus on the negotiation.

"Magic done," Curly said holding up one hook-nailed finger.

"Yes, we are aware we violated the rule." Arabela said. "By taking the wrong prize you have forfeited payment."

"Prize right," Curly held up a second finger. "We take woman."

"Why this woman? She did not commit the crime."

"She not belong to anyone," Curly said, holding up a third finger and nodding as though he had given proof.

"Why do you think that?" Arabela tried not to relax her focus on the negotiation; this was a critical point. "What is it about her that tells you she does not belong?"

"Not smell same as others."

"If she does belong to someone, will you agree that you are at fault?"

They huddled again, and then Curly turned back, and with clear reluctance said, "yes, need proof."

"She belongs to me. She is my sister."

"No, Lady of Summer Lands has no sister."

"She is a secret sister," Arabela leaned forward. "This is something no one knows."

"Why she not smell of you?"

"Maybe because she also belongs to someone else," Arabela said. "If she belonged to someone else would she smell the same as me?"

"No," Curly's response was sullen. "Who else?"

"To Sir Jode," Arabela said, leaning in close. "They are to become one."

Madeline stared at Jode and Arabela, knowing she should maintain the lie, but hoping she wasn't being committed to something.

"How we know this true?"

"I can bring forth a witness," Arabela offered. "I can call them from the top of that hill. You can watch me all the time."

"How you call?"

"I wave this handkerchief and one will come."

Curly pulled Mo forward. "No, this one will take scarf and wave. You stay here, no tricks."

The Dray took the scarf from Arabela and ran to the top of the hill; he waved the scarf and waited. A few minutes passed and he ran back to the camp. Simon appeared on the rise.

"Man come," Mo announced, pointlessly.

As they waited, Madeline tried to understand what she needed to do. There had been no clues from Arabela or Jode; in fact, neither had looked at her beyond their first glance when she was dragged out of the tent.

"You called," Simon said as he strode into the clearing. "Can I be of some assistance?"

"You know this person?" Curly asked, pointing to Madeline.

"Yes, I've known her for a long time."

"Who she?" Curly asked watching Jode and Arabela closely.

"Her name is Lady Madeline Higginbottom of the Far Lake," Simon simply answered the question.

Madeline could tell from his blank expression he also had no idea what was going on. She trusted his ability to act on the fly; it had served him well in the old world when faced with impatient or untrusting clients.

Curly turned to Arabela. "Where is Far Lake, I not know it? Is it true place?"

Jode answered for her. "It adjoins my lands; it has been a favorite hunting area for generations. It is not unusual that you would not have heard of it, most people believe it is part of my land."

"What more do you need?" Arabela asked. "We have proven you were in the wrong. You must now release Lady Madeline and allow us to return to our party."

"Why magic happen?" Larry shouted from behind the rest of the group. "Forfeit this prize, but should have other prize."

"By taking the wrong prize you forfeit any prize." Jode stepped towards Madeline and pulled a knife out of his belt. "We will leave now, this negotiation is over. Or, would you prefer we spread the word that you are incompetent?"

"You take," Curly's voice was sullen. "No tell. Us need to eat, if you tell, we be cast out."

After freeing her hands and feet, Jode helped Madeline to her feet. She rubbed the circulation back where the ropes had been tied, then followed them back to the top of the rise. She didn't speak, fearing to ruin her freedom by accidentally saying the wrong thing in hearing range of the three Dray.

As they topped the hill, Madeline looked back and saw the three small creatures watching them.

22

They rode back to camp, Madeline sitting behind Arabela in the absence of her own horse. The trail was rough, and because each horse carried two riders, they were forced to proceed at a walk. Madeline wanted to get back to camp as quickly as possible. Camp was clean water, food, and clean clothes, in her mind.

"Can we go a little faster?" She asked.

"We go as fast as is safe," Arabela said. "Do not think I am satisfied with our pace, this delay in our travels is hazardous to our quest."

"I'm sorry," Madeline said, "I couldn't have done much about being kidnapped by those smelly beasts."

"No," Arabela said, "I did not expect you to be able to do anything. It has happened, and now we must minimize the damage."

"How long was I gone?" Madeline worried, had she been unconscious for days?

"A day."

"How can that be so significant? One day delay isn't that much."

"We cannot afford any delays. Remember we must be done before the next full moon."

"So," Madeline still wasn't clear. "We skip a village, we travel faster. It can't be that hard to catch up."

"Any sign of hurry on our part may attract Sayer Goddard's attention. That would be a disaster."

"Okay," Madeline said. "I'll take your word for it, for the sake of our peace agreement."

"Thank you for that," Madeline felt Arabela relax slightly. "I am not blaming you. I apologize if it seemed that I was. If there is fault, it lies with me. I should have left Blu to protect you."

"Stop," a raspy voice called from the side of the trail. The Fay and Sylph slid off the backs of the horses and Simon and Jode drew their swords as they dismounted. When all was still, the three Dray popped into sight; their hair quills standing on end, hands clenched into fists, almost vibrating in anger.

"You lie," Curly spat, "not your sister." He pointed at Madeline.

"What do you mean?" Madeline said, sitting up as royally as she could. "I demand to know why you accuse Lady Arabela of such a thing."

"You stranger," he pointed at Arabela, "she say. You stranger, you not know danger."

"Why do you think that allows you to call her a liar?" Madeline put her best cross-examination face on, right eyebrow slightly raised, head tilted upwards so she could look down her nose. "That is a very serious accusation."

"Sister to Lady Summer Lands cannot be stranger." Curly tried to copy Madeline's posture and failed when he placed his fists on his hips and stamped his right foot.

Madeline forced herself not to laugh; this behavior could be perfectly acceptable here in this situation. The sight, though, reminded her of a client's four-year-old brat who had kicked the client because the meeting was taking too long.

"Why cannot?"

"Would know," Curly shook a finger at Madeline. "Would know danger, would know protective magic, would know why taken."

Arabela tapped Madeline's knee, Madeline took it as a signal to stop talking. The rest of the party had drawn up around the two women. Jode and Simon stood swords in hand ready to fight if needed. The Fay and Sylph stood holding the reins of the horses. Madeline saw the Sylph looking down at the ground, stepping lightly in place, fidgeting.

"Are you saying that you are reneging on our deal?" Arabela asked.

"No deal," Curly screamed. "No deal, you lie."

"You followed us after agreeing to the deal. Why?"

"Thought there was trick. Humans trick Dray all time."

Madeline recognized the situation. They were stuck in a circular argument, and it was going to go on as long as it stayed in the 'you lied, no I didn't' stage. While Arabela and Curly traded opinions on the deal, Madeline tried to come up with a way to break the cycle. She sorted through her memories of the negotiations and realized there was a loophole, a fine distinction that might work. She tapped Arabela on the knee away from Curly's sight. Tag team arguing at its best. Arabela stopped responding to Curly's argument.

"Please," Madeline said, "help me to understand. You are right, I am a stranger and I don't know the finer points of your bargaining rules. It seems to me that Lady Arabela has told the truth from her viewpoint, it seems a lie to you."

"Lie is lie, no viewpoint," Curly snapped.

"Well, you think that because I am a stranger I cannot be her sister," she waited for him to nod. "If that is so, she lied," again a wait and a nod. "If sisters are able to be strangers then she didn't lie, and the deal is good."

"Yes, but cannot be true."

"Lady Arabela and I are sisters of the soul. Do you know what that means?"

Curly checked with Larry and Mo. "No, what is sister of the soul?"

"We do not have the same parents but we share the same fate," Madeline felt the rightness of her words, that surprised her. "Without her, I cannot fulfill my destiny. Without me, she will not be able to fulfill hers. We share a fate."

Curly pursed his lips. "Wait," he said and promptly the three Dray disappeared.

"They will discuss this idea," Jode said stepping back to his horse. "It is their belief that a deal is sacred. If they cancel it with no real grounds they will be cast out by the rest of their people, they will die without the support of their clans."

The Sylph stepped forward and spoke quietly to Arabela. "Please, lady, I remind you of the offer I made. I will willingly serve these creatures if it would allow me to erase the stain of my error."

"Caver," Arabela said. "I will not trade your freedom to the Dray. There is one thing I still have to offer if the deal is not accepted. Remember how they treasure a secret."

"We decided," The Dray popped back. "Deal is not clean. It is tricked."

"And, your decision for settlement?"

"Three choices," Curly held up three fingers, "cancel deal, return prize." He tucked one finger down and looked at Arabela hope painted all over his face.

"No," she said.

"Add to price for prize?"

"And, the third choice?"

"Change deal," he said. "Start again."

"What would you take as an added price?"

"What you offer?" Curly crossed his arms on his chest and waited with a smile of triumph on his face.

"A secret," Arabela held out her hand and there was a blue bead in the center of her palm, "one secret of the house of the Summer Lands to be given in return for the prize."

"One secret each," Curly offered back, "three secrets forever."

"No secret is forever," Arabela said. "Two secrets and we will give you the right to tell the secret in one year."

"Three secrets," came the counter offer, "one year rights."

"Three secrets," Arabela agreed, "six week rights. That is my final offer."

"Wait," The Dray disappeared again.

"That is the weirdest negotiation I've ever seen. They just disappear when they need to talk." Simon stood shaking his head and chuckling.

"Do not be amused, Sir Simon. It is quite serious." The Fay spoke for the first time. "If the Dray come back and reject the offer we will have to return Madeline to them and start all over again. This may result in the delay of days rather than hours."

"Done," Curly shouted as the Dray snapped back into visibility, "Three secrets, six weeks."

Arabela asked Madeline to dismount. She produced two more blue beads and passed them to Madeline. "You must present the beads. When you pass them over tell him that the key is home."

Madeline walked to the three Dray who stood in a row with their right hands out. She placed a bead in each palm and then told them the key. They bowed and popped out of existence. She hurried back to the horse and allowed Jode to lift her up behind Arabela.

"What was that all about?" She asked as they started campward again.

"Each bead is a spelled secret. In six weeks they can say the word home over a bead and it will reveal the secret."

"So," Simon asked from behind. "How does that make the deal good?"

"Dray are captivated by secrets. They will return to their clan with these three beads and will enjoy six weeks of high status. The secrets of the house of The Summer Lands are valuable, indeed." Jode answered.

"But won't they just tell everyone in six weeks." Simon asked.

"By that time it will not matter," Arabela said. "I would have preferred that Dray not be the ones to tell these things to the world but Lady Madeline is vital to us and the rights to those secrets are not."

Once they reached smoother ground, they pushed the horses to a gallop. The afternoon had passed while they rode, when they got back to the camp Blu waited with one Eldman and two horses.

"We sent word to the village that you would not be staying, you have had an unavoidable delay due to matters of court," Blu said. "The camp moved out at dawn as scheduled. If we hurry you will be able to make a short visit and then join camp before dark."

23

After a flying visit to the village, they returned to the camp and left their horses in the care of the grooms. The rest of the camp was well into the evening distractions, drinking and gaming, Madeline saw people playing a few interesting games of dice and stones just outside the bright firelight.

"Food will be brought in after we have bathed," Arabela announced. "Lady Madeline, do you wish to forgo your weapons practice? You can catch up tomorrow before we ride?"

"No, I'll get my throwing knives and practice before I bathe, please don't wait for me to join you for dinner, just leave some for me when I get back. I need to burn a bit of energy."

"It may be a good idea for you to speak to Blu," Arabela said. "He can help you relax enough to sleep."

"I'm sure I'll have no problem," Madeline replied. "Practice is more important than talk at this point."

"If you change your mind, please call through the door."

"Allow me to escort you to the training area." Jode said. "Arabela, if you have no further use for me I can attend to Lady Madeline's sword practice as well."

"And, I'm going to change and head out to some friends if that's okay," Simon said barely waiting for agreement before he rushed into the tent.

"It seems we all have separate plans." Arabela waved goodbye to the guard, Caver, and AaLa as they stepped away. "Let us say goodnight now, then. I will spend some time with Blu before retiring. You will find food left for you out here in an hour?"

"Thank you," Madeline and Jode said together.

"Madeline," Arabela said. "I think this idea of sisters of the spirit is an excellent one. Your profession in your old world must have been interesting if it required such imagination. Goodnight."

Thanking Arabela for the compliment, Madeline went into her room, retrieved her weapons, and tied her hair back with a black scarf, curls flowing down her back. A large tub sat beside her bed, a servant laying out tomorrow's clothes looked up as she entered. "You will want to bathe," the woman said pointing to the tub. "I'll call for water."

"No," Madeline knew she would work up a sweat with exercise. "Is it possible to have something clean I can sleep in as well as clean clothes tomorrow? I want to throw these into the fire after practice. The smell of the Dray is soaked into them." She remembered how embarrassing it had been when she had to stand apart from everyone in the village to avoid making people gag.

"Yes, I'll lay out a dress for you," the woman said. "There are no nightclothes available, I am sorry."

"Not a problem," Madeline nodded towards the tub. "I will look forward to being clean later."

The woman grimaced. "I will find some herbs to scent the bath they will remove the stench of Dray. You will probably want to wash your hair as well, I'll make sure there's a fire built outside so you can dry it. Remember, one hour, or the water will be cool."

Madeline promised to return on time and hurried out to meet Jode. He stood waiting, his tall form standing facing away from her, she stopped for a moment to enjoy the strong shoulders and nice butt, the loose white shirt and black riding pants gave him the look of a romance book hero. "Hmm, I guess the difference is he's real, the book cover is a model."

"Lady Madeline, did you say something?" Jode turned.

"Oh, nothing," she felt her cheeks burn in embarrassment, or lust, or both. "Shall we go? I have strict orders to be back in one hour."

"The same orders were given to me," Jode gestured for her to walk ahead. "Hot water is difficult to create in camp and no one wants it to go to waste."

"I'm not sure I could practice more than that anyway," she admitted. "I'm feeling the weight of the day in my bones and muscles."

"This is a good time to practice," Jode said. They had reached the edge of the camp; a wooden post stood a little further away than yesterday's tree. "An enemy will not wait until you are rested before attacking."

Madeline laid her weapons out on the cloth holding her throwing knives, "which first?"

"Knives," Jode untied his sword belt and used it to mark the line for her to start from. "Throw each one twice and then I will count out a pace for you to learn speed. We will spend half our time on knives and half on sword. You are better with the sword so it won't matter if we have to cut that short."

"Makes sense," she stepped up to the line and placed all the knives in the ground at her feet. The first throw missed by three feet. Of the first ten knives, she threw only the last six hit the post. She retrieved them and started again, this time thinking about the effect of her fatigue before throwing, nine sank into the wood.

"Now," Jode said handing her a mug of water and a strip of dried fruit. "When you have eaten, place the knives in the ground in a row, two inches apart. When you are ready, you must pluck the first knife, and throw in one move, do not stop to set your body up for the throw: pluck, stand, aim, and throw. Move to the next knife when you have finished the movement, continue until all the knives have been thrown."

Madeline chewed on the fruit while she looked at the row of knives, she would have to step to the side every other throw. She swallowed the fruit and gulped some water, before bending at the waist, she plucked the first knife, stood, drew her arm back and up, and threw the knife, bent at the waist, repeated the throw, and took a half step to the left. It took her ten seconds to throw all ten knives. She stood at then of the row and realized that each knife had hit the post in a line, from six inches from the bottom to four inches from the top.

"Holy shit," she said before she thought. "Did I do that?"

"You have a skill with edged weapons it seems," Jode smiled at her and nodded his head. "You are tired. I think we should stop before you hurt yourself."

"No, I'm all right." She didn't want to skimp on the training; if she had been better prepared the Dray incident may not have happened.

"I don't want to see you hurt," Jode insisted. "These knives can cause serious damage if you are careless."

"So," Madeline felt her patience slipping, "whoever attacks me will make sure I'm fully rested first?"

"No, but there is no need to take foolish chances."

"I am still alert enough to be careful," Madeline wasn't sure that was entirely true, but didn't really want to stop practice.

"Get your knives, then, we will pull you back and see how well you do."

She repeated the knife practice six times, each time a foot length further away. On the sixth attempt, only four of her knifes reached the post, three of those bounced off. Her arm was burning with the effort.

"Rest your arm," Jode said. "I will get your knives. It's getting dark; we have time to practice with the swords before we are done."

Madeline rolled her shoulders and stretched her arms while he retrieved and wrapped her knives in the cloth again. Unsheathing her sword, he handed it to her. "I will show you some moves, you can practice these on your own. Tomorrow evening we may have time to spar a little."

They stood beside each other, a sword's length apart. Madeline felt the heat of Jode's body on her side; she clenched her teeth to restore her focus. Ignoring the stench of the Dray, she followed him through a series of movements that mimicked a thrust and parry fight. After she had the movements down, they practiced until both were glowing with sweat. "If your task involves a swordfight I think you will be on even terms," Jode said as he started a second set of moves.

"I'm surprised how much I remember from the fencing lessons I took back home," she said, carefully following his lead and stepping forward, sword held over her head point out; her arms and shoulders screaming in pain. "It's really a matter of concentration for me."

"You concentrate better than some of my most experienced men at arms," he said, stepping back at rest, sword held blade up in front of his chest.

"Whew," she was only able to hold the final position for a couple of seconds, her arm shaking as she dropped the point towards the ground. "I'm done. Are we going to be late for the hot water?"

He wiped his face on his shirtsleeve. "We should be back just as the water arrives." Madeline's hand was still shaking with fatigue so Jode took the sword and sheathed it for her. "There is a tear in your sleeve," he said, accusation in his voice, as he pointed to a slice in the fabric.

"It didn't draw blood," she poked a finger through.

"That does not matter," Jode pulled her hand away from the tear. She could see his face tighten as he touched the fabric. "It could have been serious. A fraction of an inch and you could have sliced your hand off."

"Yes, but I didn't," she snapped, her hand warm from his touch and a yearning building to lean into him. "I probably should have stopped after the first set, but it's okay. I'm not hurt." She took her weapons from him and carried them back to the tent, walking with him in an uncomfortable silence.

"Would you prefer to have your meal in your tent?" Jode asked when they arrived. "I can have a tray sent in if you wish."

"No," Madeline was feeling reluctant to be alone. She told herself it was residue from the kidnapping, not reluctance to be apart from Jode. "I'm sorry, you were right. I was too tired. I'll listen to you next time."

"Do not make promises you cannot fulfill," Jode smiled. "As you say, there was no real harm."

She felt warmed by his smile. "I would like to eat here, with you if that's okay. I, um, would like to talk about…" what? Talk about her feelings, no, she didn't need to do that, "…you. Would you tell me about your life while we eat?"

"I'm sure there are more interesting topics, but if that is your desire, I will be happy to talk of my family and my people. Ah, see here is the water," he pointed to a team of ten people carrying steaming buckets of water. "Go, and enjoy your bath, I'll be here when you are done."

Inside her room, the tub was half full of water, the woman from earlier stood beside the bath and directed the men to fill it with most of the buckets of hot water. She had them leave the last two smaller buckets and told them to leave.

"Now, take off those stinking clothes and I'll set them to soak while you clean yourself." Madeline dropped her clothes and stepped into the water, hot but bearable. "Here," the woman said and handed Madeline a bowl of what looked like sandy soap and a rough cloth. Then she poured a powder in the bath and the scent of lavender and violets filled the room. "I'll be back in a few minutes to wash your hair for you."

“Wait, what is your name,” Madeline called as she worked up a lather. “You have been so kind.”

“Thank you my lady, I am called Alice,” she picked up the pile of clothes and walked out of the room.

The water turned gray as Madeline scrubbed away the grime of the day. She was looking at the buckets of clean water when Alice returned.

“You must feel better,” she said taking the soap from Madeline. “You look all clean and pink; the smell of those awful Dray is almost gone.”

Alice lathered Madeline’s hair and then made her duck beneath the water before lathering it again. “Now stand,” she ordered, taking a small ladle and pouring hot water over Madeline’s head until it ran clear and one of the extra buckets was empty. Alice directed Madeline to move to stand in the empty bucket then repeated the rinse so that the last traces of dirty water were diluted by clean.

“You are almost presentable,” Alice said, picking up two towels and handing them to Madeline, “dry yourself, then as much as you can your hair. There’s a brazier outside which will dry your hair completely before you sleep.”

“I feel perfect,” Madeline said as she finished rubbing her hair to dampness. “I don’t smell anymore, it’s like I’ve been in a spa.”

“I do not know what a spa is lady, but let’s get you oiled and dressed so you can join that handsome Sir Jode.”

Madeline giggled, and then rolled her eyes at the silly sound. “He is handsome, but there’s no reason to get me all prettied up for him.”

"A man sometimes needs encouragement."

"No," Madeline pushed the pot of oil away. "That is the last thing he needs."

"Why?" Alice stepped back in surprise.

"It's complicated," Madeline reached for the clothes.

"I do not think so, but, you should still allow the oil. It will keep your skin healthy and the insects away."

The small jug of lavender scented oil was sitting on a stool; Madeline applied a thin layer to her body while Alice massaged a tiny amount into her hair. When they had finished, Madeline was considering crawling between the sheets on the bed. Then her stomach growled in protest.

"I guess I do need to eat before I go to bed," she shrugged into the white dress and tied the ribbons under her breasts to create an empire waistline. "I hope the food is ready, and I could really use a glass of wine. Thank you, Alice."

"You do not need to thank me," Alice said smiling and blushing. "You go; I'll make sure this is cleaned up. I've put your clothes for tomorrow on the stool. Put the dress on the bed in the morning and I'll get it after you leave."

Madeline found her slippers, putting them on before making her way to the space in front of the tent. Jode sat at a small table waiting for her, a brazier glowing nearby. As she stepped away from the curtain, he rose and came towards her, eyes fixed on her face.

"You are beautiful," he said.

"Jode, don't"

"No, do not deny me the privilege of admiring you."

Madeline lowered the hand she had raised to quiet Jode. "Okay, I guess I appreciate the compliment. You're looking pretty hot yourself."

He had changed to deep red pants that hugged his form, and he looked good. His shirt was another loose open necked affair but this one was a cream color and looked so soft Madeline had to stop herself from reaching out to touch him. "I will also accept the compliment," Jode bowed. "Come; sit near the fire before you catch a chill."

Madeline sat with her back to the brazier, making sure her hair hung down so it would dry as quickly as possible. Jode joined her, sitting across the small table and pouring wine into black pottery mugs. The food looked and smelled like the best food she had ever had served to her. There were small bowls of bright vegetables, beans, carrots, and radishes. There was a plate of sliced dark bread in the center of the table and beside it a bowl of butter. Another plate held slices of sausages and cheese. For dessert, there was a bowl of bright shiny berries and tart thick yogurt.

"Tell me about your home," Madeline said as she reached for bread and sausages. "Do you have a castle, too?"

"My home is not as large as Lady Arabela's. And it lacks the homely feeling that a family brings," he picked at the vegetables. "I am not there often."

"You have never married?"

"No," Jode placed some of the cheese on sausage slices and nibbled, "I have spent my life so far in service, first to Alric Lord of the Summer Lands, and now to his widow."

"No children?" Madeline tried to sound casual, she wasn't supposed to care, or rather didn't have a right to care.

"No," Jode answered. "I would not have children if I was unmarried."

"Really," shit, was he a virgin? "It isn't necessary to be married to have children where I come from."

"Neither is it here, Lady Madeline. If I had sired a child I would have married the mother, it would not be right otherwise."

"Interesting," Madeline said, "and what if you didn't love her."

"I would be obligated to support her and raise the child. What would love have to do with the situation?" Jode sighed. "Until now I hadn't thought of the prospect of marriage without love as anything other than a duty. Now that I have met my true love I see that it is fortunate I am not married."

"Yes," Madeline felt tension she hadn't known she was carrying release in the confirmation Jode was unencumbered. "I mean, yes it is fortunate you haven't been forced to marry out of duty."

"My family is not important enough to worry about marriages of political advantage," Jode looked at her, his gaze intent on her face. "And you? Why aren't you married?"

Madeline laughed. "I haven't even come close. I guess men find me a bit intimidating."

"Weak men perhaps," Jode smiled. "Are you determined not to be married?"

"I've never thought of it that way," Madeline pushed her plate away and poured them more wine. "I've never liked the idea of losing my identity in marriage."

"Why would you do that?" Jode seemed genuinely baffled.

"Well," Madeline sipped her wine. "I don't know why it happens, but most of my friends who got married ended up changing. Some of them even stayed in bad marriages because they didn't remember who they were as a person."

"I still do not understand what you mean," Jode said leaning forward. "Are the women kept away from the world? Are they sequestered in a harem?"

"No," Madeline thought for a few minutes. Jode waited patiently, watching. "In my old world there's this concept that we are all only half a person, that we need someone to complete us. I don't feel like a half a person. If finding my true love means I'll stop being a whole person, I don't want to find him."

"Why would someone fall in love with a half person?" Jode clearly couldn't understand the concept. "Love is the attraction two people feel. Love is the thing that keeps them together when they disagree, when they are apart, until they die."

"Yes, that's what it is supposed to be."

"Then why do you resist my love for you?" Jode took her hand. "I do not see you as a half person, Madeline. I am not a half person either. If, at the end of the quest, you choose to leave, I will not stop loving you. I will survive here, I will be happier for knowing that you love me."

Madeline felt tears rise, and swallowed the rest of the wine in her mug to cover the pause while she composed herself. "And, if I choose to stay?"

"I will not make you marry me, if that is your worry," Jode rubbed her hand. "If you stay, you are your own person. You will have land and income; you will not have to rely on a husband to support you."

"You're right, I find you very attractive. I don't know if I love you," she said, fearing that was a lie. "If I say yes, if you court me, how will I be able to make the right decision at the end?"

"How will you make the right decision if you do not allow your heart to be free?" Jode released her hand. "I am sorry, I said that I would not make you decide, and here I am pressuring you."

Madeline took his hand back, "Don't. You're right; I need to know how I feel before I decide. Regardless of what I can do, here or back home, if I do love you it should be part of my decision."

Jode became very still. "Are you agreeing that we should court?"

"Yes," she felt the rightness of her words as she spoke. "If I love you, then I love you. I warn you though; I am not going to be an easy person to court."

"I would have it no other way," Jode placed a kiss on her hand. "Now that we are courting we should not be alone together. I will speak to Arabela and she will find us an appropriate chaperon."

He kissed her hand again and walked towards the center of the camp. As she watched him leave, Madeline felt an unfamiliar peace and warmth wrap around her.

She muttered, "that didn't really work the way I intended. If I'd known he would leave I would have decided no."

She stretched her arms above her head then fluffed out her hair; it was completely dry. The warmth from the brazier was dropping as the wood burned into embers but it was enough to make her drowsy. Taking a ribbon from her pocket, she braided her curls for sleep. A servant arrived to remove the plates and cups. Madeline wished him a good night and went through the tent curtain to bed.

24

Jode wandered towards the music coming from near the goblin camp. He knew that he would find Simon there, working with the small group of musicians, creating unfamiliar but pleasant sounds. He felt relaxed despite the difficult day. Madeline agreeing to be courted had lifted a veil of confusion from his mind. Her refusal had been difficult to understand, but it seemed he had underestimated the difference between their two worlds.

As he walked, he thought about the rules and games of courtship; it would be difficult to follow the normal process while they were on the quest. He laughed as he realized there would be less difficulty because of the quest than there would be without it as Madeline's attention was on her task, not on his actions. Her expression when he said they needed a chaperon was probably a good indication that he was going to find out a lot more about her culture than he already had. He wondered what the courting rules were in Madeline's world.

"Sir Jode," Yorr called as the band played the closing notes to a sweet tune. "Join us we are in need of your voice."

“Hey, Jode,” Simon said turning away from the flute player, Dass, Jode believed was her name. “Good timing, we need a neutral opinion to help us make a choice.”

“What choice will that be?”

“The choice of name for the band,” Simon drew Jode into the center of the six band members. “We have three options. Tell us which you think is best.”

“I will try to assist.”

“I favor the name Flight of Song,” Asla said.

“The Goblin Army,” Buck and Urr said at the same time.

“And the third name,” Jode asked. “I must hear all before I suggest the decision.”

“The Pathfinders,” Simon said. “It’s the name of my original band back home.”

“All are excellent choices,” Jode stalled. “Flight of Song is an uplifting name, and describes clearly some of the music I have had the pleasure of hearing.”

Asla smiled, “thank you. I think then we have our name.”

“Ah,” Jode said, “but, Goblin Army is a strong name and will serve you well throughout the life of your band.” Urr and Buck slapped each other on the back and started to play their instruments. “No,” Jode waved them back, “it seems to me that Pathfinders is also an excellent name, it describes your journey bringing new music to the land.”

"So," Yorr said. "Which one should we choose? It must be one we can use forever. Our name should reflect our position as the first band playing the new music."

"May I offer a fourth option?"

"Sure," Simon replied. "Anything that helps us get going would be great."

"It seems to me you were formed simply because Sir Simon was brought here to help fulfill the quest. If he had not come, there would be no new music."

"True," Zora said. "Our name should reflect that." The other band members nodded agreement.

"Then your name should be the Questers or the New Questers."

"It's not bad." Simon said. "If we were in the other world we would be a folk music band, but we're cross genre and in a whole different world, so why not?"

"The New Questers," Yorr said. "Yes, the New Questers, it sounds right, it feels right."

"Then so be it." Asla said. "Sir Jode, would you sing for us again tonight? We miss your voice in our music."

"Guys," Simon said before Jode could answer. "Practice the last few songs while I chat with Jode about that. We'll just sit over here."

Here, was a couple of boxes set on end as temporary seating. The six band members returned to the circle of instruments and plucked, sawed, and blew them to test the tuning. Then Yorr counted off uno due tre, the piano started and a deep violin sound sawed across. Then Asla's voice floated out of the music, the hours grow shorter as the days go by."

"That is an interesting tune," Jode said sitting down. "What is it called?"

"Lovers in a Dangerous Time," Simon said. "It needs a male voice, like most of this music, it's written from a man's point of view."

"An interesting coincidence," Jode muttered.

"What," Simon turned from watching the band, "hey, what's up? You look more relaxed than I've seen you for a few days."

"Lady Madeline has given me permission to court her, and we travel in a dangerous time." Jode's voice was matter of fact but Simon could see a light shining from his eyes.

"I'm not sure that would relax me," Simon laughed. "You be careful."

"I was hoping you could advise me on the finer points of courtship in your world," Jode said. "I do not wish to simply approach this from my customs. I believe I would be more successful if I included some familiar courtship rituals."

Simon slapped Jode on the arm. "I'm sorry, I know that look. You're already lost so there's no hope of talking sense into you."

"I can only hope you are wrong," Jode said. "I'm not used to this feeling of uncertainty; I usually know exactly what to do."

"Get used to feeling uncertain. The only advice I can give you is treat her like she has a brain. She won't appreciate you protecting her, or fawning over her."

"This is not new information," Jode shrugged. "How do you court such women in your old world?"

"It's not about how things work in the old world, Madeline is different. She's going to give you a challenge, not because she plans it but because she is terrified of commitment. I think the best advice is to find something that makes you happy outside your relationship."

"Yes," Jode sighed. "What would you suggest?"

"We need a singer," Simon grinned. "I saw you the other night, you loved being in the band. What's the problem?"

"I am not able to travel with your band of musicians, I have duties."

"I'm sure Arabela will release you after the quest."

"It's not that," Jode shook his head. "I am with Lady Arabela because I choose to be not because she commands me. I have other obligations. And, if I am successful I will have a wife to tend to."

"You might want to avoid using that expression with her."

"I do not understand."

"Man," Simon shook his head. "She is not going to want to be tended to."

"You know what I mean, surely," Jode frowned.

"Yes," Simon said, "but she won't. You must have noticed that she is sensitive about anything that might make her feel dependent."

Jode laughed, "this is very much like trying to walk silently through dead leaves. I take your point."

"Madeline will not be happy if you give up something you love for her," Simon said, returning to the subject of Jode's occupation. "She will find her own interests if she stays. You'll need to have your own too, or she'll make you crazy."

"She has spoken to you of plans for a future here? That is wonderful; she is not set against this world."

"Yes, she has thought of a few things, but don't get your hopes up. She's thinking of making a change even if she goes home." Simon saw hope drain out of Jode's face.

"I would prefer to have fallen in love with someone who has fewer decisions to make. It feels as though I have no certainty, no way to step forward."

"Look, she hasn't decided as far as I know. If you sit around waiting for her to decide, you'll probably drive her to go back. I'm telling you, you need to find something to do. Join the band, man."

"I will join with the New Questers," Jode agreed. "I only commit for the time we have in our journey and when I am not training Lady Madeline, or serving Lady Arabela."

"Fair enough," Simon pulled papers from his pockets, "here're the words to the songs they know so far. We'll run through them tonight. I'm thinking we might have a concert to celebrate our victory. So you need to be ready."

Jode flipped through the sheets of paper; there were more than twenty songs. "Very well, we should get started."

"Yep, and, Jode," Simon paused.

"Yes, Sir Simon?"

"You might want to check with Madeline if she wants to hear the Lady stuff; her answer might be no. You can drop the Sir with me." Simon walked to the band members and waved them to stop playing.

Jode followed reading through the words on the pages.

25

The morning brought a fine rain that seemed to hang in the air rather than fall. Madeline rose with the sound of the camp stirring; she stretched the kinks out of her arms and back, and then dressed quickly, looking forward to her training session. Alice, or someone, had placed bread and honey on the stool; a mug of caf steamed beside the plate.

Madeline took a slice of the bread and spread the thick almost black honey on it before hurrying out, sword belted, knife bundle tucked into the belt. The area in front of the tents was empty but people were hurrying to break camp. She ran to the practice ground and saw Kapeni waiting for her.

"Good morning," the Eldman said. "I have brought your cloak. It is good that you will get a chance to practice with that encumbrance."

Madeline put the last bite of breakfast in her mouth and chewed as she took the offered cloak. "Good morning, Kapeni," she said, undoing the ties then wrapping the cloak around her damp shoulders. "Is Sir Jode not joining us for practice?"

"He has other duties this morning. He asks me to tell you he will wait until you are ready to ride out. You are to meet him and Asla, a Fay woman of his acquaintance, at the paddock after practice. The others will have ridden ahead."

"We had better get on with it, then. I don't want to keep anyone from their ride today."

The two worked through sword movements until Madeline was able to pull thrust and defend without entangling the blade in her cloak.

"Until you are stronger I suggest you slit the cord on your cloak and let it fall if you find yourself in a fight. It is better to be cold and wet than to be impaled because you were unable to draw your blade," He said. "Now, join Sir Jode, you can practice your knife throwing when you stop for luncheon."

She thanked him, turning to go to the stable area; she saw Jode and a Fay woman, standing at the edge of the space holding three horses.

"The stables were being packed while we waited so we decided to join you," Jode said handing her the reins for Glory, the roan shook herself and snorted; she was clearly ready to get going.

"Thank you," Madeline said, vaulting into the saddle. "I hope I didn't keep you waiting."

"Not at all, your training is the most important thing. We will catch the others before they reach the village and still be able to finish training." Jode helped the Fay woman into her saddle, and then mounted his own horse. "May I introduce Asla; she has kindly agreed to join us today as our chaperon."

Madeline turned, shook hands with the scaled woman, then followed Jode at a walk until they reached the road. The way was wide enough for three horses; Asla rode between them, ensuring her duties as chaperon were fulfilled.

"I would like to learn this method of mounting a horse that you use," Asla said. "It seems much more useful than waiting for someone to assist you."

"Sure, as soon as we stop I'll teach you," Madeline leaned around Asla to speak to Jode. "Why is my training so important?"

"It is the only thing we can do to prepare you for your task."

"But you don't know what I'm supposed to do," Madeline said, then brightened, "unless, you have more information?"

"No," Jode answered. "There are other things we could do to prepare you if we had more time. But since we do not have that luxury, the skill that seems to be easiest for you is use of sharp instruments."

"You should be happy that is all you have time for," Asla said. "If they had time to develop your magical talent, yes, Jode, we know she has some kind of talent." She said acknowledging Jode's raised eyebrow. "Anyway, if they had time to do that you would be fasting and meditating not riding out on this beautiful day."

Madeline looked around her, the trees dripped with the misty rain that still fell. Her cloak had gained five pounds with the weight of the water. The horse's legs were spattered with mud from the road. There were no birds singing, no buzzing insects. The world had closed in on itself in a gray, wet, quiet blanket. "I haven't heard irony before in this world," she commented.

"What is irony?" Asla asked, "I do not recognize the word."

"It's a form of humor," Madeline racked her brain for the dictionary definition. "It's saying one thing but meaning another. Like when you said, it's is a beautiful day."

"But," Asla said, "I meant that, do you not enjoy the weather?"

"Asla's people come from a desert area," Jode said. "Any day when water falls from the sky is a beautiful day to her."

"I guess that makes sense," Madeline laughed, "I come from a place with much the same weather as this. We call it a rainforest environment. It rains a lot."

"A paradise then," Asla sighed. "But, I suppose that I would find it less beautiful if it rained more often. I must admit it is quite cold."

"Uh huh," Madeline agreed tired of the subject of the weather. "How do you know Jode?"

"Lady Asla is part of a musical group that I have been spending time with," Jode said.

"Yes, Sir Jode has been singing with our group, the New Questers, he has a beautiful voice, we are lucky to have him with us."

"Sounds like something Simon would like to be involved in," Madeline thought back to her discussions with Simon about his musical background.

"Indeed," Asla said. "He brought us together and gives us wonderful new music to perform."

"Oh man," Madeline rolled her eyes. "Simon has set up a rock band?"

"I do not know what rocks have to do with it." Jode said.

"No," Madeline waved her hand to dismiss the thought, "a different meaning of the word. I knew he was working with musicians at the castle but not that he'd gone so far as to form a band."

"Further, perhaps than you imagine," Asla looked sideways at Jode. "Sir Jode is considering joining our group after the quest."

"No," Jode said. "I have not promised anything. I may not be free to decide that."

"In my world," Madeline said, looking over at Jode who was blushing, "musicians are considered to be the most desirable of men."

"It is so here, also." Asla said. "In fact many women will actually lock their daughters in their rooms when a roving group of musicians arrive."

"Yes, we have that expression too," Madeline giggled. "Lock up your daughters, though most parents would not actually do it."

Jode coughed, his face deepening in color, "I would not take advantage of a young woman. Lady Madeline, please believe me I am an honorable man."

Asla and Madeline burst in to laughter at his obvious discomfort. "I believe you," Madeline was finally able to say.

"I am sure that is true," Asla added.

"Are you really interested in doing this, this singing in a band?" Madeline was surprised that Jode would consider such a different life from the obviously respectable and responsible one of knight.

"Yes," Jode said. "But it is not my decision alone. As my betrothed you would expect me to maintain a respectable position in society."

"Hold on, I don't remember agreeing to a betrothal."

"No," Jode answered quickly, "that is not what I meant. I meant if you were to become my betrothed."

"Wait," Asla jumped in, "are you implying that my profession is not respectable?"

"Ladies," Jode held up a hand in surrender. "It appears I have been clumsy in my words. Musician is a very respectable and valued profession. I would be proud to count you as one of my close friends, Lady Asla. You are welcome as a guest in my home whenever you wish to grace us with your presence." Asla smiled and nodded her acceptance of his apology.

"And, Lady Madeline, I would not make such a decision without consulting the woman I have given my heart to; regardless of whether you are my betrothed or not, you still hold that heart."

"Very pretty," Asla said. "Lady Madeline, how can you not be charmed by this man?"

"I didn't say I wasn't charmed," Madeline said. "It would make me happy to hear what you would do, Jode. Whether or not I'm here, no matter my advice or preference, what is it that you want to do?"

"I am drawn to sing for this New Questers group," Jode confessed. "I am considering accepting Sir Simon's offer of a position in the group."

"Then," Madeline said, "that is what you should do. I will not stand in your way. My decision to stay or go will not change because you have chosen your path. Jode, it will make me the most happy to see you happy."

Madeline trained with Jode that afternoon during the village meeting. Asla watched from the sidelines giving encouragement as they danced around each other with their practice swords. "I must be getting fitter," Madeline said during a pause, "I don't feel any pain in my muscles."

"You are developing the right muscles for this fighting," Asla said. "Sir Jode, do you think her form is improving?" He was saved from answering, if not from blushing, by a messenger announcing lunch.

After the meal, the whole group rode leisurely back to the main camp. The mist had dissipated, but the day was still chilly. Madeline watched as the servants ran back and forth, pitching tents, building fires, starting dinner cooking in large pots over the flames. The movement was like a well-choreographed dance; no one tripped or bumped anyone else, tables appeared and were covered in drinks and snacks as if by magic.

"Come, Lady Madeline," Arabela called. "Let's watch the guards train. I think you have done enough for today."

"Who will be training?" She asked as they walked towards the empty space beside the paddock.

"The four guards, Jode, and three of the Eldmen." They reached a roped off area where several small barrels had been placed as stools. There were a group of people huddled at one end of the row of seats. They were chattering and passing notes back and forth.

"Are they placing wagers?"

"Yes," Arabela said. "Did you wish to participate?"

"No, I have no idea how to figure out the betting system and I have no money, but thanks."

"Perhaps in the future," Arabela smiled. "If you wished to place a bet on Sir Jode, I would be happy to provide the funds."

"No, thanks all the same. I think it would be better if I didn't encourage him to foolishness just to win me some money."

"Ah well, you probably know best. Do not count on him to not be foolish when he sees you watching him."

"I've seen him with a sword."

"No," Arabela said shaking her head. "You've practiced with him. You have not seen him dance with the blade."

"Why do I think you've set me up?"

"Probably because you are a wise woman," Arabela chuckled. "I challenge you to resist loving him after this contest."

Madeline groaned, this was not going to help, she just knew it. The first contest was in knife throwing. The Eldmen and one of the guards took turns hitting a target from increasingly further distances. When someone missed, they stepped out. Kapeni was the winner; he threw a blade a distance that was so far she could not see the target; she only heard the hard thunk as the knife penetrated the wood. The group of bettors rapidly passed paper and coins around and then sat back for the next competition.

Four guards appeared in the centre of the cleared ring. They whistled and two goblins ran out with small colored balls that were placed in a circle around the men. The guards pulled whips out of their belts and cracked them over their heads at the same time. Then each one lashed his whip and caught a ball sending it spinning towards the goblins. The crowd applauded politely. Madeline was impressed with the skill but kept looking around for Jode.

"Pay attention," Arabela nudged her.

The goblins picked up the balls, then at a shout threw them at the group of soldiers. Three balls were flicked down by the whips, the fourth hit one of the guards; he swore then left the circle. This was repeated until only one guard was successful in hitting the thrown ball. The crowd whistled and yelled their approval, or disappointment, as they settled the round of bets.

Madeline looked around and noticed the audience had tripled during the whip exhibition. As she watched, the heads turned as one to the right; the bettors finished their wagers and settled quietly for the next event. Turning in the direction of everyone's gaze, she saw a tall man, one of the guards stride to the center of the arena. He took a staff from one of the goblins and drew a circle in the dirt. When he was finished, he tossed the staff back to the goblin, bowed then walked to the far side of the circle standing just inside the line.

Jode walked into Madeline's line of sight. His blond hair tied back in a tail, his sword hung across his back. He wore a white shirt, a black and dark green kilt that swung about high black boots, which rose to an inch below his knee. Madeline sucked in a deep breath, "Damn."

Arabela laughed quietly, "Yes, he is well presented isn't he?"

"Good thing we have a chaperon, I guess."

"Sir Jode would never be improper," Arabela assured her.

"It wasn't his behavior that I meant. That is one fine looking man."

Arabela smiled and patted Madeline's arm.

The two men stood facing each other, then, at some unseen signal, made a short bow and drew blades. They walked around each other for a few turns; Madeline realized they were looking for the first opening. Suddenly the guard stepped forward and lunged at Jode. Madeline saw the blade was not a practice blade, dulled on the edges, but a real blade, if it made contact it would draw blood.

She watched as the two men tested each other lunging and defending, no contact made. Jode spun and dove as though the blade was an extension of his arm. The other man was as skilled as Jode the fight went on for several minutes before one of them found an advantage. The guard pushed Jode's blade away and lunged forward to cut his chest. As he passed, Jode spun around, slashing at the guard's side. Jode's shirt was sliced open on the side, no blood showed. The guards' shirt was sliced across the back, no blood there either.

"I can't watch this," Madeline whispered. She felt dizzy at the thought of Jode being cut. "I have to go."

Arabela grabbed her arm and held her to the seat. "Do not distract him. What is the problem?"

"Someone is going to get hurt," she couldn't bring herself to say Jode. "They are using real blades."

"Of course they are," Arabela squeezed Madeline's arm. "They are in control. Do not worry; if blood is drawn, the attacker is disqualified. Do you think I would put any of our party in danger for sport?"

Madeline let out a shaky breath. "No, not when you actually say it. But, it looked like they were really fighting." She swallowed the fear in her chest.

"I am sorry," Arabela said, "I didn't think. I should have told you the rules. This is a display of control. The winner will have sliced the shirt off the other; if either loses control enough to draw blood, he loses."

"Okay," Madeline turned her eyes back to the fight. "Hasn't anyone been hurt or killed in this type of fight, ever?"

"Not killed," Arabela shrugged. "A few scars but no death."

Madeline watched as the two men continued the contest, each scoring cuts until their shirts were in ribbons. The guard was in the worst shape; Jode had sliced the fabric until only a tie at the neck held it together. Jode spun again and flicked the point swiftly cutting the tie and tangling the man's sword in his sleeves as the shirt dropped over his shoulders. They retreated to their original positions and bowed, grinning at each other as the crowd cheered.

"See," Arabela said. "No one was hurt."

Jode turned to the two women and bowed deeply, his shredded shirt exposing his muscular chest gleaming with sweat. He rose, turned and left the circle.

"Hi, ladies," Simon appeared at Madeline's side. "He is going to make a great rock star. Don't you think so, Madeline?"

"He sure knows how to play the crowds," she nodded toward the bettors. "It looks like he was the favorite."

"We should return to the tents," Arabela said, drawing Madeline up. "Dinner will be ready soon and Sir Jode and Simon will be hungry I'm sure."

"Actually," Simon said. "Jode and I have something else we need to attend to. We may not join you this evening."

"Then Lady Asla should be told," Arabela said. "I'm sure she would like to know if she doesn't need to act as chaperon."

"Yes, well," Simon said backing away. "She knows already. Have a lovely evening, ladies."

"Do you know what is going on?" Arabela asked. "I assumed Sir Jode would want to dine with us and bask in his success."

"I think he is going to be spending the evening exploring his future career," Madeline said. "I'll let him tell you about it. Come on let's get back I'm famished, all this training is giving me a big appetite to go with the new muscles."

The two women walked back to their tent where bowls of steaming stew waited on the table. The chairs held dry warm shawls to take the chill off while they ate. "Tell me," Arabela said. "What do you think you will want to do after the quest is finished? It seems that Sir Simon has found his path and Sir Jode may also be changing his."

"Yeah," Madeline put her empty bowl down and picked up the wine mug. "It seems that this quest is leading to a lot of life changes."

"Surely if you return to your world you can return to the work you were doing there."

"I could, it would be a pain to figure out how to explain where I was for all this time, but I could go back to being a lawyer. I'm pretty sure I'd make partner this year."

"Do not worry about explaining your absence," Arabela waved her hand in dismissal. "Blu can return you to your time shortly after you left. No one will know you were gone. You'll have to explain what happened to Sir Simon, though."

"I'll just say he quit," Madeline shrugged. "It seems he was going to anyway. So, what if I don't return, will people miss me?"

"They will remember you, whatever usually happens in your world when someone disappears will happen. Is there someone who you care about there, someone who will worry?"

"I was just curious." Madeline leaned back in the chair. "I don't have many friends, and no family. I was an only child of only children; I guess they'd miss me at work for as long as it took to find a replacement."

"It sounds like a lonely life."

"Not really," Madeline realized that was true, at least true before. How would she feel knowing Jode was here missing her? "I don't want to go back to that life anyway. Wow, it feels good to say that. If I go back I would do something completely different with my life."

"Then why not do that here?"

"It's a big change, I don't know if I'm prepared to make that kind of decision. What about you? When Sayer is dead with what will you do?"

"You know I have the responsibility that we will not mention."

"Yes, but that is not really going to fill your time."

"As you say, these are big decisions," Arabela said. "I am, perhaps, as unprepared as you to make such large decisions."

"Okay, I get that." Madeline felt the weight of the events fall on her shoulders. "If I knew what I was supposed to do, maybe it would help. But, then again, more knowledge isn't always helpful."

"These decisions we have to make," Arabela said, passing the empty plates and mugs to the waiting servant. "They are decisions of the heart, decisions we feel. They are not decisions of the mind."

"I'm not used to making decisions that way."

"No," Arabela said, "perhaps it is time you became more comfortable with your heart and stopped worrying about your mind."

"Should I say the same thing to you?" Madeline refused to be pushed. "Should you let your heart decide your future?"

"Perhaps," Arabela chuckled. "Then again, perhaps the problem is that neither of us really knows what our heart wants. It is because the choices we have are all good."

"Maybe you're right." Madeline pulled the shawl around her. "I think I would like to walk around before I go to bed. Would you like to join me?"

"No, I need my rest," Arabela headed towards the tent. "Talk to Blu, he may be able to help you. Good night."

Madeline nodded and walked towards the edge of camp, the pent up stress of watching Jode fight was making her restless. She found Blu staring at the flames of his campfire, yellow robes pulled tightly around his small frame. He looked up as she walked into the circle of light.

"Lady Madeline, please, join me I have been waiting for you," he pointed to a stool on his left. "I fear the time is growing short. We will be at our destination in two days."

"I'm not ready," Madeline said.

"I think you are overly worried. How is it that you know you are not ready?"

"I don't know what to do. What if I don't have the right skills? What if I hesitate at the wrong moment? What if I rush in too soon?" The questions poured out of her with no thought.

"Do you have such little faith in the prophecy? Or, he paused "are you talking about something else, perhaps?"

"I don't know," Madeline shrugged. "There are so many things coming to a head. I think I'm talking about the prophecy, but it is also about my own choices."

"Let us walk," Blu stood pointing to the edge of the camp. "I find it sometimes helps to move the body while you try to sort the mind."

The priest only came to her shoulder; Madeline was not used to being the tallest person in any circumstance. She tried not to bend over as she talked to the priest while they walked towards a lighted area. People were practicing with bows and arrows. The archers stood in the last slice of sunlight, and fires lit the targets, but between them, there was growing shadow. Soon they would be shooting through full dark.

"See the arrows," Blu said. "They are made for the one purpose, to fly through the air."

"I thought arrows were designed to kill things." Madeline said.

"No," Blu said. "Their purpose is to fly straight and true. The archer chooses to aim at a target, or at a living being. It is neither the arrow nor the bow that makes the decision about the where the arrow lands."

"Are you comparing my situation to the arrow?" Madeline expected a Zen-like answer, no answer at all really.

"No," Blu shook his shaved head. "You are the arrow, the bow and the archer."

"Great," Madeline looked to the sky. "Let me figure that out. So, I have been made for a specific purpose, the arrow. I am able to make that purpose into action, the bow. And, I can direct that purpose to more than one end, the archer."

"I am impressed," Blu turned to her, looking surprised. "Not many of our own people would have made that connection so quickly."

"I spent a year trying to be a Buddhist," Madeline explained. "I didn't have the patience to really be one."

"Patience is not always a virtue in this world we inhabit," Blu nodded, apparently Buddhist translated to something here.

"You said I may have magical talent," Madeline said.

"Yes," Blu paused to watch a flight of twenty arrows rise and fall in their progress to the targets. The sky was still light enough to follow the path, but only barely. "I sense that you have power, but it is sealed away. Would you like to pursue the path to unlocking it?"

"I don't know what that means. I don't wish to become a priest, or priestess."

"Priest, the word does not denote gender. You do not have to become a priest. Lady Arabela possesses power and is not a priest."

"So, if I stay here I could study magic?" Madeline added that to her list of choices. "Having more options isn't really helping me make a choice."

"In the end, when you make a choice, you will realize there are no options, only the one path."

The sound of a flute rose from off to the side of the archers, it seemed familiar to Madeline, but she was not able to name the composer. Simon's work she thought, he had eclectic taste and a perfect memory for music. The flute was joined by a single drum sound. She looked over to the side and saw a group of five musicians standing in a circle. She waved at Jode, Simon, and Asla who were standing to the side.

"Sir Simon has chosen his path," Blu said. "He did not seem to find the decision difficult."

"Simon seems to be able to take leaps of faith that I cannot."

"The path to the right decision does not always have to be a smoothly paved one. Sometimes the path must be difficult because there is so much at stake."

"I guess I have to make this choice on my own. No one can tell me what to do, and if I'm honest I wouldn't really listen." She looked over at the band.

"Join your friends," Blu said. "I will contemplate the arrow's flight for a time."

Madeline walked behind the line of archers to join the musicians, her skin heating suddenly. "I can't be having hot flashes," she muttered shaking off her wrap. The wind picked up and the archers started to put away their bows. A sound like creaking tarpaulin rose from the far side of the clearing, to the right of the target. The archers turned quickly re-stringing bows and pulling arrows from the quivers on the ground.

Madeline drew further back allowing the archers room for whatever they needed. She was about half way between the priest, now sitting alone just at the edge of the fire light, and the band who were drawing closer together, instruments silent. Dread rose from the people like a damp chill finding its way into her bones.

The archers drew their bows and held the pose. The sound changed, a screeching call cut through the night. Madeline watched as Blu suddenly rose and started to move towards the crowd. A pair of clawed feet appeared; she stared as what looked like a pterodactyl swooped down and caught the priest between its talons. Blu rose with the beast a whoosh of wings lifted them ten feet up and forward. Arrows flew at the beast's head, tail, and wings, not one came close to the feet and Blu. There was still enough light to see the arrows impact. One wing crumpled and the thing dropped the tiny robed figure. Madeline saw four men run out to catch Blu before he hit the ground. They tipped him onto his feet, then all of them ran for the shelter of the larger group.

The flying lizard circled the group trying and failing to gain height with only one working wing. People scattered in small groups, Madeline joining them her eyes still on the sky. Another volley of arrows whished up and two found the beast's eye. It folded into a circle as it fell; people scattered from underneath. Two figures didn't run far or fast enough and were caught under the slamming weight of the creature as it crashed dead to the ground.

The sudden silence after the crash felt to Madeline as though the world had emptied of everyone but her. She couldn't hear her own breathing, and couldn't take her eyes away from the huge body. She knew that two people were under the creature. One had been a goblin; the other, she thought was Asla. Asla, the woman she had spent a whole day with, someone she had thought a friend, dead. Jode pulled her into his arms and the first sound she heard was his heart beating. She felt the warmth of his body seep in to hers replacing the icy cold of shock.

"It is okay," he whispered. "You are fine, you are safe."

She took a deep breath that turned into a sob. "It was so fast."

"It is better that it was fast," he said rubbing her back, comforting her. "Morge do not eat dead flesh."

"Is Simon okay?" She pulled back from his chest, not ready to face the reality of the moment, but reluctant to hide from the horrible events. "Who else was hurt?"

"Simon is unhurt," Jode said, "at least his body is unharmed. The two who were killed were his friends."

"Let me go and help," she pushed out of his embrace. "I can't just collapse, people will need help."

Jode opened his arms and let Madeline go. She walked to where Simon was standing. He didn't acknowledge her presence; he stood staring at the carcass. She could see tears in his eyes. She turned him away from the sight and reached up to put her arms around him. "It's done, Simon. Please don't keep looking at it."

26

The clearing filled with people. A mob ran to the carcass and started wrapping ropes around it. Others brought warm blankets and wine for the witnesses, handing them out to the people standing around staring. Madeline watched as the bustle and hurry turned into organized activity. She and Simon stood, arms around each other, watching people pulling the carcass off the two crushed bodies.

"Come," Arabela's voice spoke gently. "This is not the place to be. You should come away and let people clear up this horror."

"No," Simon said, not turning away from the sight of his friends. "I need to see this. I should help them with the bodies."

Simon pulled away from Madeline and joined the group who were wrapping the dead musicians in white sheets. He touched each one on the forehead before the wrappings were sealed.

"What will happen to them?" Madeline asked, taking the proffered blanket, "the bodies?"

"We will build the pyres and they will be cremated before we leave."

"And the beast?"

"The Morge? It will be cut into pieces and left for the scavengers; it will be bones by tomorrow night."

"It happened so fast," Madeline shivered. "I was going to join them. I was half way there. Oh, Arabela, it could have been Jode. He could have been under that thing when it fell."

"Yes," Arabela said, wrapping her arms around Madeline. "But it was not. We will miss the two who are gone but, they are gone and we are here. Lady Asla would not want you to be so sad; neither would the goblin, Yorr was his name."

"Do you not morn them?" Madeline kept watching as people took the bodies to the edge of the light. Others were running with arms full of firewood. "Do you just shrug it off and forget them?"

"No," Arabela gave her a squeeze. "You are frightened. This is part of our world, I do not know what your own death rituals are but this is part of life. They have gone to the next life."

"I have never seen people die before." Madeline watched Simon help lift one of the bodies to the top of a pile of firewood. "I can't just watch. Look at Simon he's helping; I can do that." She started towards the group around the bodies.

"There are enough people there," Arabela drew her back. "Come back to the tents, Jode will join us. Let him help you with this."

Madeline took a deep breath and went with Arabela. When they returned to the tents, the two women sat on a low bench that sat in front of a brazier. Alice was waiting for them and she brought caf and a small jug of strong smelling liquid.

"Drink a few sips of this. It will make you feel better, if only for a short while." Alice poured the clear strong smelling liquid into tiny cups.

"What is it?" Madeline felt her eyes water with the fumes.

"Eldmen brew, they call it howl, it will clear your mind." Arabela sipped, as if to show Madeline it was safe.

Madeline took a deep breath then exhaled, lifted the cup and shot the contents back in one movement. She swallowed and felt the burn slide down to her stomach; she held her breath for a moment, afraid to inhale in case she started coughing. It made tequila seem like chamomile tea.

"Whoo," she finally said, "I can hear my blood moving in my veins. That's some powerful booze."

"It has brought some color to your face," Arabela said. "Are you feeling better?"

"I don't know if I feel better, but I guess I'm not feeling so shocked," she admitted. "I still can't believe it, it happened so fast. Where is Jode?"

"He will be here," Arabela said. "He has some duties before he comes."

"Tell me what you meant when you said they have gone to the next world."

"We believe that life exists on several worlds," Arabela said. "We don't know what that next world is, but we believe it exists. What is your belief?"

"As I said, we have many beliefs." Madeline said. "It doesn't help, though. We are always sad when someone dies."

"We do not have time, we will do something when we return from the quest," Arabela poured second cup of howl.

"So, you don't do anything to mark their passing, or say goodbye."

"Yes, but our rituals are varied. We believe in celebration of life, we do not linger in sadness."

Madeline sighed, "I didn't think about people dying. I guess I knew that we would have to kill Sayer, but I didn't think about the real danger to other people."

"Part of life is danger." Arabela said, passing the full cup to Madeline. "We live in a world that is full of creatures like the Morge, and people like the Dray. Life and death work together to keep the world balanced."

~~~

Simon and Jode stood beside the pyres, watching the flames as they reached the wrapping and started burning the bodies of their friends. "I am sorry you lost your friends," Jode said, watching the fire. "We will miss them in the band."

"I had a friend die once, it was a car accident. I watched as he stepped out into the path of the car," Simon saw Jode start to ask for a definition; "it's a vehicle like a wagon but faster. It happened just like this. One second he was waving goodbye, the next he was a bloody battered shell in the middle of the road."
~~~

“I am sorry,” Jode patted Simon’s arm. “They are moving to the next life now.”

“It is not a consolation.”

“No?”

“You believe in reincarnation?” Simon saw puzzlement when he looked at Jode. “That spirits come back in other forms after death, like Asla will come back as a butterfly, or something.”

“No,” Jode smiled at the thought, “no, not a butterfly. They will move to another life as who they were. Lady Asla will return in the form of another Fay, Yorr as a goblin.”

“Will they know who they were?”

“No.”

“I guess we’ll think of a way to honor them in our music.”

“That would be fitting,” Jode pulled Simon away from the fire. “Are there others who wish to join the group?”

“Jeez, they are barely cold.”

“Warm or cold, they are gone. If we are to honor them with music we will need more band members.”

“It doesn’t seem right, finding replacements.”

“No,” Jode said, “not replacements. You cannot replace people like a broken chair or sword. If we try to replace the two who were lost we would not grow.”

“I think we can find two more musicians. Yorr said he had a cousin who played as well as he did. It still doesn’t feel right.”

Simon held up his hand to stop Jode arguing. "I know it is necessary. I guess it's a heart versus mind problem. Don't worry I'm not going to break up the band. I understand it's important, maybe more important now, to keep going."

"Yes, and I do understand. I, too, feel regret that we have lost them. I know Yorr's cousin is called Gurn," Jode nodded. "And I know of a woman who can sing. Perhaps she will agree to join us."

"Let's talk to them tomorrow." Simon shrugged. "If that's okay, I mean."

"It is perfectly okay," Jode said. "We will be continuing on tomorrow, the quest must be completed. I'm sure Arabela will plan something for when we get back. Something that will be fitting to celebrate the lives they lived."

27

"Everyone is so depressed they look like they are about to lie down and give up." Madeline said as they rode out the next morning. "We need to get this quest over with."

"I want that as much as you," Arabela snapped back. "I am not willing to throw away our chance of success by rushing headlong into a battle."

"Unless you think that some vision will come from the sky to instruct us over the next couple of days, delay won't help."

Arabela shook her head and turned away to investigate a clearing off the side of the road. "We need a safe place to stop for lunch."

"Jode," Madeline called back to the two men riding a few horse lengths behind. "Help me convince her to speed up our progress."

"I cannot," Jode shrugged. "It is for Lady Arabela to decide how we proceed."

"Fine," Madeline turned her horse around and started back to the main body of the camp. Jode started to turn his horse around to follow.

"Let her go," Simon said. "You will only end up being yelled at."

"Yes," she called back over her shoulder. "Stay there, both of you. I need to spend some time with other people."

"Let it be man," Simon repeated. "When she's in this mood she's just looking for a fight."

"I will trust your experience," Jode said, turning back to follow Arabela into the clearing.

~~~

Madeline wandered back around the wagons and files of people walking. The faces around her were solemn; there was no chatting, no interaction at all between the people. She kept riding until she came to the wagon that carried Blu. The priest always rode behind closed curtains; Madeline thought it seemed more like retreat today than privacy. His driver was slumped on the front seat, the horses plodding along without his attention. They were following the wagon in front, which was following the one in front of it.

The entire camp seemed to be in motion. Blindly. Automatically. It was as though someone had wound up clockwork toys and set them in motion. The whole camp felt only a few steps short of coming to a complete and final stop.

The curtains of Blu's wagon were firmly drawn closed. Madeline did not want to call to him in case she was violating some custom. She rode forward to the driver.
~~~

“Do you know if the priest will be available to talk soon?”

“Probably,” the driver said not looking up.

“Do you think it will be possible to speak to him when we stop to eat?”

“I don’t know.”

Madeline gave up; the camp was like a funeral march. She hadn’t been with them when camp moved before but she couldn’t believe the lively group of people they joined every night was so morose during the day. No matter what Jode and Arabela said, these people were mourning and needed to have a chance to grieve.

She rode forward again to catch up with Simon. “I need to talk with you,” she said leaning close so he would hear her voice without her having to raise it.

“We’re sending people to stop in the clearing ahead. Arabela says it is large enough to hold the camp for a short break. How about we talk while people are eating?”

“Good enough,” she said. “Meet me on the road as soon as everyone is in the clearing.”

“You want me to tell Arabela to meet us, or Jode?”

“No, just you and me,” She looked around. “We’ll talk to them later, but right now you are the only one who might understand.”

“Fine,” Simon looked back as the first wagon appeared around the corner. “I’m guessing it will take a half hour. I’ll pick up some food and drink and meet you back here.”

Madeline watched as the wagons passed. The people were looking down and dragging their feet. She wanted to go up to them, hug them and tell them it was going to be fine; a feeling that came as a shock. The final wagon pulled into the clearing and she dismounted and led her horse to the back of the last wagon, a water wagon designed to allow the horses to drink without having to find a stream.

Simon appeared around the side of the food wagon, he handed her a bun filled with meat and a mug of water. They wandered back to the road where they were visible to the grooms tending the horses but far enough away that they would not be overheard.

"What did you want to talk about," Simon asked around a mouthful of sandwich.

"Have you been watching people today?"

"Not really," he admitted. "I've been kind of wrapped up in my own thoughts. No one seems to be talking much anyway."

"No one is talking at all." She nibbled her sandwich knowing she needed the nourishment but not feeling hungry. "I think they are mourning for Asla and Yorr."

"I've asked about that and they don't seem to have that concept here."

"I know that Arabela and Jode say they don't, but I think we might have misunderstood."

"They were pretty clear."

"No," Madeline said, wrapping the last of the sandwich and putting it in the pocket of her jacket. "They said that there would be a ceremony after the quest was completed not that people didn't need to mark the passing of the dead."

"So? I can't imagine you really care about these people, isn't that violating some rule you have about not getting involved?"

"Stop it." Madeline felt her throat close, in anger or grief she couldn't tell. "I am not that much of a hard hearted bitch. Look, I think we need to do something and do it tonight. Another day of this will kill any hope we have of fulfilling this quest."

Simon shrugged, "I don't think we should just barge in on their customs."

"I don't think we can just let it be either," Madeline felt her impatience and frustration bubble up. "Look at them. Everyone is discouraged, what would happen if we had to go after Goddard right now?"

Looking around, Simon saw the whole camp silently going about the business of their lunch break. People serving were walking head down with platters of food held out for anyone to take; grooms were feeding and watering the horses; wagon tenders were checking their vehicles for signs of damage. All the action was right, the silence was not; this camp had always bubbled with sound before.

"I don't disagree with you. If we had to fight right now, my best bet is we would lose a lot more of our friends because they didn't have the heart to fight. My point is that it's not time to barge in and tell people what to do."

"I know, but I have to do more than just ask what we should do, or wait for something to break."

"What are you thinking we should do?"

"I know if I ask, the answer would be to wait. Arabela is just as affected as everyone else." Madeline pointed to where Arabela was sitting alone picking at the sandwich in her hand. "And, Jode is worse. Any other time he would be here, with us, making me train or trying to talk me into loving him. I can't even see where he is."

"Okay," Simon held up his hands in surrender. "Look, if we were at home I'd suggest a wake. The rest of the band can play sad music, people who knew the deceased would talk about their memories of the lost lives. Everyone would cry and get drunk and then start getting over the loss as they got through the hangover."

"I've been to a wake, and it sounds like a good plan to me." Madeline said.

"Well, I think the first objection would be that we can't just have everyone get drunk. We would need to have someone on guard." Simon said, starting to think about the details.

"We can ask for volunteers."

"No, we should ask people who didn't know Yorr and Asla to volunteer," Simon said. "You know that Jode would volunteer, and as you pointed out, he is as badly affected as everyone else."

"Okay," Madeline sighed. "What else?"

"Arabela isn't going to like the idea of a delay. You're going to need to convince her that it's worth it."

"It doesn't need to be a long delay," Madeline said, "you know, we may end up moving faster tomorrow if we have the wake tonight."

"Remember to tell her that. If we have the wake tonight while we would be stopped anyway the only delay is us being a bit slower on the trail tomorrow."

"We can make up the time. I need to get her to agree to that." Madeline felt her mood change as they came to a workable solution.

"Just don't bully her." Simon's face was serious, the usual teasing absent from his tone.

"Come with me," Madeline said. "Help me convince her, them, really. I think Jode will need to agree to this too."

"Okay," he paused, "do me a favor?"

"What?"

"Remember they were my friends too. I feel like shit, and I'm willing to tell you that but others won't. Don't use me as the reason we need to have this wake."

"Simon," Madeline reached over to hug him. "I forgot they were part of your band. I'm sorry. In such a short time, you made friends here and now they are gone. You've integrated so well, it's been just over a week that we've been here and you have already lost people you love."

Simon hugged back and then drew away wiping his tears with the back of his hand. "Yeah, well. I guess I'll be okay. Just be sensitive to people's feelings. If you go home, we still have to live through the aftermath of this damn quest."

Before Madeline could approach Arabela to discuss the idea, the camp was called back together to commence the afternoon leg of their journey. Simon and Madeline mounted and moved their horses forward until they rode on either side of Arabela.

"Arabela, do you know where Jode is?" Madeline didn't want to jump into the discussion too quickly.

"I believe he is traveling with the musicians," Arabela said. "If you wish to be with him, drop back and I'm sure you'll find him there."

"I would prefer it if he joined us here," Madeline gestured for Simon to drop back and bring Jode to the front. "I would like to discuss something with both of you."

"If you cared for him you would allow him to be with them, he needs to be with people who understand the loss he feels. The dead ones were his friends."

"I know, how could you think I didn't know that?"

"I'm sorry," Arabela said. "I am sure you know all you need to know about Sir Jode."

"No, I'm sorry," Madeline swallowed her rising anger, recognizing it as a form of grief. "I spoke without thinking. I may not have known Asla and Yorr very well, but I did like them. I do feel their loss."

"It is too bad you will not be here for the celebration of their lives."

"Why?"

"It seems to me you have decided to leave us when your part of the quest is over. It would be better to send you back as soon as that is done."

"Why do you think that?"

"You do not seem to want to talk about anything beyond the quest." Arabela turned and looked at Madeline, "everything you do is focused on understanding what you need to do to finish your task as soon as possible. You do not even want to discuss what your life could be like if you stayed. You make Sir Jode court you with no expectation of success."

Madeline was shocked at the anger in Arabela's voice. "I'm sorry you think that," she said. "I don't like to think too much about my options because I want to concentrate on what I have to do for you, for the quest."

"Are you sure?"

"Yes."

"Consider this," Arabela looked behind them as if to make sure no one would be able to hear her words. "You may not wish to consider your options because you are afraid of the possibility you might want to stay here, that you are afraid to take such a large step into a new life, that you are willing to settle for a familiar life in your old world rather than a strange life here."

"You don't know me well enough to say that."

"True, but whose fault is that?" Arabela seemed to deflate, the anger that drove her to speak so plainly, evaporating. "If you choose to let us know you, perhaps you will come to know us."

Madeline started to answer but heard the sound of two horses approaching. Her heart squeezed in her chest at the sight of Jode. He looked faded, his skin was gray, his blue eyes sunken in large dark circles. His tall frame somehow diminished as he slumped in the saddle.

"Okay, we're all here," Simon nodded to Madeline as they rode alongside.

"You wanted to discuss something with us," Jode asked.

"Did you sleep last night?" Madeline didn't expect him to say yes.

"I sat vigil for the departed." Jode said. "It is our belief that the spirit does not go until the fires burn out. Someone must watch to ensure the fires stay lit until the last of the remains have burned to ashes."

"Is that part of a ceremony?" Madeline asked thinking that it was as good a place as any to start the discussion. "If you were not here, on the road, with a deadline, would more be done?"

"Yes," Arabela answered. "We have ceremonies for the departed. People sing songs about the life of the dead friend."

"The ceremony is different for each of the people. Eldmen chant the dead to the next life creating a magical protection for them. The Fay wail for days fasting until the official mourners all become too weak to cry. The Sylph sit in silence for two full days, they meditate on the departed life; the goblins hold a feast to celebrate the person's successful completion of this life."

"So, none of the people here would normally just carry on after the fire?" Simon asked. "Death is a significant change regardless of what your belief is?"

"No one is arguing that," Jode said. "This is not a normal situation. We have no time for two days of silent contemplation, or fasting and wailing."

"If we don't do something we won't get any further than the camp tonight," Madeline said. "Look around you. People are sleepwalking. They have no heart for the quest, they are sad and discouraged."

"What do you suggest?" Arabela asked. "we need to hold a wake tonight," Simon said, not waiting for Madeline to answer.

"What is that?" Jode asked.

"It's a celebration of the lives of friends lost. People tell stories about the departed and there's crying and laughing. Often there is significant alcohol consumption but we don't need it," Madeline said. "In fact it would probably be better if people weren't suffering hangovers the next day."

"And, you think that one night will get people back to normal?" Arabela's tone was disbelieving.

"No, not back to normal, but at least on their way to living their own lives again," Simon answered.

"I can't think of a reason not to try, my lady," Jode said his voice low and thoughtful. "It can do no harm. Look around you, as Madeline suggested, there is no hope in the people. Without hope, how can we defeat Sayer Goddard? Without hope, how can you protect those under your rule?"

Arabela looked around at the others and sighed, "what will we need to do? How much will we need to prepare?"

"It's not difficult. Please, let me talk to Blu and we'll work it all out. All you need to do is gather the people when we stop for the night," Simon answered. Arabela agreed to her part and Simon dropped back to talk to the priest.

~~~
~~~

Sitting beside Jode waiting for the wake to begin, Madeline reflected on how easy the arrangements had been. Four Eldmen had stepped forward and said they would mourn their companions the next day. The rest of the camp sat in small groups around a rough circle. The remaining members of the band sat together across the circle from Madeline and Jode; Simon was talking quietly to them.

Blu stepped up onto a platform and the quiet murmuring of the crowd stopped. He held his arms out in front of his body and bowed to the band.

"It is time to say goodbye to our friends," Blu's voice carried despite the distance between him and the waiting people. "I will start the evening by expressing what I will miss about Lady Asla and Sir Yorr; perhaps others will come forward to share stories as well. We will continue the evening until all who wish to have had a chance to speak."

Madeline expected to recognize the tune as the musicians started to play. She was surprised to find that the somber notes were unfamiliar. The tune was of this world. The oboe and bassoon played sounds that seemed to weave around each other, and as Blu started to talk, the music formed a song of his words. Wakes she had attended back home lacked the layers of sorrow and beauty that she heard tonight.

"I did not know these two before we were brought together by the quest," Blu said. "That does not mean I did not grow to love them as companions. I have listened to the sounds of the new music that Lady Asla sang each evening on the journey, and I will remember that sound for my life. Each time I hear the new songs, I will think of her voice floating on the night air.

Sir Yorr has been a faithful companion to me as well. I know that his music was important to him. What you may not know is that he also rode along side me most days; we discussed philosophy, and tradition. His company has made the journey enjoyable."

Jode patted Madeline's hand and rose to stand beside the platform. Blu bowed again to the band and stepped down. Madeline watched Jode step onto the platform. He stood for a few minutes, it seemed like an eternity to her as she saw him take control of his emotions. He bowed to the band as Blu had and cleared his throat.

"Many of you know me," he started. "You know me as a man of sword and armor. Few of you know me as I once was, as a youth, someone who was committed to becoming a bard and a troubadour."

Madeline blinked with surprise. Jode seemed so fitted to being a knight, he was the ideal knight, tall, blond, handsome, that it hadn't occurred to her that he was ever destined for something else.

"When my older brother died I was bound by duty to put aside my own desires and take his place as my father's heir. I put aside the music that filled my heart with pleasure and learned to love the arts of war and battle instead. It was Lady Asla and Sir Yorr who reminded me of other choices; this life of a knight did not mean I could not live my other life. They were unyielding in their efforts to sway me to become a troubadour. I will always thank them for that; I will miss them every time we perform."

Jode bowed again and returned to Madeline's side. She took his hand and held it in her lap, wanting to keep him close during the evening, not wanting to leave him alone in his sorrow.

Simon spoke about the talent of the two departed friends. Other members of the band followed one after the other. Then each of the Fay members of the camp stood and spoke of Asla's virtues, and the goblins of Yorr's.

Madeline felt her tears flowing and heard others sobbing as the evening proceeded. The sorrow of the group was evident and the first steps to relieving the pain were well underway. Finally, there was no one standing at the platform waiting to speak. It was time to get the laughter bubbling, time to start the second part of the process, remembering the two friends as people not as idealized paragons. She hoped when the laughter started, the healing would begin. It was vital that tomorrow morning dawned with the camp able to look forward and not just inward to their sorrow.

She nodded to Simon. He turned to the band members and said something to the Eldman, Zora; the music slowly faded. Madeline started towards the platform and the band started playing again, this was something she recognized, not cheery by any means but definitely not a dirge; Simon had directed them to play Con Te Partiro.

Madeline stood on the platform and bowed to the band. She looked around the circle of people and smiled. "I feel your sorrow as well, but I know that Lady Asla would not wish us to cry overly long. Although I did not know either of them well, I was looking forward to becoming friends with Lady Asla. She had agreed to become my chaperon. I thought it would be helpful to become friends with her if she was to fulfill that role. In our first day, she helped me to tease Sir Jode into blushing. I will miss her, but I wish to celebrate her now, not mourn her passing. She has gone to her next life; we should go on with our current life."

Madeline stepped off the platform and a goblin woman replaced her. As Madeline walked towards Simon, she heard a story about how Yorr had carried out a long and involved prank on the leading family of the goblins.

Looking over at Jode who was sitting watching the woman tell the story, she saw a small smile on his lips as though he was anticipating the ending. Madeline needed to talk to Simon, she was feeling lost; there was something bigger that she was mourning, and he would know how to help her.

"Okay, guys," Simon said to the band before following Madeline to the outside of the crowd. "Play what we talked about and I'll be back soon."

He followed Madeline to a patch of grass just behind the group of people. They were still in the camp, still under the protection of the sentries but had a modicum of privacy with everyone's attention on the speaker.

"Okay, what's up?" Simon asked, as they settled on the grass. "I liked your speech; it seems to have started people feeling better."

"Yes, that's going according to plan."

"So, why aren't you cuddled up to Sir Jode?"

"Everything people have talked about, the way they felt about Yorr and Asla, it is the way I was starting to feel about them. It has made me think."

"About your life, yes, that usually happens at a wake, you know that."

"That's why I need to talk to you. I don't want to make my decision with all of this emotion weighting it down."

"I get that," Simon shrugged. "So what do you need from me?"

"What do you think people are saying, or will say about you when they realize you won't be coming home?"

"You mean if they have a wake for me?"

"Yes, I guess that's what I mean. Like we'll be dead to them back there, at some point they'll realize we're gone."

"I hope people will miss me for a while, I guess," Simon thought about the question. "You know I had lots of friends there, at least I thought they were friends. Now, I'm pretty sure they were acquaintances. The people here mean more to me already than the people I've known for years."

"Is that a good thing?"

"Yes, since I'm staying. I think the people at work will figure I took off and then move on. It will take about a week," He laughed.

"Really, and it doesn't bother you?"

"No, my friends probably will fight over who gets my winnings from the Survivor pool and then move on," he brightened. "Hey if you go back will you contact them?"

"That's the thing," Madeline looked down and picked at the blades of grass. "I don't think I am going back."

"Jode is going to be really charged about that."

"Don't tell him." Madeline heard the panic in her voice. "I haven't completely decided. I don't want to get his hopes up. It's just that listening to all the things people said about Asla and Yorr, made me wonder what will people say about me. People back there?"

"The office," Simon took her hand to stop her picking the grass completely bare. "They will miss you because of the clients. They don't care about you. I'm sorry but they don't."

"I figured you would say that. I know it's true and I think I should feel hurt. I just kind of feel relieved."

"What about your friends?"

"I don't have any," Madeline said. "I was too busy to keep up friendships. I don't have any family, before you ask."

"So, why are you even considering going back?"

"I don't know," She threw the broken blades of grass over her shoulder. "That's what I realized; I don't know why I want to go back. It's like I spend so much time thinking about back, that I haven't really thought about forward."

"So, start thinking about staying here."

"I shouldn't be staying here just because I have no reason to go back. It's not fair to anyone."

"Yes," Simon said. "I think you need to figure out what you are going to do with Jode. If you don't love him or if you aren't going to commit to him, it will be hard on both of you if you stay."

"It's not that I don't love him."

"Do you want my advice, or just my ear?"

"Tell me what you think," she laughed, "I'll ignore it if I don't like it anyway."

"Ha, you ignore me whether you like what I have to say or not."

"Yeah, yeah. So, what do you think I should do?"

"Stay."

"That's it? No advice on romance, no career ideas?"

"Hey, you have time to figure that out if you stay. Start with the decision to stay and figure out the rest."

The music was becoming more cheerful and Madeline could hear people laughing out loud. She stood and pulled Simon to his feet. "It sounds like your band needs you. I'll think about what you said. Thanks, it helped to talk with someone who doesn't need anything from me."

"Yeah, I need to sing a few songs before the night is over." They walked towards the crowd, Simon turned to the band, and Madeline to cross the field to join Jode.

"Madeline," Simon called. "If you go I will miss you. I think of you as a friend. You aren't alone here."

"Thank you. I would miss your friendship too. Who would have thought that, hey?"

Smiling, Madeline returned to Jode's side as the band started the next song, Michele my Belle. He wrapped his arm around her as she sat; she felt the warmth of his body seep into hers.

"I would like to talk with you, Madeline."

"Yes, I'd like to talk with you too, let's go somewhere more private."

"No," Jode held her back as she tried to rise. "We have no chaperon, we must talk here, where people can see us if they choose."

“Really, I’m not sure I’m comfortable talking with all these people about.”

“They are concerned with their own business at the moment. It is important that we maintain our reputations. Do not worry, no one will listen, look, they are starting to dance anyway.”

“Okay, I’ll trust that we have some privacy in the crowd.”

“This evening has made me think about more than just our friends,” Jode started. “My heart is sore at the loss of people I cared for, but I am willing to have it hurt again so that I can start to heal all at once.”

“What is it that will hurt you?” Madeline thought she knew the answer but wanted to make him say the words. It might give her time to think of an answer.

“I do not think I can wait any longer for your decision on our future.”

“It is not a good idea to make commitments after such emotional times.”

“I need hope, at least.” Jode stood, “I know I said I would be patient. But life is so fragile; I need to know if you love me.”

“You know it’s not that easy for me, it’s not just about love, it’s about everything.” Madeline felt her stomach tighten and her throat clench with fear that she would say the wrong thing, that she would say yes to make him feel better. “It has been difficult for me today as well. I have been thinking about my home, about the people I left behind, who I will leave behind if I stay.”

“And,” Jode asked.

"And, I don't know. I can't make this decision now. Please do not ask me to."

"Am I still to wait on your deliberations?" He leaned away from her.

"I'm sorry; I can't make that decision today." Madeline stood and took his hands in hers. "I have other decisions to make that must be made without a commitment to you. I must also decide what I will do here as a profession. I cannot simply be a wife; I need something to challenge my mind, to enjoy when I am not with you."

"Then you have made a decision?" Jode smiled, "you are staying?"

"I have not made a firm decision. As I said, I have other decisions to make first. And, I have to survive my role in the quest."

"Do not think you will die in the quest. It is not good to think of death in these circumstances."

"Okay, I won't. Please don't ask me about our future. I can't think of that when I'm so worried about what I need to do in the next two days. If you make me talk about it, if you make me decide before I'm ready, then I will just break off our relationship now."

"If that is what you wish." Jode stood, "If you have no more use of me then I will join the other musicians. It is difficult for them to make up for the two lost ones if I am absent as well." Madeline nodded unable to speak for fear she would simply tell him she loved him, and wanted to stay here forever with him. That frightened her more than the upcoming battle.

~~~

The next morning dawned fair and clear. The camp broke quietly but with a sense of life, people spoke softly but walked with a spring in their step. The wake had been successful. Those who hung their head today did so with a slight uneven weave and a greenish tinge to their skin; hung over not heartbroken. Madeline and Arabela walked together to the horse paddock and helped the grooms saddle their mounts. Walking the horses to the edge of the camp, they waited for the rest of the riders to join them.

"You were talking to Sir Jode last night," Arabela said. "Have you come to an understanding?"

"No, he tried to make me decide, but I'm not sure of anything," she fiddled with the reins as they talked. "I don't know if he is even pressuring me to stay really. I know what he says but it seems to me all he wants is a decision one way or another."

"You are being obstinate," Arabela sighed and shook her head. "You will lose his love if you keep him waiting."

"I shouldn't make such a big decision just because I am afraid of losing one of the choices."

"What are you afraid of? He is a good man; he has a beautiful and rich estate. You would be able to do whatever you wished to entertain and interest yourself."

"It is not just about love, it is about changing everything I know." Madeline heard her voice tighten with anger. "You are all blind to the fact that I have to give up everything if I stay."

"So, what is it that is so valuable about your life in that world?"
~~~

"I don't know. Damn, if everyone stopped pushing maybe I could figure it out. I had friends who married and ended up divorced over stupid things. If I end up wanting to get out of a marriage here I would have no one and nothing."

"If you wished to end your marriage to Sir Jode he would provide for you."

"Yes, that's what is supposed to happen in my world too. But, it comes down to fights over money. The relationship that starts in a sense of wonder and hope ends in a fight over who has to pay who, and how much."

"It does not happen that way here."

"That maybe true, but I am not going to jump blindly into marriage. I don't want to find myself facing divorce here. I want a marriage that will last forever."

"You are really quite an idiot," Arabela snapped. "If you wish to stay married to Jode then you will. If you are willing to work through the difficult times and accept that you are both flawed you will stay together until death takes one of you to the next life."

"Fine," Madeline said squeezing her knees to signal Glory to start walking. "If it's that easy then I am an idiot. But, I'm an idiot who won't be pushed. I think I'll ride further back in the line." She turned Glory's head toward the end of the line of horses, joining Simon about half way down the line.

"That looked like you were fighting," He said as she turned Glory to ride beside him. "Please tell me you weren't alienating our hostess and the woman who will be my patron if I'm lucky."

"She was antagonizing me," Madeline said.

"Really? How?"

"Telling me I shouldn't keep Jode hanging, accusing me of being stupid, or spiteful, or a coward, just because I can't make a decision."

"So, which one is it?"

"What?"

"Stupid, spiteful, or afraid?"

"Asshole," she shook her head, "confused I think is more like it, or perhaps overwhelmed."

"She's right, you know."

"About what?"

"You need to decide and you need to tell people."

"Fuck off, I thought you would understand," She tried to turn Glory so they could ride further back in the line but Simon stopped her by grabbing the reins.

"I do," he said. "What you don't seem to understand is that you are asking them to go into battle with too many things on their minds."

"No, I'm not. Arabela is taking them, and me, into battle."

"Yes, but you hold a lot of power in that situation. Jode should only be worrying about the next day or two, but he's not. He's worried about what you will do. He's trying to understand if he will have a new life to look forward to. If you say yes to him, he knows his next steps with you and can put aside that worry. If you say no, he'll be heartbroken, the guy loves you to bits, but he knows how to deal with that."

"So it's all my fault," she felt the anger and frustration reach explode out of her control. "Because I need to take some time to think out my future, I'm the bad guy?"

"You already know what you want to do," he hissed at her keeping his voice low. "You told me yesterday. I have seen you be a right bitch to people, but this takes the cake. This isn't about just you; it's about all these people."

"Let me go," Her voice was calm and cold. "I don't want to talk about this; I'm going to ride at the end of the line."

"Fine," Simon let go of the reins and watched her ride back to join the Eldmen at the end of the line of wagons.

"Sir Simon," Urr's voice came from the region of his boot. "Please, we need you with the band. There is a terrible argument going on. We need you to help stop it."

At the head of the line, Arabela and Jode rode side by side. "You should leave this to me," Jode said. "It is my heart that is at stake."

"You are not accustomed to this type of decision," Arabela said. "It is better if you let me talk to her. I will make her understand that she must marry you."

"I do not wish her to marry me because she has been ordered to do so."

"Of course not," Arabela laughed. "Most men do not wish to know that their wives have been obtained through any other means but true love."

"With respect, Lady Arabela," Jode said quietly, his body held stiffly in the saddle. "I am not a child. I am aware that there are traditions of expedience, political or otherwise, in uniting houses. I do not wish to have a marriage of expedience. I would rather she be willing than not."

"An admirable goal," Arabela ignored the first statement. "And, if she decides to go back to her world. Would you prefer that?"

"If she believes it is the right thing for her."

"You would be heartbroken, how will you recover from losing her? You should not worry so much about what happens after, just how to get her to be your wife."

"Allow me to decide what I should or should not worry about." He nudged his horse into a faster gait; "I think I shall ride ahead and ensure the road is safe."

He trotted ahead and was lost around a bend in the road. Arabela dropped back until she was riding between two of her guardsmen; it was not safe for her to ride out of protection. She knew Jode was taking advantage of the fact that she wouldn't follow him because she wouldn't endanger the rest of the group.

"My lady," one of the camp servants approached with a flask of water. "Please, take a little refreshment."

"What happened to your face?" Arabela asked as she reached for the flask. The woman's hair was loose and tangled, as though she had ridden through a windstorm. Her face was marred with a fresh scratch across the right cheek.

"It is nothing," she put her hand over the scratch, "a disagreement over duties."

"Ask Blu to look at it," Arabela said passing the flask back to the woman. "It would be unwise to leave a cut like that to become infected. Have someone bring water to the men as well." The woman nodded and ran back to the supply wagon.

~~~

As the sun reached the high point of its path, the camp stopped for a rest break. People ran around with platters of bread, dried meats, and fruit. Others ran behind with jugs of water and wine, grooms took the horses to a nearby stream to be watered and their hooves and legs checked for injury.

Madeline felt the hustle and bustle of the camp rub on her nerves like sandpaper on skin. She took a sandwich and a mug of water to a slight rise off to the side of the camp. The relative peace of the space allowed her to relax and enjoy the break. As she ate, she watched the others about their duty, there seemed to be more bumps and shoves than usual. She saw a couple of the grooms standing nearby while they waited for the horses. They started shouting and swearing at each other for no reason she could see. The stable master cuffed them both across the side of the head. They stopped fighting, but threw looks at each other that guaranteed the fight was to continue later when no one was looking.

There was a clatter of metal falling and a young serving girl stood looking down at a pile of platters that she had dropped when another server had crashed into her. The plates were empty but it looked like she was going to be in trouble for clumsiness; the cook was marching towards her with a fist raised.
~~~

Madeline ran forward to get between the cook and the girl. "Stop, it was an accident," she said putting her hands out to stop the man moving forward. "It was an accident," she repeated firmly.

"Too many damn accidents today," the man said, and then stomped back to the cook wagon.

Madeline helped the girl pick up the platters and take them to the team of dishwashers. As she did she observed more arguments and fights than she had in her entire time with on the journey.

"It looks like the wake didn't quite do the job," she muttered. "Emotions were released but not soothed. I think we need something else before this explodes into a full, camp wide, fist fight." She went in search of Blu, thinking that the priest was the best option for a calm observation and a plan to resolve the problem. When she found him, he was standing beside his wagon talking to two men who had drawn knives.

"It is not in our best interest to fight each other," the priest was saying. "Put away your knives, we may need both of you if it comes to a battle."

The priest was patting the men's arms as he spoke. They kept their eyes on him and seemed to relax their posture at his words. The two men apologized, sheathed the knives, bowed and turned to walk away in opposite directions.

"What is going on?" Madeline asked.

"There is too much tension," Blu said, taking her arm and walking her around his wagon, pointing at small conflicts all around. "The people know that there is tension between you and Lady Arabela, between you and Sir Jode. Tension in the leaders transfers itself to the people. It is worse now because the stakes are so high."

"I'm causing this?" Madeline was amazed that he thought she had that much influence. "This is because Arabela, Jode and I are having a disagreement?"

"Not all," Blu said. "But you must remember both you and Arabela have power, magical power. When she was a child her training focused on containment; you have not received such lessons."

"Can you train me?" Madeline was horrified that she was at least partially to blame. "Can you shield me or something? If this continues we won't have a chance."

"No, there is no time to train you and I can't shield you because it might interfere with what you are supposed to do."

"Well, how do we stop this?"

"Make peace with yourself if you can." Blu stood with his arms folded across his chest. "Make peace with Sir Jode and Lady Arabela."

"Okay," Madeline hoped peace wouldn't require a decision. "Do you know where they are?"

"Over there," Blu pointed to a group of people who were shouting at someone in the center of their huddle. "They are trying to resolve an issue between the Fay and the Sylph. Come, I'll take over the negotiation to free them to talk to you." They made their way through the crowd by excusing themselves as they wiggled into the gaps between Fay and Sylph.

"Please," Blu said in a surprisingly loud voice. "Gentlemen, ladies, I will hear your complaint. Allow these three to pass they have important business. Now, one at a time, please, tell me what this is all about."

Jode and Arabela allowed her to guide them to the edge of the crowd without protest. When they were clear, Madeline saw Simon moving towards them. She called him over and they retreated to the shelter of the trees.

"It is not right that I leave Blu to settle that dispute," Arabela said, looking at the crowd but not moving to go back. "Not right, but he will do a much better job than I would."

"What the hell is going on?" Simon said. "It's like everyone just decided to take offense at the mere presence of others." Madeline passed on Blu's comments.

"So, you need to reach some sort of compromise," Simon said. "As far as I can see, you keep arguing about the same thing."

"We have had many arguments, what is a single thing?" Jode asked.

"Madeline," Simon answered. "It's always about whether or not she's staying, and whether or not she will marry you."

Arabela looked at the expression on Jode's face and laughed, "you are certainly very focused."

"And, Lady Madeline is willing to make her decision for the sake of the people?" Jode eyes lit up in hope. "I am happy to hear what she has to say."

"No," Madeline said. "I'm sorry I don't think it's about that."

"I had to ask," Jode said.

"Well, the tension for me is because we keep talking about it. It doesn't help to keep going on about what I should or shouldn't do."

Simon held up his hand to get their attention. "Look, I think she's right. Forcing a decision will only push these feelings underground and that's likely to do more damage than a brawl. What if we agree not to discuss it until the quest is done."

"Until I have to decide?" Madeline shrugged. "I think I can find other things to talk about for a day."

"It is perhaps wise to discuss other topics," Jode conceded. "I am happy to agree to discuss anything but our future. Perhaps we can return to your training as a substitute topic."

"If you can put the subject aside I suppose I can do so too," Arabela said. "It is less important to me what you decide, Madeline. It does feel somewhat easier not having to think of ways to help you with your decision."

"Okay," Madeline said. "So, do we need to cut our fingers and mingle our blood to make a pact?"

"How perfectly horrible," Arabela shuddered. "Why would you damage yourself that way?"

"Old custom on my world," Simon laughed. "Look, just shake hands and walk back together. It might be a good idea for you to wander around the camp together encouraging people to pack up and get going."

"Yes," Jode said. "A show of harmony will probably do the trick."

28

"Wake up," Alice called to Madeline at sunrise. "You are to meet with Lady Arabela at the priest's wagon in a half hour."

She jumped out of the bedding and put on her sword belt, sliding the throwing knives into pockets sewn into her shirt and the side of her pants. The weight of her weapons distributed evenly making it possible to move as if she was not carrying several pounds of sharpened steel.

"Here," Alice said handing Madeline a mug and a sandwich. "Eat this as you talk. There may be no other opportunity until this is over."

"Thanks," Madeline looked around the tent room that had become home in the last ten days. "Are you packing up?"

"No. We will be here when you return. I will lay out a dress for you to wear at the party to celebrate victory. There will be a bath waiting for you if we have enough notice."

"And, what if…" Madeline started to ask.

"Do not contemplate anything other than victory," Alice said in a rush. "You will be victorious and you will all return to celebrate."

Madeline nodded and ran towards the meeting. Blu's wagon was in the center of a cleared space. All of the armed men stood in a circle around the clearing, all except Jode, who stood waiting for Madeline to arrive. There was a small round tent set up in front of the wagon; around the tent were piles of stones and incense.

"Good morning," Jode said taking her hand and leading her to the tent. "We will be meeting in here; it is protected from spying eyes and ears. It is time to decide what we will do."

"Do we have any more information?" Madeline avoided asking the real question, what was she supposed to do.

"Not as far as I have been told." He held back the tent flap, then followed Madeline inside.

The others sat in a circle with two spaces empty. Blu, Simon, and Arabela sat side by side; Jode and Madeline sat beside each other to complete the circle. Blu welcomed her and then reached around to close the tent flap with ties of blue and yellow ribbons.

"Now no person or creature outside will know what happens inside," He said. "It is time to discuss plans."

"I am willing to go now," Arabela said. "If we ride quickly he will have no time to prepare."

"What if you could end this by agreement," Madeline asked. "My skill lies in negotiation, maybe that's what I am here for. If you could do this without bloodshed, would it not be better?"

"I do not think Sayer Goddard will negotiate," Jode answered. "The Scree do not give up so easily."

"In my world we had long standing wars that were resolved by negotiations," Madeline looked to Simon for help. "Do you think this might be like that?"

"No," Simon said. "I know you think this is like the troubles in Northern Ireland."

"Yes," Madeline said. "No one thought England and Ireland could agree to a permanent peace."

"I know, but there are a lot of things that are different."

"Tell us," Arabela said. "I agree with Sir Jode that the Scree will likely not agree to stop the feud. But, if you have a way of doing that, I am happy not to shed blood, even Scree blood."

"Two countries fought bitter wars for generations. Parents passed hatred to children; children killed people for things that had been done to their grandparents and great grandparents." Madeline tried to paint the picture.

"Yes," Simon jumped in. "It was like a blood feud between two countries. But, here's the problem with applying that logic to this situation. The troubles were not about personal issues. They were solved because it wasn't personal; no IRA fighter was trying to kill a specific Englishman. They were able to put down their weapons because the problem didn't exist anymore. The economic situation changed, the rest of the world did not take sides, and they applied pressure to both England and Ireland for a peaceful resolution. And, they were both human. That's not the case here."

"Fine," Madeline conceded, it was difficult to argue the similarities against such facts. "It isn't the same. I was reaching for an example. Thanks for shooting it down."

"I'm not shooting down the idea, just the example," Simon sighed.

"It is not worth arguing over such a thing," Blu said. "But arguing is what we need to do. Within this tent, it is required that disagreements are aired and discussed. It will not affect the rest of our people; it will not escape the protections."

"Okay," Madeline shrugged. "I'm out of ideas."

"I think it makes sense to heed Lady Madeline's advice," Jode said. "It is not sensible to discard her suggestion simply because she is unable to provide an example."

"Thanks," Madeline felt warm at his approval. "Why haven't we really discussed this before?"

"We have all hoped for new information." Arabela said. "You are not the only person who wished to know your role. It does not matter, though. Often the best plans are made at the last minute when everything is known. If you plan far in advance, too many things can change."

"What do you think we should do?" Simon asked turning to Arabela. "This is your quest after all. You probably have the most to lose. What would you do if we weren't here?"

"I would call Goddard out to battle my champion. Sir Jode would fight Goddard, or his champion, and we would settle for the winner."

"Okay," Madeline jumped in. "I'm not going along with that one."

"Do you not believe I can win against a Scree?" Jode asked. "I am the best warrior in the land. I could dispatch the best Goddard could bring to the field."

The thought of losing Jode to treachery rose like a shadow in her imagination. "You said you can't trust Goddard to abide by an agreement. That means he probably wouldn't fight fair."

"You are right to argue against the plan," Blu said. "The prophecy was clear, you are critical to the success."

"I do not wish you to be placed in harm's way." Jode placed his arm around Madeline.

"Yeah, yeah, both of you are interested in keeping the other safe. I think we all get that." Simon said. "You know you can't though, right?"

"Yes," Madeline said.

"I do," Jode said.

"Well, we must agree on a plan, and it will put someone in harm's way. It may put all of us there before we are done," Arabela said, her frustration showing in the sharpness of her tone. "I think there are only two choices. We fight, or we negotiate."

"There is a third option," Blu said. "You can try to negotiate first. Then attack if it is not successful."

Madeline said, "I think you should try. If you are right then we don't need to attack openly. We can try to sneak into the keep and kill Goddard quietly. If we can do that without leaving any trace we were there, would it solve the problem?"

"Proof or otherwise, if we kill Goddard his people will not retaliate. There will be a long and hard battle for the leadership of the family it will be years before they are ready to attack anyone else," Jode answered.

"It is not our way," Arabela started. "And, that is a good thing. Blu, is there any lore or custom that says we cannot do as Madeline suggests?"

"No," the small priest answered. "Not that I am aware of. I will meditate on this until dark; I will have an answer for you then. Now, go and spend the day together, practice your skills, think of the details of your plans, discuss them quietly so that you do not bring attention. Goddard may be spying on us when we leave the tent."

"Until dark, then," Arabela stood and cut the ribbons holding the tent flap closed. "We have only two days until the moon is full."

They followed her out of the tent and stood watching as the priest laced a blue ribbon through the holes from the inside.

Arabela dismissed all but two of the guards, setting them at the door of the tent. "I suggest you all spend the day practicing your skills as Blu said. I will be in my tent thinking about this negotiation. I will need to have something I can give to Goddard if this is to work. Something he will value and cannot take forcibly from me."

Simon walked away to the edge of the camp where the goblins had set up. "I'll be hanging with my guys," he called over his shoulder. "It's not like I have skills to hone."

"Come," Jode said. "I suggest we spend time on the practice grounds. It is an hour or more before the midday meal. We have time for you to learn some new skills."

"Really?" Madeline thought she was as skilled as she was going to get before the fight. "You think I have time for that?"

"Yes," Jode took her arm to draw her along to the clearing. "This is a skill linked to the dance; it will help you to survive if you lose your weapons and have to face an armed opponent."

They reached the clearing where few of the guardsmen were working through a sword exercise and others were testing the strings of their bows. Jode asked her to wait at the entrance to the space while he talked to two of the guards. When he returned they followed him, exchanging comments she couldn't hear but brought broad grins to their faces.

"Lady Madeline, I have asked Alan and Booker to demonstrate the skills I need you to learn." He directed the two men to stand apart a few feet away. "When you have seen what they have to show, I will take you through a few warm up exercises. You won't have time to warm up if you need this in battle, but there is no need for you to hurt yourself while we practice."

He clapped his hands twice and the two men circled each other once, then Booker rushed at Alan pulling a knife from his belt as he did. Alan sidestepped then spun around as the attacker passed. He completed the spin and feigned stabbing Booker in the lower back. The two men bowed and return to the starting position. Alan charged the second time, this time low and aiming at Booker's stomach. Booker spun and kicked the knife out of Alan's hand as he passed.

"It's like a bullfight." Madeline said, "I saw one on National Geographic television a few weeks ago. It's not that different from sword defense. Can I try?"

"I would like you to warm up first," Jode insisted. "Get your sword and we'll go through the standard movements. I'll ask Alan to come back and take you through the defensive movements."

"Why not you?" Madeleine felt disappointment fill her.

"I must admit I am not an expert," Jode looked down as if embarrassed and then looked up at her with a grin. "I do not often find myself without my sword so I have not spent much time practicing. I think it would be better if you worked with someone more familiar with the art."

"Fine, let's warm up then."

The two spent a half hour walking through the sword practices. By the end, they worked through the motions in perfect synchronization. Madeline felt as though they were dancing and didn't want to stop.

"I think you are sufficiently warmed up." Jode stepped back and summoned Alan back to the area they were using. "Please, give me all your weapons, Madeline." Unbuckling her sword belt, she handed it with the sheathed sword to him. Then Madeline started pulling knives from the pockets in her shirt and pants. When she finished, she felt considerably lighter and Jode stood with his arms full of very sharp metal.

"Lady Madeline," Alan said, "let us walk through the movements so I can explain them. Then we can do them quickly until they become instinct."

He stood in a low crouch and waited until Madeline copied the stance. "Good, now, when you see an opening, or when the opponent attacks, show me what you think you will do?"

Madeline stepped forward and swung her arm around as though to stab him in his side.

"No," Alan spun away slapping her hand as he went. "I would have cut you badly if I was armed."

"So," Madeline rubbed her arm, he had made solid contact with her. "What should I have done?"

"Protect your body, and cut outward not inward." He made the movements to illustrate the concept. "That way it is more difficult to turn your momentum against you."

"Start again," she said, crouching.

Alan crouched and attacked without stopping. Madeline spun away from him, feeling the breeze as his hand passed her body. She lost control of the motion and fell.

"More control," Alan snapped. "Don't look at your feet when you move; watch your attacker."

Madeline pushed away the frustration she felt at her inability to pick up the skill as easily as she had the sword. She kept trying, and eventually was able to avoid his strikes and not fall down from the momentum. Alan nodded his approval of her performance and made to leave.

"Wait," Madeline said. "What if more than one attacker comes at me?"

"I would suggest you run as fast and as far as you can," Alan responded. "You may survive a few passes but two men with swords will attack in pattern, they will force you to try to dodge in two different ways. You will find yourself impaled quickly."

"Good advice," Jode added. "Madeline, I hope with all my heart you are not put in a position to fight with or without a weapon, but, you are as prepared as we have time for."

"Okay," she thanked Alan and then put all of her weapons back into place. "I guess I should practice my throwing now. Jode, Do you want to come?"

"Yes," There's a target set up, I'll have the archers stop so we can use it."

"Why didn't you teach me to shoot an arrow?" She asked curious as they approached the archers.

"Look at the archers," Jode pointed. "See the way their shoulders are built?"

Madeline noticed that, male or female, human or other, the archers had strong broad shoulders and big arm muscles. The smooth movement as they drew and released the arrow from the bow was impressive in the way it strained the muscles.

"I guess I would need much more time than we have," She sighed. "What if I hadn't known how to use a sword before I came? Would I only have throwing knives? I don't think that would have been enough."

"The sword is your best weapon, true. But, if you had not the skill we would have trained you to use the knives without throwing them. Tell me, why you took so many different classes. It seems you have a little knowledge in many things."

"I never found anything that kept my interest enough to keep at it when it got hard. I have to admit I was worried when I saw how quickly people here learn," she said. "I thought you might have too high an expectation of my abilities."

"You have learned well," Jode said. "It is, perhaps, because of all the classes you took."

"I suppose I have more incentive to keep going when it gets hard. If I give up here it could cost lives, not just a bit of money."

"Will you teach me knife fighting this afternoon?" Madeline brightened. "Defense was good but, another way to fight will be a benefit."

"Of course I will teach you. After you are able to throw from this distance," Jode placed a stick on the ground. "This is further than you have thrown before. Sink all of the knives into the target three times and then I will show you how to hold the knife for a fight and you will show me how you think you would fight with it."

Madeline looked at the tree in the distance. A red ribbon was circled the trunk and several knives were already stuck there. Jode signaled to two men who had approached the tree to pull out the knives that she would be throwing and they hurried back behind the stick.

Patting the pockets holding her knives, Madeline thought about the pattern of movements she would need to make to reach for and throw all of them; in a real fight, she would not be pulling the knives from the ground but from their hiding places. She closed her eyes, took three deep breaths, and then opened her eyes to focus on the target.

She reached for the blades on her hips first, throwing one then the other right at the target. Then she pulled the knives from the front of her shirt, and finally the knives from the diagonal pockets on the back of her shirt. All of the knives hit the target and stayed in the wood until she pulled them out. She returned them to their pockets as she walked back to the stick.

"Well done," she heard the two men say.

She reminded herself not to get cocky and then repeated the performance; all the knives sank into the wood again. This time one of the men ran to pull the blades from the wood and return them to her. Jode had not spoken for the entire performance.

Madeline held one knife in her hand and placed the others in the ground. This time she pulled them from the ground and threw them in one smooth motion not waiting to see the blade land before throwing the next. All blades made contact.

"Are you using magic?" Jode asked as the two men retrieved the blades.

"I don't think so," Madeline remembered the danger of using unprotected magic. "I hope not. What does magic feel like?"

"It is different for everyone. But, I think you would feel something. If you do not think so, then you are probably not doing so."

"Will you teach me knife fighting now?"

"No," Jode took her arm. "You need to eat something. You are pale, and I am afraid you are about to fall over."

Madeline laughed, but agreed with him about eating. "I guess it's been a while since breakfast."

They took water, meat and cheese to a group of boulders by the stream. They were in sight of everyone but not close enough for anyone to overhear. While they ate, Jode talked to her about the techniques of knife fighting, demonstrating the proper way to hold the knife so she would not cut herself too badly.

"The most important thing to remember is that knife fighting is fast," he said, putting their plates down on one of the boulders. "You must act on instinct. If you try to think, you will be stabbed before you decide what to do."

"Swords are like that," Madeline said, holding the knife in her hand and trying a few different passes at an imaginary opponent.

"Yes, but the knife is not as heavy. The follow through is shorter and the recovery is immediate. Here, let's try without the blade."

He made her hold her hand as though she held a knife and then they started fighting. Madeline copied his stance while they circled; legs and arms wide. Jode suddenly rushed her and she spun away trying to stab as she did. He grabbed her hand and twisted her back to his chest, holding her with one hand and miming slicing her throat with the other.

"Try again," Jode said, releasing her. "This time keep your arms in when you spin so I cannot grasp you."

"Okay," Madeline said, breathing heavily from the exertion and his closeness. "But, am I supposed to be learning not to get into a knife fight with someone so much bigger than me?"

"You've learned the first lesson then," Jode laughed as he circled her. "Let's see if you can at least pretend to damage me."

They fought for almost an hour, circling each other and attacking, sometimes Madeline would start the attack, sometimes Jode. Mostly Jode would win but towards the end, Madeline started to use her smaller size and speed to her advantage. Ducking in under Jode's reach, she was able to cut him, well pretend to, and dodge away. On the last pass, she was able to contact his leg in a way that would have hamstrung him if they had been using knives.

"Very well done," Jode gasped out. "Your advantage in a real fight is your short stature. It is a good strategy to give many small cuts; it will drain your opponent quickly when moving so fast. You might be able to survive a fight."

"I think I'm better off running if I can, though." She said, panting. "The odds are against me surviving long enough to get in the cuts."

"Yes," Jode said, "I would prefer you run. I would really prefer you were not required to be in a fight at all. But since we have no guarantee of that, you are at least as prepared as we can make you."

Madeline felt her heart squeeze at the thought of not surviving a fight. It came home to her that this wasn't a game. They were practicing fighting because she might have to do just that, she might have to stick steel into another person so they wouldn't do it to her. She watched as Jode turned to pick up their plates and the simple task a vision of their future flashed in her mind. Jode and her, in twenty years, at home, cleaning up after a meal. She felt an overwhelming knowledge that she couldn't leave this man.

And, that she couldn't leave it up in the air. This man who loved her was doing everything he could to prepare her, not to protect her. Her fears about losing herself in a man's life were stupid in the face of his actions. That realization seemed to bring a brightness to her world.

"Jode," her voice was soft and seemed to be caught in her throat.

"We should be getting back to the tents," he said turning towards her. "We will want to clean up and change for dinner."

"Jode, please, just listen for a moment before we go back. I'm afraid we won't have time to talk until it's over."

"I do not wish to hear anything that might lay a curse on the outcome."

"Please," Madeline said. "I have to say this."

"I am listening," he stood very still looking at her, his focus on her face.

"I have made my decision," she paused and swallowed to ease her dry throat. Now that she had decided to say it, she was afraid to say the wrong thing.

"Yes," Jode looked down, apparently not willing to see her say the words.

"I love you," she blurted out. "You must know that already."

"I had hoped, but no, I did not know it. I am overjoyed to hear you say the words." He kept his eyes on the ground, "is that the only decision you have made?"

"No, that would be cruel to say I love you but don't know if I'm staying. Do you think me cruel?"

"No, I do not think that," He looked up at her, shock on his face. "I could not love you if I thought that."

"Relax," she smiled to soften the word. "I have decided to stay. I think I want to study magic."

Jode looked around to see if anyone was paying attention. Everyone nearby was rushing about on camp business so he put the plates down and pulled Madeline into his embrace. She reached up and drew him into a kiss; the first time she had kissed someone she loved. His lips were firm and warm; the scent of his skin filled her senses.

He pulled her tighter to his chest and she could feel his heart beat against her. Jode straightened and lifted her off her feet. He leaned away from her and stared into her eyes. "We should not be doing this," he said before he kissed her again.

They drew apart at the sound of a cough; Blu was standing watching them. "I am sorry to interrupt you," the priest said with a smile. "I think you should make arrangements immediately to replace your chaperon."

"Thank you for protecting our reputations," Madeline said, as Jode placed her back on her feet.

"Not at all," the priest laughed. "I only interrupted to save us from a pile of broken plates from people bumping into each other as they avoided watching you."

"Have you finished your meditation?" Jode asked.

"Yes, I have already notified Lady Arabela and now I will tell you before I seek out Sir Simon. It is not a good idea to have a formal announcement; the fewer people know the details the better. I am approving the plan proposed by Lady Madeline, the signs are all positive, not a guarantee, of course. But then there never are guarantees in battle."

The priest bowed and left them standing together beside the stream. Jode picked up the plates and mugs again and nodded towards the camp. "We should return, perhaps you could ask your servant to act as chaperon tonight?"

29

The next morning the all met at Blu's wagon. The priest sat them in a circle and carried out a short ceremony of protection.

"Now," he said taking his hands from Arabela's and Jode's heads. "You will be safe from magical treachery, but you must be alert for a more practical attack. Be ready to ride back to camp to avoid danger."

"What about Simon and me?" Madeline asked. "You didn't do anything to protect us."

"That is because you are not coming," Arabela said.

"Wait," Madeline couldn't believe the words she heard. "I'm not sitting here waiting for something to happen. I'm supposed to have a role, a critical role."

"You must stay," Blu answered for Arabela. "You may have already completed your task when you created the plan. If not, you will be needed after this step fails."

"How do you know I'm not needed to make the negotiation work?"

"You may be, but you do not have to be there to help." The priest held out a long stick of what looked like bone. The stick was carved intricately in a pattern that reminded Madeline of Celtic knot work. The pattern radiated out from the center, a mirror of each twist above and below. The only difference was the pattern above the center dyed red and the pattern below blue.

"We will observe the events and you will have one opportunity to speak instructions," he explained. "When the rod is broken you must not speak to either of them unless it is vital."

"But, negotiation is based on back and forth, a dialogue." Madeline said, confused. "What is the point of only speaking once?"

"You will only speak once; these two will not be able to answer." Blu passed the rod to them, the red end to Arabela and the blue end to Madeline. "It would be better not to speak if you are not sure the information is needed."

"How long will they be gone?" Madeline asked.

"If Goddard is not willing to speak with us we will return within two hours," Jode said. "If he will talk, then it may be much longer."

"Are you ready?" Blu asked.

"Yes," Arabela and Madeline said at the same time.

The priest pulled a curved knife from a fold in his robes. He placed the knife under the center of the bone and whispered a word Madeline could not hear. The knife twisted and the bone snapped perfectly in half, a thread of purple smoke rising and dissipating quickly.

"Now," Blu said. "Go, and remember to keep the rod in your possession. We will hear everything you say, you will only hear what Lady Madeline will say once."

Jode and Arabela left, walking towards the horse paddock. Simon, Blu, and Madeline watched as they rode out. Jode's voice provided a running commentary on where they were and what they saw. Blu motioned them to enter his wagon while they wait, "I will have someone bring refreshments. Lady Madeline, please remember as long as you hold the rod you must not speak to either Sir Jode or Lady Arabela. To be sure, please use the name of the person you are addressing before you say anything."

"Blu," Madeline said immediately, "Do I need to hold the rod all of the time?"

"No, but when you do not touch it we will not hear their voices."

"Simon, do you have any advice? If I can't speak to them until something is critical it's important to know what might be critical."

"My advice," Simon shrugged. "You won't know or you will. I think they both know more about the situation and the people than you do. That means your contribution won't be about whether someone is lying or not, or something is valuable. It will be about your experience. I think you should wait until you think they might be missing a key question, something only you would think of."

"It would be better if you didn't speak rather than speaking foolishly," Blu added.

"Blu, what do you mean?" Madeline tried to keep half her concentration on the words coming from the two travelers. "Is there a price for using this magic to speak to them?"

"Yes, but not how you probably think. The price will be giving Goddard the knowledge you are here and you have unknown potential. If he knows that, he may offer to give up his feud for the price of you. You would be putting them in a position of weakness. You will be putting Sir Jode in a position where he would have to decide for his heart or for his duty."

"Blu, I will not do that."

For the next hour, they listened to Jode talk to Arabela about mundane issues around their estates. He gave instructions to their escort regarding their duties. She talked to him about his love of music, asking what his plans were for the time after the quest. They were clearly staying away from any specific discussion of Simon or Madeline. She appreciated it, something about listening into the conversation felt wrong. Even though they were aware that she could hear, it felt like spying.

"We have arrived at the edge of Goddard's estate," Arabela announced. "The escort is going forward with the banner of discourse. If Goddard comes out he should abide by the rules." Madeline pressed her lips together to avoid speaking; it was excruciating not to ask questions.

"The gates are opening," Jode said. "It seems Goddard is willing to talk. He comes on horseback with three escorts. It will take him a few minutes to arrive."

The three in the priest's wagon waited, listening to the horses shift, the birds sing in the trees, and finally the sound of approaching horse hooves.

"Goddard," Arabela's voice called. "I thank you for coming."

"Get on with it woman," the man's voice was deep, and rough, and loud. "I came to hear you out, not to exchange pleasantries."

"Very well," Arabela's voice became more controlled as she spoke. "I have come to ask that the blood feud be ended."

"It is ended," the laugh that followed made Madeline's skin crawl. "Your weak husband's line is ended. If there are no more Summer Land heirs then the feud is over."

"And, my people, will you leave them in peace?"

"Why would I? The Summer Lands are fertile and my people are hungry."

"Your feud was with my husband's family not with the people of the Summer Lands."

"You have come to beg for peace," his voice sounded surprise. "Pledge the lands to my rule and they will be left in peace."

"I cannot do that. You know that is not within my power. Only a crowned ruler can do that; we are a free state."

"No, you have come for revenge. That is why you are here." He paused, the three listening heard horses snort and stamp. "But, you would not trust my word, so you must be going through the motions of avoiding war."

"We could find a way to bind you to your word."

"No, you ask me to give up the prize of the Summer Lands after many generations of feuding. That was the agreement, the prize; the survivors would take the lands of the dead."

Madeline started to shake her head and Simon placed his hand over her mouth. "Tell me first."

"Simon," Madeline whispered, rubbing her burning skin. "There is something wrong, he is stalling. I think this is a trap, I feel it in every breath. This is a trap."

"Tell them," Blu said. "Only they will hear."

"Arabela, leave, it is a trap. I don't know what is about to happen but I know it is treachery."

"I see we will not come to agreement," Arabela said, interrupting Sayer in the middle of a taunt. "I trust you will honor the rules of discourse and allow us to leave?"

"Go," Goddard said, "I will meet you over the corpses of your people."

The three listeners heard the sound of horses retreating. "Thank you for your advice," Arabela said quietly. "We will be back…" The sudden sound of an arrow hitting a tree cut off the words. The horse hooves started to pound rapidly; Madeline realized the party was fleeing.

"Arrows," Jode said, "they are shooting from the trees, they seem to be only in one place; the arrows are coming from the same tree all the time. We are not injured." As soon as he spoke the sound of a man's painful cry came through.

"Jode, Jode," Madeline called.

"They cannot hear you." Blu said.

"One of the armsmen was struck," Arabela's voice came through. "Jode has dropped back to help him. I think we are out of range. We will ride hard to join you in any case. Expect us in the next half hour."

30

Horses exhausted, they returned to camp leaving the wounded man with the other guardsmen. In no better shape than the horses, Jode and Arabela took the food and drink that a servant offered then joined the others in Blu's wagon.

"We made a true effort at negotiation," Arabela said, then took a long draft from the water mug. "You heard everything?"

"Yes we did," Simon said. "You did try, but you were right, he had no intention of making an agreement, or holding to any agreement he pretended to make."

"Our next attempt must be successful. We have only until tomorrow moonrise to complete the quest. If we are not successful tonight we will have one more chance tomorrow."

"The plan?" Madeline asked. "We need to get the details memorized so that we are ready for whatever happens."

"You will not be joining us," Jode said in a tone that offered no argument. "You have already saved our lives that must be why you are here."

"Sure," Madeline snapped. "I was brought here to talk you into putting yourselves in danger so I could get you out of it."

"Sir Jode," Blu interrupted before Jode could respond. "I believe that Lady Madeline still has her task to complete."

"Do you know what it is?" Madeline turned away from Jode and stared at the priest. "Have you learned something?"

"No," Blu shook his head. "But, the quest is not complete; we cannot assume you have done what we brought you here to do."

"Okay," Madeline's disappointment was obvious in the way her shoulders dropped and her smile faded.

"But," the priest continued, "we have learned something about you, something that might help us to understand your task."

"What is that?"

"Your talent is, or includes, prescience; the knowing of things to come."

"True," Simon said. "How did you know they were about to be attacked?"

"I just knew," Madeline thought back to the experience. "It's like I could feel the presence of other people, not their bodies, more like their intent, an intent that didn't have a body. Does that make sense?"

"Yes," Arabela answered before anyone could speak. "If my guess is correct you feel the future. I don't know how far, only a few minutes if today is an example. But you felt the attack before the attackers were there."

"She has the same talent as your grandmother, then," Blu said, "that is most interesting."

"Well, we can investigate my possible talents after we've finished." When Madeline saw the reaction of three faces, she realized she had not told anyone else about her decision. "If you will teach me, that is. I guess I should say I've decided to stay if you will allow me. I would like to study magic, at least at first, maybe I'll find another interest later. But, that's not important right now."

"I will teach you," Blu said. "Now, as you say, we have more urgent topics to discuss."

Simon looked at the others then said, "we sneak in. I think that's the best way."

"How? Won't there be guards. Won't he be on alert?" Madeline asked.

"You would think so, but they are arrogant, the Scree," Jode said. "They will not expect us to come in a small group. They will be preparing for an attack on the camp; they will think we are preparing to leave."

"And, if we have a distraction, they will not notice four people," Madeline nodded, this was a good plan, she could feel it.

"Two people," Jode said.

"Three," Madeline said.

"You are not coming," Jode said firmly.

"I am. I feel that I must be there." Madeline lied; she had no premonition, "you, me, and Arabela: three people."

"Why not me?" Simon asked. "I don't want to sit around waiting to hear what happened."

"For this to work, we need a distraction," Madeline answered. "You need to have a concert, a very loud concert; I'm talking heavy metal loud."

"So they will be looking at us, not for you."

"And, the noise will cover any sound we might make," Arabela said. "It is a good idea, this distraction."

"I can't make it loud enough from here to distract them."

"I can help with that, Sir Simon," Blu offered. "We need to move people closer but not so close as you think. I can increase the amplification spell we use in the castle; the sound will carry loudly for a large distance."

Simon grinned and rubbed his hands together, "and, what about creating some light effects?"

"Light effects? Ah, you mean fireworks," Blu smiled in response to Simon's question. "I see what you are planning. I can create fireworks of many kinds. That will provide them with a great distraction, Scree enjoy explosions and bright lights."

Madeline rolled her eyes at their enthusiasm; she pictured a future for the music of this place that would put the loudest craziest concert back home to shame. "What will we be doing while Simon is distracting them?" She asked.

"I have been thinking of that very question," Jode said, apparently not willing to argue with Madeline any more. "If they are distracted, we should be able to find Sayer Goddard alone. He will not share his enjoyment of the show with others. If we can find him alone, I will kill him and then we will leave. His body will be found after we have left."

"It sounds too simple a plan," Arabela said. "What if you cannot kill him? What if something happens to you?"

"You will be there to make sure we are not seen. If I am not able to kill him, you or Madeline can do so."

"Do you think you can kill someone?" Arabela turned to look at Madeline, "it is not easy to take a life."

"I cannot say for sure. But, if Sayer Goddard had hurt Jode, I think it likely I would kill him regardless of your quest."

"You should rest," Blu said standing up. "Sir Simon and I must work with the New Questers to ensure the distraction is perfect. Sleep until dusk. When it is dark you will ride out."

31

They left the camp at dusk, the three who would enter the keep dressed in black, hair tied under black caps, faces smudged with dark color. The Scree would have a very difficult time seeing them in shadows.

Simon, Blu, and the band members, stopped just inside the tree line at the edge of Goddard's land. The show would start a half hour after Madeline, Jode, and Arabela left, allowing them to cross the open space and enter the keep before the band captured the attention of the inhabitants.

"Remember," Blu said, "we will keep the music playing until you return, but lights will stop every half hour after the first hour. You will have time to run to the tree line if you leave the shadows of the keep as soon as we stop."

"We will hope to return in the first break," Jode said.

The group huddled together, hugged each other and whispered words of encouragement for a few moments before the time came to start. Slipping to the edge of the last tree, the three looked towards the keep, no sentries patrolled the walls or grounds. The keep had slit windows around it from what would be the second floor; lights shone through one or two of them. On the top of the keep, a light flickered but there was no silhouette of a watcher to worry about.

The keep itself stood like a monolithic monument to defense from a slight rise ringed by a single road. The only entry through a wide gate, now closed, only a small door standing open.

"You wait beside the doorway, while I watch to see when the guard is distracted, and then we will slip inside," Jode said pointing at the gate. "There will be a staircase to the right; the guard will be in a small room under the stairs. No matter what happens, run up the staircase and through the arch into the corridor. There will be places to hide inside."

Madeline looked at the approach; trees provided cover until the last stretch of open ground, about a half kilometer by her estimation. "The moon rise will shorten the shadows from the trees," she commented. "We will have a longer run in the open as we leave."

"Yes," Arabela said. "We need to go now, you follow Sir Jode. I will make sure we are not followed."

They ran through the trees for what felt to Madeline like fifteen minutes, a jog that was easy for her to keep pace with, but it made noise as they trod through the leaves and needles carpeting the ground. When they approached the end of the tree line, Jode signaled her to stop. Arabela came up behind and they stood in the shadow of a large tree, taking time to catch their breath and watch the keep again. There were still no sentries or watchers from the top of the keep.

"He is sure that we will just leave," Jode said in a low voice. "He will regret that arrogance."

"If I stand here too long I'll stiffen up and won't be able to dash the last stretch," Madeline bounced on the balls of her feet, not quite running in place; she remembered seeing joggers doing that at red lights. "Are we about to go?"

"There's no reason not to," Arabela answered, "it will not get darker and the music will start soon."

"Madeline, can you run that far in one attempt?" Jode asked. "If not, we can run to that group of shrubs and then rest."

"No, that will make the distance twice as far and give them twice the opportunity to see us. Besides, we need to be there before the music starts; let's just go."

"There is no one looking," Arabela confirmed, "we should run together and quickly."

They left the safety of the trees together, Madeline mimicking the low loping strides of the other two. The distance was less than she had estimated, only about two hundred meters, it was the longest two minutes she had ever experienced. No one shouted alarm, no lights came on, and she had no feeling of danger. Standing beside the doorway, Madeline looked up at the wall which was not straight, it leaned slightly out as it rose. From the top of the building, they would be out of sight.

Jode held his hand out palm facing them then lowered it, the signal to wait. He slipped into the doorway and disappeared. Madeline waited for disaster, but there was a roll of drums and a high piercing shriek. The concert had started and nothing had gone wrong, yet. The first song started to unfold; The Stones, Sympathy for the Devil, good choice. By the time the lyrics started, Jode was back reaching for Madeline to pull her inside through a tunnel. "The guard was asleep. He will stay that way. And no, I did not kill him, I have no wish to start another feud; he will stay asleep for a few hours. That is all." He pointed up a staircase, "stay close to the wall as you go, no one will be able to see you in the gloom."

Arabela led them up the stairs and through an archway into a corridor that circled the keep. The rooms ran along the outside wall. Madeline realized the tunnel was the thickness of the rooms and this corridor. As they slid into a nook, they heard footsteps of several Scree, both male and female, running from the other sides of the keep to enter rooms facing the music. Madeline could hear the screaming voice, probably Simon, supported by the ooo ooo of the rest of the band. The song was ending; the light show would start with the next one.

Jode tapped her shoulder and pointed to another staircase at the end of the hall, it rose to the next level, there were no other people coming. As they ran past to the open doorways, she could see heads crowding around the slit windows to see what was going on. As they climbed the stairs to the second floor, Madeline saw the next stairs were at the other end of the corridor. This pattern repeated four times until the stood in a small entry room that led to the open roof.

Arabela stopped and made them wait until she was sure there were no footsteps following them. The music changed and a flash of white stars rose from the forest. The sound was a rhythmic electronic beat, Madeline wondered how they had accomplished that, and then howls and shrieks started keeping time. Another flash of stars, this time green, and the lyrics started, a high voice, It's close to Midnight… Simon had a flair for soundtracks, she thought. The three stepped out of the room and looked around the corner of the building. Sayer Goddard sat on the wall watching the show, his arm around a boy who looked to be about five years old.

"See, son," Goddard said. "See how they foolishly celebrate. We will crush them."

"I like the music," the boy said.

Arabela pulled them both back into the room. "It is not over."

32

Drawing back into an empty room, they huddled in a corner out of sight of the doorway, away from the window. There seemed to be no doors on any of the rooms.

"We can't kill him and his son," Madeline said. "I will not kill a child."

"It would not be right," Arabela agreed. "I would not have embarked on this if I had known about the son."

"We cannot go back without resolving this," Jode said, "by coming we have awakened his interest in our lands."

"I'm sorry," Arabela said. "I did not know. He must have kept the boy a secret from all his enemies."

"Look," Madeline said. "It's no point being sorry; we have to figure out what to do. Do you think he will be open to negotiation now that you have found out about his son? He seems to care for the child."

"It is a boy, of course he cares," Arabela snapped. "He might agree to a peace to save the boy from an assassination. It would not occur to him that I would not kill his son given the chance."

"What guarantee will we have that he will keep his word?" Arabela asked.

"None," Jode said. "You know you cannot trust him."

"What if you took the boy into your care? If you took the boy, and promised to keep him safe, would Sayer keep his word?"

"Yes," Arabela smiled, "this is a good idea. I could raise the boy to be less brutal, perhaps. But, how would we get Goddard to agree?"

"He would have to think the boy's life in danger; it would have to be the only option to keep the boy alive," Jode said.

"Then we pretend to attack," Madeline said. "When we have them cornered we will offer this solution."

"What does your instinct, your talent, tell you?"

Madeline closed her eyes to remove the distractions, the sound of the 1812 overture rolled through the keep. She could not feel any danger; there was no confirmation or denial that the plan would be successful. "Sorry, nothing."

"We have to try," Arabela said, her quiet voice loaded with desperation. "I cannot let this child live to continue the blood feud."

"We go back to the roof, then," Jode said, checking the outside passage, and beckoning them forward. When they stepped back onto the roof, the boy was no longer at his father's side. Sayer Goddard leaned against the low wall and watched as a spray of blood-red fire burst through the trees and the sound of cannons roared from the drums.

"Stay here," Jode whispered under the cover of the noise, "do not come out of the shadow until necessary. Your talent will tell you if you need to come." Madeline drew into the shadow of the corner of the roof; she had a clear view of side where Sayer stood. Jode strode forward, Arabela slightly behind. "Goddard," Jode called loudly. "We have come to end the blood feud."

"Stupid humans," the Scree lord laughed. "Are you come to kill me?"

"If that is what will end the killing, yes," Jode said. "Are you prepared to die tonight?"

"I am prepared to fight," Goddard said, reaching into the shadows at his feet, he picked up a long blade. He stepped forward and Madeline could see that his reach was much longer than Jode's. She remembered the exhibition of skill; reach was not always a guarantee of victory. She hoped he relied on force rather than skill; skill was the only advantage Jode had.

"Do you fight for your Lady? Or, is she willing to fight her own fight?"

Arabela stepped forward, "Sir Jode is my champion, he will fight for me."

"Coward," Sayer taunted her. "If you were truly thirsty for revenge you would want to taste my blood by your own blade."

"We humans are not as brutal as you Scree," Arabela said, taking a step closer.

Madeline felt her skin burn with warning. "Stop," she shouted coming forward.

It was too late; Sayer's hand snaked out and touched Arabela. There was blue chalk on the end that left a smudge on her forehead. She crumpled, unconscious, to the ground.

Madeline kept moving forward, her skin still burning, knowing the danger was not over. She took three steps and saw a short blade swing around the corner of the building; the boy was back, and aiming his sword at Jode's hamstring.

"Look out," her warning was in time. Jode swung around and blocked the blade with his own. He reached over the boy's blade and lifted the child by the back of his shirt. Sayer Goddard stopped moving, his eyes following Jode's every move.

"Your son, I believe."

"Put him down," Sayer said, lowering his own blade. "He is only a child."

"Yes," Jode nodded and looked at the boy who was trying to grab Jode's sleeve. "But he is your child."

"What is it that you want?"

"Release the spell on Lady Arabela to start with."

Sayer flicked his fingers and sprinkled white chalk over Arabela's hair. She moaned and pushed herself up from the floor. "Let the boy go, we can fight this out between us," Sayer's voice still held contempt. "He does not need to be hurt."

Arabela nodded and took the boy from Jode. Madeline motioned her to step into the shadows. "Wait," Madeline said, ignoring the burning feeling on her skin, the warning of her talent. "There may be another way."

"Who is this?" Sayer said. "I do not know this woman."

"It's not important," she answered, standing beside Jode, out of his way should he have to use his sword. "I have a suggestion that would mean we all walk away."

"How can I trust you?" Sayer snarled, his eyes searching the shadows. "How can you trust me?"

"If you are willing to listen, I think you will hear the answers to your questions."

"Speak woman, I am not accustomed to waiting."

"If both you and Arabela revoke the blood feud then it is over."

"It is over," Sayer said. "This is about revenge. Unless, ah now I understand. That weakling Alric left her with child."

"Would it matter?" Madeline asked, trying not to confirm or deny his suspicion. It was always better to let opponents assume things, it left them open to persuasion, or threat depending on your point of view. "You were going to attack the Summer Lands anyway; Lady Arabela is trying to avoid war."

Sayer was still trying to see his son. "If I was to agree not to attack, how would I know she would forego her revenge?"

"She is not warlike; it is more in her nature to live in peace. Is she in the habit of breaking her word? Are humans known for their treachery?"

"True enough. I can think of ways to make her swear an oath that she could not break. How do you know I will not break my word?" This time he turned to look at Madeline, leering at her. "Scree are not so weak, we are celebrated for our treachery."

"We will take your son back to the Summer Lands. Arabela will raise him, safely, in trust of your word."

Sayer didn't reply, he stared into the shadows again. There was a lull in the music; they could hear the boy struggling against Arabela's grasp. Sayer stepped forward; Jode drew his blade; Sayer stepped back. Madeline's skin felt like it should be smoking; there was still more danger here. She didn't understand what it could be. Sayer had his sword out but didn't seem to be about to attack. His other hand was behind his back he seemed to be muttering something but the music swelled again. The song was Very Superstitious; the next one would signal the start of the half hour of darkness. They needed to get away soon.

Another scuffle in the corner, Madeline turned her head to see what was happening. Arabela swore and the boy started running towards his father. Sayer flung his arm out from behind his back a fine spray of red chalk dust floated towards Madeline. She saw it as she turned back to him, and side stepped out of the reach of the dust.

Jode stepped forward, "no, damn you," he shouted raising his sword. It looked to Madeline as though he was aiming to cut off the chalk-covered hand.

The boy ran between Jode and Sayer. Sayer stepped back to avoid Jode's blade. The boy jumped for his father and the added momentum toppled them over the wall. The scream and thud were only barely audible over the music as the song wound to an end.

"Are you unhurt?" Arabela asked, stepping back into the light, rubbing her ribs. "He kicked me so hard I think he may have broken a rib. I am sorry I should have held onto him, even so."

"Did any of the chalk touch you?" Jode said, stepping carefully around the red stain on the stones. "It was a curse."

“No, I used the defensive moves you taught me. I’m fine.” She stepped towards the wall.

“Don’t look.” Jode said, holding his hand to her while he peered over the edge. “They are both dead.”

“Then it is over,” Arabela said.

“We should go,” Madeline could still feel heat in her skin. There was still danger. “Will you be able to run if your rib is broken?”

“I will make it, do not worry.”

They ran quietly down the stairs past rooms, where people were muttering about the lack of fireworks. Out the door to the keep and across the open ground, they stumbled into the trees and waited until Arabela caught her breath. Moving more slowly through the trees, they met up with the musicians. Blu bundled Arabela into the wagon and had one of the musicians ride her horse back to camp. The concert ended with a burst of light and Leonard Cohen’s Closing time. By the time the last notes settled, the players were already on their way back to the camp.

33

People stepped forward to take the horses as they returned to camp. "They will want to celebrate," Simon said, as they walked away. "Should we set up for a party?"

"No," Arabela said. "We will have a small celebration tonight, and then a large one when we arrive back at the castle. We will send a couple of riders ahead to prepare. You should not be worrying about entertainment, without your music we would not have been able to succeed."

"Thank you, but I think that might be an exaggeration." Simon blushed.

At the centre of the camp, there was a platform set up; Arabela stood on it. She told everyone to get a drink and then toasted their victory. "We shall return to the castle with as much speed as we can so that we can properly celebrate the end of this threat."

When she stepped into her room in the tent, Madeline burst into tears. "There, dear," Alice said, patting Madeline's back. "It will be all right. You have done a hard thing, but it was the right thing. Come, there's a bath here and clean clothes to wear to bed. Have some of the food while you soak."

~~~

The camp was stirring as she stepped out of the tent door the next morning. Her skin was still burning; she hoped it was just a side effect and would fade over time. There could be no further danger in the middle of the camp. They met for breakfast in the space before the tents; it was a quick meal and jug of caf. "Will we travel with the camp from now on?" Madeline asked.

"Yes," Arabela answered, "but we will still move faster. There is no need to stop for meal breaks every day; we can eat in the saddle. We will stop an hour or two later in the evenings and leave and hour earlier in the mornings. It will not be as pleasant a journey but we should be back in three days not the six it took us to get here."

Servants took the empty plates and men started to collapse the tents. The four of them walked to the paddock to get their horses saddled. "Will we be able to travel together," Madeline asked Jode as they stood waiting for the saddles to be brought. "I mean, will Arabela be our chaperon until we find someone else?"

"We will all ride together. Both Lady Arabela and Sir Simon will witness our propriety."

"So, when we get back what happens?"

"We can discuss that as we ride," Jode said. There was a sound of a scuffle coming from the far side of the paddock. "Now what?" Jode turned towards the sound.
~~~

"It seems to be coming from that group over there," Madeline pointed. "Is that a woman? Do you know her?"

A woman Madeline didn't recognize from the camp ran towards them. She held a knife, her hair streaming behind, and her robes billowing out around her frame. As she ran, she shrugged off people who were trying to stop her and aimed directly for Jode and Madeline; both reached for their weapons.

"You," the woman shrieked pointing her finger at Madeline. "You killed my lover." Madeline felt frozen in place, her skin on fire. It was the woman from the vision. The Scree woman moved quickly towards Jode, slashing at his arm with a long blade. He tried to ward her off, but his sword was on the side of his body next to the horse, he couldn't draw it.

The woman reached under Jode's defenses and started to stab him. Madeline felt her hands reach for the throwing blades; she took one in each hand and drove them into the woman's back. The Scree grunted and folded at the knees, her blade hit the ground; she collapsed in a heap.

Madeline's hands dripped with crimson blood. She looked at Jode; blood ran from cuts on his chest and arm, too much blood. She screamed; the little priest ran into the paddock. Jode staggered towards Madeline but didn't make it; he collapsed beside the dead woman.

Madeline's skin had stopped burning, but now she felt like the world was fading from her; a cold dampness covered her body. She strained to hear the people who were calling to her. The grayness increased and the world disappeared from the edges of her vision. She felt her knees give way and tried to gain control; arms grabbed her and stopped her from falling. She heard Simon's voice as if from far away. "I've got you, don't worry. Everything will be okay."

How could everything be okay? Jode was dead. She hadn't protected him; He was dead and it was her fault, at the crucial moment, she'd frozen, been too late.

34

The world came back in waves of sight and sound. She heard Arabela's voice calling her back to consciousness, "drink this, it will help."

She sipped the liquid, it tasted of peppermint; it did help her feel more aware. She looked around, the light was dim and she felt motion.

"Where…"

"You are in Blu's wagon. We were worried she had hexed you."

"No, I'm fine, where is Jode?"

"He is over there," Arabela pointed at the other bench where Jode was laid out, Blu kneeling on the floor beside him. The priest was sewing the deep cuts on Jode's chest.

"The woman?"

"Dead," Arabela paused.

"What, there's something else."

"We know why you were brought here."

"Why?" Madeline kept her eyes on Jode's still form. "Why did I have to come here?"

"That woman was Sayer's other wife. She carried his unborn twin children." Arabela waited for Madeline to realize the importance of her act. All Madeline cared about was the sight of her love lying on the bench, not moving.

"If you had not been here, she would not have come out. We would not have known about them," Arabela explained. "Blu says they would have been formed enough to live outside the body in another few days. That is why we had to act so quickly."

"How do you know there are no others?" Madeline asked, her voice dull with grief.

"Blu searched and found none. In fact, he found no trace of any living family member for Goddard. The other Scree acted swiftly. The keep ran with blood by dawn."

"Can you send me back?"

Arabela sat back clearly surprised. "Yes, but I thought you wanted to stay. You said you loved Sir Jode, you wanted to study magic."

"There's no point now. If Jode is gone I would rather go home and be miserable in familiar territory."

"Gone?" Arabela smiled and brushed Madeline's hair back. "He is not gone. Blu provided him with some pain killing herbs. He is in a deep sleep so he won't feel the pain. He is very much alive."

Madeline blew out a shuddering breath. Looking over at Jode, she felt relief and warmth flood her body. He was alive and they would be building a future together. "Okay, then, I guess I'm staying."

ABOUT THE AUTHOR

I was born in the UK and moved to Vancouver BC in 1967. I've been writing for decades but recently became more focused on getting published. I started with National Novel Writing Month in 2009 and Off Track is the result of that crazy month.

I do write a different genre under the penname P.A. Wilson. Alice tends to the nicer stories, and young adult - although someone always has to die, they are more romance than anything else. Under P.A. Wilson I write gritty mystery, urban fantasy and other more dark stories.

Other books by Perry available at PaperBox Books

Closing the Circle by P.A. Wilson

8544122R0

Made in the USA
Charleston, SC
19 June 2011